MOVE
THE
SUN

The Signal Bend Series
Book One

by Susan Fanetti

THE FREAK CIRCLE PRESS

Cover design by Flintlock Covers
FlintlockCovers.com

ISBN-10: 1502382431
ISBN-13: 978-1502382436

Dedicated with tremendous love and great thanks to my Freaks,
especially Lina Andersson, Jessica Brooks, and Sarah Osborne.

And most especially to my infinitely patient and unfailingly encouraging daily writing partner, Shannon Flagg, without whom Signal Bend simply would not exist.

Women, I love you. You make me happy; you keep me sane.

We're all still Freaks.

Yet my wings were not meant for such a flight—
Except that then my mind was struck by lightning
Through which my longing was at last fulfilled.
Here powers failed my high imagination:
But by now my desire and will were turned,
Like a balanced wheel rotated evenly,
By the Love that moves the sun and the other stars.

Dante, *Paradiso*, Canto XXXIII

PRELUDE: 1989

Mena's car was in the driveway, but the house was dark.

Not a light on anywhere, as far as Johnny could tell. He'd worked late, but it was only 8:30. They should be home. The family life was nothing if not routine. Routine was critically important to Mena. He'd expected to see the familiar glow of the TV through the living room picture window. He parked his sedan next to his wife's station wagon and walked to the front door. He tried it; it was unlocked.

Johnny Accardo had been career Army, a Green Beret, in fact, and had done three long tours in 'Nam. He was retired now, working a damn desk in a damn office building, but he still knew when a situation was wrong, and this one was. On high alert, he opened the door and walked into his own dark house.

Everything was quiet, and nothing seemed out of place, but he couldn't shake his sense of foreboding. As he checked the living room and dining room, then the kitchen, he tried to think of harmless reasons his family could be gone on this school night, with the car still here. Maybe Mena had taken Lilli for a walk and lost track of time or even gotten lost—entirely possible if Mena was having an "up" day. She often got an itch to go "adventuring" on her "up" days, and on occasion he'd had to track her down miles and miles from home.

He'd check the rest of the house, but then he'd need to do a search through the neighborhood. He doubted they were with a neighbor. Mena didn't much like people, and she wasn't confident of her English, so she didn't socialize. But they might be wandering the streets in the dark. He could imagine his little Lilli, already far too serious and grown-up

5

at ten years old, trying to cajole her mother into heading home or seeking help.

So far, everything in the house was still normal, but he couldn't relax. He walked down the hallway and checked his office. Nothing. He started to call his wife's name, but something, an instinct to be quiet, stopped him. He checked his daughter's room. Her school blazer and bookbag were lying on her bed, so she'd come home from school. Otherwise, her room looked untouched. As always, she'd made her bed and tidied up before school, in accordance with house rules. Her favorite stuffed animals were arranged in a row across her pillows, staring blankly at him in the dim light coming through her windows.

He closed her door. He peeked quickly into her bathroom. Clean, quiet, empty.

As he approached the door to the master bedroom, his sense of doom nearly overwhelmed him, and with sudden clarity he understood exactly what he feared—and with the next thought, he knew what he would find.

Heart pounding, he strode straight through the master bedroom and turned the corner toward the en suite bath. He stopped in his tracks. The bathtub was directly across from the door, and he could see, even in the unlit room, that his wife was lying dead in their tub, naked, her wrists cut long and deep, her blood tainting the water and caking on the edge of tub and on the tiled floor.

"Oh, Jesus. Mena, *dolcezza*—no!" He reeled into the bathroom and dropped to his knees at the tub, pulling his wife's cold, stiff body into his arms and weeping. She'd been dead for hours, lying here in the frigid, bloody water. Hours.

He had no idea how long he knelt there, crying into Mena's stiff, sticky hair, but his tears finally abated. As the first blast of grief moved past, he thought of Lilli. Did she know? Where was she? Had Mena sent her to a friend's before she'd done this thing?

He kissed his wife, so lovely and fragile, so deeply loved, on the mouth and laid her body back in the tub. He had to call the authorities. He had to clean this room. He had to find his daughter and figure out what to tell her. He would have to make a new life for her. He had no more time for grief. He stood and turned.

And then, clear to him now even in the twilit room, he saw her. Lilli, curled tightly into herself and wedged between the toilet and the wall, her arms around her legs and her head on her knees. Her school uniform was blotchy with dark stains. Blood. She hadn't made a peep.

Instantly, Johnny understood. Lilli had come home from school and found her mother like this. She'd wedged herself into that corner and sat there for hours, alone in the deepening dark with her mother's bloody, bare, cold, dead body.

Mena had done a terrible thing. She had abandoned the husband and daughter who so loved her. But Mena was broken and lost, and Johnny could forgive her for that. But leaving her mess for their daughter to find? Innocent and alone? He would never forgive her for that. Never. He slammed and locked the door on his grief.

He squatted down near his little girl. "Lilli? Lillibell? It's Papa. Come to me, *cara*. Come to me."

He heard a tiny whimper, but she didn't move. His heart lurched in his chest. "Oh, *bella*, let me take you out of here. Come to me."

She looked up, and he could see how huge her eyes were. She was terrified, in shock. She whispered, "Papa? Papa, Mama's hurt." She sounded years younger than she was.

He reached out and tried to take her hand. She had her hands locked around her legs and wouldn't, or couldn't, release them. He'd seen this in villages in 'Nam after the VC, or sometimes other US troops, plowed through—children hiding under beds and behind chests, or in holes in the fucking ground, too scared and shocked, too traumatized, to accept help when it arrived. "I know, Lilli. Let's go into the kitchen and call for some help. Will you help me do that?"

She looked at him for several long moments, her eyes wide and frightened. Then she nodded and held out one small hand. He took it in his and pulled her into his arms. He gathered her up and carried her away from that godforsaken scene. He closed the bedroom door on his way out and took his daughter into the kitchen, turning lights on all the way. It was just the two of them now.

CHAPTER ONE

Following the stilted British intonations of the GPS, Lilli turned off the interstate and made a left at the light at the bottom of the ramp. Another fifteen miles or so down a lazy, neglected stretch of macadam, nothing to either side of her but farmland, and she passed a wooden sign offering her a "Welcome to Signal Bend!" She figured the sign had once been quaint, brightly painted, with a vaguely Scandinavian aspect, but it had been some years since it had seen any upkeep. The welcome it offered seemed weary.

She followed the GPS into Signal Bend, Missouri. The whole town seemed as weary as its welcome sign. Lilli supposed it was a typical Midwestern town, just far enough from the limits of a city to be rural, but just close enough that the suburban spans of superstores, megaplexes, and gallerias drained the life from the local economy. A geographical limbo that meant a long, slow, weary death for most towns.

She could see that it had once been bustling, and a few blocks of the main drag were making an attempt to capitalize on its quaint history, with antique shops, a couple of cafes, and an actual ice cream parlor lining the street on both sides. But there was a grimness under the pastel surface.

She pulled up in front of a small green bungalow with a large picture window dominating the front of the house. The door was mostly glass; a sign proclaiming "Come In, We're OPEN!" hung from a suction cup in the center. Painted in gilt on the picture window, the words "SIGNAL BEND REALTY, MAC EVANS, BROKER" told Lilli she'd arrived at her destination before the GPS figured it out and announced the same. She turned off the portable unit and slid it into the pocket of her leather jacket.

As she closed the door on her black 1968 Camaro SS, she was startled by a thunderous roar of engines behind her. Three men on huge black Harleys turned the nearest corner and headed down the main drag—which was called, appropriately, Main Street. They wore basic black helmets, black sunglasses, and black leather kuttes. The rider in the lead—big and broad-shouldered, with a dark full beard and a dark thick braid running down his back—noticed her ride, then noticed her, and nodded, giving the throttle a little goose, all in the span of time it took to roll past her.

Patches covering the backs of the three men's kuttes declared that they were the Night Horde Motorcycle Club, of Missouri. Their emblem was the bust of a horse—probably a stallion—with a flaming mane. Lilli smirked. Subtlety did not tend to run deep in the MC world.

She turned back and headed into the realtor's office.

The office was obviously a converted house, with the living room apparently serving as the reception and main work area. It still had the air of a home, with floral wallpaper and a dark green, sculpted carpet that had been around awhile. There was a small desk right inside the door; Lilli assumed it was for the receptionist, or the secretary, or the assistant, or whatever they called the likely underpaid, likely young woman who usually sat there. It was empty now. She didn't see anyone, in fact. There were two other desks deeper in, but neither was occupied.

"Hello?" she called out.

From even deeper in, she heard a man's voice call, "Yeah—one sec!"

In more like sixty seconds, the owner of the voice trundled into view. "Hi—Lillian, right? I'm Mac." He held out his hand.

Lilli shook it. "It's Lilli. Hi."

She had never met Mac Evans in person, so she took him in now. He was average in almost every respect: say, mid-forties, about her height, so five-nine or so. Slightly balding, light brown hair, cut in a classic, conservative style that had been around since at least the middle part of the last century. Rimless glasses over brown eyes. Little beer gut forming. Wearing khaki Dockers and a pink oxford shirt. Lilli saw a navy blazer hanging on the back of the largest chair behind the largest desk in the room. The only feature by which Mac might leave any memorable impression at all on most observers was his nose—large, long, wide, and hooked, with nostrils probably an inch long. It drew one's eye, to say the least.

"So, Lilli. Why don't we sit. I've got a few papers for you to sign, and then I can hand over the keys to the rental. You're sure you don't want me to head over with you, do a walkthrough, make sure everything is as promised before you sign?"

She was sure. She was signing regardless, and she wanted to get the keys and get started. She sat in the chair facing his desk. "Nope, I'm good." She smiled at him. "I trust you."

He smiled back, charmed. Guys like Mac were easy to charm. "Well, that's refreshing. The world needs a little more trust, if you ask me. And you won't be sorry, I promise." He passed the few papers she needed to sign to finalize her rental agreement, and, when she signed and passed them back, he handed her two keys on a ring with a glow-in-the-dark plastic fob. "The brass key is the house key, the silver the garage."

Lilli took the keys and stood. Mac walked her to the door. "Is there anything else I can do for you?"

11

"Actually, yes." She smiled again. "I'd love a recommendation for a good place for breakfast. I didn't even see a McDonald's as I was coming into town."

"Nope, no McDonald's. Not a lot of those chain places here in Signal Bend. We have the A&W; that's about it. Oh, and the 7 Eleven, for gas and sundries. Where you really want to go for breakfast or lunch is Marie's. Good pies, fresh baked daily. And the fluffiest waffles you ever will eat. For dinner, there's the Chop House. Those are my recommendations." He gave her what Lilli figured was his best flirty smile. "In fact, I'd be happy to buy you dinner at the Chop House tonight, welcome you to town."

"Wow, Mac, that's really great. But I've been driving all day. What I really need is a quiet night. Rain check?"

He took the rejection in stride. "I'll hold you to it. You have a good night, now."

Thus released, she went back to her car and drove to her new home.

~oOo~

It was a prefab, a glorified double-wide trailer, elevated from trailer park status by the fact that it was attached to a foundation. She had rented it without seeing it in person, because the satellite photos she'd found online showed it was tucked back into woods, with the nearest neighbors a good half mile away. It was rented furnished. It had a large, detached garage. And it was in the right location.

She parked her Camaro in front of the garage doors. No remote opener. So she got out, unlocked the door, pushed it up, and drove in. She pulled her duffels out of the trunk and headed in to check out the digs.

It was clean, and smelled as if it had been recently aired out. Mac had had the place prepped for her. She was impressed, she had to admit. The place was sparsely but adequately furnished in a random style that Lilli immediately thought of as 1970s garage sale chic. She took her duffels and dropped them in the largest bedroom. It had a small en suite three-quarter bath. Must be the 'master suite.' Funny.

There were linens and blankets stacked at the foot of the bare queen-size mattress. But no. Lilli would not be using linens for which she didn't know the history. Sheets she had packed, but she was blanket-poor. She'd pull her bedroll out of the car for tonight, and she'd find a place she could buy a couple of blankets, maybe a bedspread, tomorrow. She needed to stock the kitchen, anyway.

Tonight, though, she meant to drive around a little, find a burger—not at the Chop House—and start getting to know the town. Maybe find a bar. Even the shittiest towns at least had a bar. The shittier the town, the livelier the bar, in her experience. People with shitty lives liked their beer on tap. She went into the en suite bath and gave her face a quick splash, then checked her look. She'd do.

~oOo~

The GPS was no help to her finding local businesses. If it could have shrugged at her, it would have. So Lilli simply drove around, got to know her surroundings the old-fashioned way. It was better, gave her bearings much more quickly.

She found a couple of diners and cafes, but at 9:30 in the evening, they were already closed. She found the Chop House, but wanted to avoid that in case Mac Evans had kept his taste for steak even after she'd declined his invitation to dine with him.

13

There wasn't a lot of traffic on the roads. This was the kind of town where the few traffic lights still swung from wires strung across the intersections. These people mostly kept farmers' hours. 9:30 was the deep dark of the night. Even the streetlights seemed dim and sleepy.

Eventually, though, she came upon a brightly-lit building that screamed old-style honky-tonk. It had the clever name of "No Place." The gravel lot was more than half full on this mid-week night, and there was a line of bikes, all big, black Harleys, arrayed near the front door. When Lilli stepped out of the Camaro, she could hear the music coming through the walls: high-steppin' country. No surprise. Didn't sound live—that was no surprise, either, on a weeknight in the sticks.

She ran her hand over her long, dark ponytail and strolled on in. Hopefully, they had a kitchen that stayed open to feed the hungry drunks, but at this point, Lilli would be content with a bowl of stale peanuts.

The music was coming from a jukebox, a huge Wurlitzer in the far corner. Lilli was sort of impressed by the sound quality, as if someone had figured out a way to juice it up. Garth Brooks was singing about his friends in low places. The setup was pretty standard: wood floor, wood walls, country-style wood tables and chairs. Long, dark, L-shaped bar, scratched and gouged from years of hard use, darkened by years of spilled booze. Big mirror on the wall behind it, the booze arrayed on glass shelves on the mirror. Straight off the Universal Studios lot. Add some swinging louvered doors and a spittoon, lose the Wurlitzer, and sit back and wait for Wyatt Earp to stroll through.

Well, except for the big, hand-lettered sign on the mirror that admonished: *This Is A CASH ONLY Establishment: Save Your Fucken Plastic For The Mall.*

The place was doing some brisk but not overwhelming business. Most of the tables were occupied, mostly with the typical farmland types—grungy John Deere caps, dark red, lined faces. Not a lot of women, Lilli noticed. Those around were, on average, fuller figured and dyed. Lots of plaid and denim. Lots of domestic beer. This was definitely not a pick up joint. It was a place for hard-working men to get drunk. Lilli noticed sandwiches and baskets of fries on several tables. Score.

She went to the bar, which was crowded with the owners of the Harleys out front—a row of six men, all wearing kuttes with the same patch: the Night Horde MC. Three of the men were leaning with their elbows on the bar; the other three were leaning back against it, keeping an eye on the room. One of those was the man she'd noticed riding down Main Street with a couple of his brothers earlier in the day. He was watching her.

She made eye contact with him, and he nodded and lifted his beer bottle. No beer on tap for him, it seemed. She wasn't sure whether he was acknowledging that he recognized her from earlier, or whether he was simply letting her know that he'd noticed her. She supposed she did stand out a bit in this crowd. She walked to the end of the bar, where there was an empty stool. The bartender, a curvy, very-not-natural redhead showing a huge rose tat on lots of cleavage, came right down and asked for her order. "Any chance the kitchen's still open?"

The bartender looked over at the old, animated beer sign on the wall. It would be "vintage," except Lilli was pretty sure it had been hanging exactly there since it had been brand new. There was a clock embedded in it. "Fifteen more minutes. What can I get ya?"

"Just a cheeseburger and fries. And a bottle of Bud. Thanks." The busty bartender offered an approving nod, popped the top on a Bud, and handed it to her before she

15

went back to push the swinging door to the kitchen open and yell in her order.

Lilli took a long swallow of the cold, soothing brew. Bud might not be the smoothest or the fanciest beer around, but it was the King of Beers, after all. She felt a tingle up her back and turned quickly to find the Biker Man coming up on her. Despite his general mien of menace, he wasn't casting an especially aggressive vibe, so she leaned back on the bar and watched him come. He stopped directly in front of her and took a pull of his beer. He was wearing black leather cuffs on his wrists and three big silver rings on each large hand: thumb, middle finger, ring finger.

He was tall—really tall, at least six-five, maybe more. Broad shoulders, with the firm swell that indicated real definition under his kutte—a kutte with several patches on the front, one of which, on his right side, read "President." Top of the food chain, then.

His beard was dark and full; his hair, in that thick braid halfway down his back, was also dark and full. Vivid green eyes. Long scar running up and across the left side of his face, from just under his nose to his temple.

He had her attention, definitely.

"You set?" His voice was deep and rumbly. Of course it was.

Lilli lifted her bottle and waved it a bit. "Yep. But thanks." He winked. "I'll get the next one, then." He took another swallow, killing his beer. Leaning in on her to set his empty on the bar, his head near her ear, he said, "I'm Isaac." Lilli could smell the leather of his kutte.

When he stepped back, she smiled at him. "Hi, Isaac." Without saying more, she drank some beer.

Isaac grinned. It was lopsided, lifting the right side of his face. Lilli liked a lopsided smile. "You know, when someone introduces himself, it's customary to return the favor." Still smiling, she raised her eyebrows, but said nothing.

"That how you're playin' it, huh? I guess I could call you Sport. That was you today, in that Camaro SS, right?"

"It was." It would be silly to prevaricate here; the town wasn't big enough to try to stay under the radar. But she wasn't about to do more than answer his questions as minimally as possible until she had gotten a good read on him.

"Nice ride. Lotta car for a girl. You were at Mac's. You movin' to town?"

Lilli now understood that this was more than small talk going on here. He wasn't just trying to get into her jeans— though she was sure he'd do that, too, if he could. He was feeling her out. His town. New resident. He was trying to understand why she was here, where she'd fit. Whether she was a threat.

"I am."

"Not many people move *to* Signal Bend. If you're looking for work, won't find it."

"I'm not."

"Damn, girl. You got a two-word limit on your sentences or something?" Just then, her burger and fries came out. The bartender brought the food out in two red plastic baskets lined with red-and-white checked paper. She set ketchup, salt and pepper on the bar as well.

"Get ya anything else?"

"Get her another Bud, Rose. And me. And put it all on my tab, hon."

Rose—the busty bartender with the big rose inked on her chest—gave Isaac a knowing grin. "You bet, Ike."

Ike, huh? Lilli turned back to him. "Thanks, Ike."

"It's Isaac. Some around here call me Ike. Never liked it, but it stuck young. You call me Isaac." Rose brought them fresh Buds as Isaac sat down on the stool next to hers and shook salt, pepper, and ketchup onto her fries. When she shot him an incredulous look, he grinned. "Hey—I paid for 'em. You're sharin'."

Lilli conceded with a nod and proceeded to share her dinner with the tall, dark, and menacing biker who'd bought it for her.

"This your version of a Welcome Wagon? You share fries with all the new people in town?" She took a bite of her burger. Oh—it was really good. Just rare enough in the middle, nice and juicy. The bun was soft and fresh.

He grinned around a mouthful of fries. "Oh-ho! She speaks in complete sentences!" He finished chewing. "No, Sport. This is special, just for you."

"And I warrant special treatment because …?"

"I like the look of…your ride." With a shrug, he took the burger out of her hand and had a bite.

She looked down the bar at his MC brothers, all of whom were watching the show. Apparently their President sharing a nosh with the new girl in town was some kind of noteworthy. She'd known staying off the radar would be impossible, but she had hoped to keep a lower profile than this.

Looked like she was going to have to play things another way.

CHAPTER TWO

Isaac was interested.

The woman sitting next to him sharing her burger and fries was a knockout, but he didn't think that was really what had his interest. Sure, he'd looked her over good, and she was in his sweet spot—tall; shiny, dark brown hair pulled off her face and hanging down her back; lively light eyes, the color of which he couldn't figure out. Great tits, just the hint of a swell of cleavage showing over the curved neckline of her shirt. She was simply dressed, too, in jeans, low-heeled black boots, a white t-shirt and a black leather jacket. The only jewelry he could see was a big silver ring on each middle finger and a pair of thin silver hoops just big enough to lie on her neck when she tilted her head. He bet that neck smelled nice.

Nothing on the left ring finger; he'd checked that out first thing.

He liked his women without a lot of frills. This one was gorgeous but didn't look like it took her two hours to get that way. The kind of woman from whom he'd never hear the boner-killing plea, *Watch my hair!* Fuck, he hated women like that. He liked his fucks to get messy. So, yeah, he could sit back and look at her all day. But that wasn't what had caught him.

He'd noticed her cage before he'd noticed her, when he, Len, and Showdown were on their way out of town earlier in the afternoon. That '68 Camaro was cherry. It was worth a lot of money, and it wasn't so usual to see expensive cars around Signal Bend. Even the out-of-towners who came out on weekends to the shops on Main weren't the ritzy 'antiquing' types. The 'Main Street Marketplace,' so dubbed by the sad, little men of the sad, little Chamber of Commerce, was really junk shops. Permanent garage sales.

So a hot chick with money was at the one and only realtor in Signal Bend. That was worth a look. He'd decided he wanted to know more while they were still riding past her; he intended to put Bart on it in the morning. But now she was here at the bar, so maybe he could get what he needed straight from the hottie's mouth.

She kept that pretty, rosy mouth closed, though. He didn't even have her name yet. She was smiling, her eyes keen and sparkling, and she was sitting here sharing her eats with him—her reticence wasn't hostile at all. In fact, he was picking up that she might well be good for a tumble tonight.

So why so cool? He wasn't a big talker, but she'd said one word for ten of his. There was something going on behind those—blue?—eyes. Woman was smart, and she was paying careful attention. That had his antennae up.

Her name and address he'd have five minutes after he put Bart on it. Probably less. But there was something else, something deeper and much more interesting, to know about her.

Taking a pull from her bottle of Bud, she looked past him down the bar and rolled her eyes. Isaac turned and saw his guys all goggling at them like the assholes they were. Dan raised his glass of whiskey, and the other four followed suit, toasting him as if they'd never seen him work a chick before. Assholes. He lifted his beer to them and turned away.

"Don't mind them. I don't let 'em out much." He watched her tip the bottle up and swallow down the last of it. The way her throat moved as she swallowed, the muscles flexing rhythmically, gave him an urge to run his fingers across that smooth, sleek skin. He barely caught it back; his

21

fingers actually stretched a little toward her, which surprised him.

She set the empty bottle on the bar. He drained his and did the same. "'Nother?"

She smiled at him—that smile said that she was on to him, and she wanted to make sure he knew it. "One more. Gotta drive home in unfamiliar territory, so I'll need my wits."

"I'll see to it you get home, don't you worry."

"I'll bet. One more. And thank you." She pulled a fry heavy with ketchup and ate it, end first. It left behind a small, tomato-y drop, and he reached out to catch it with his thumb, but, with a sly glance at his reaching digit, she slid her tongue out and ran it over her lower lip. His balls clenched hard at the sight, and his cock filled out uncomfortably. He signaled to Rose to bring two more Buds.

As Rose was nodding, Isaac heard a crash behind him and instinctively looked at the mirror behind the bar. Jimmy Sullivan and Don Keyes were going at it and, in customary fashion, pulling in the rest of the crowd, men and women alike. His brothers were fairly leaping into the fray. Okay, then. He turned to his new, nameless friend. Way too pretty to get caught up in the melee.

"You should get behind the bar with Rose, Sport. Show's startin'."

Signal Bend, Missouri was named for a particular feature: a complicated bend in the railroad which bisected the town. When, after three massive derailments, the rail line acknowledged that the bend was more than a locomotive could take at speed, they installed a signal house at the location. As hard times hit the country at the end of the nineteenth century, and the huge farms around the railroad

22

got sold off in parcels, bringing in a spate of residents to farm neighboring plots, a town had grown up around the little hut in which the signalman had lived and worked.

Eventually, Signal Bend got its own station, and it thrived as a community through the middle part of the twentieth century. Never having developed any other kind of industry but farming and the railroad, and the commerce to support it, Signal Bend began to starve slowly as interstates and corporate farms became the way. By the 1990s, the railroad had been abandoned and suburbs of St. Louis finally had started to bump up against the farmland surrounding the town. A Walmart went up less than thirty miles away, drawing dollars from the locally-owned shops. Things in Signal Bend were getting dire. The most recent recession dealt the death blow, though the dying was slow. The only people who stayed around now were the ones whose families had been here for generations and knew nothing else. Not even many of them were left.

About half the family farms were still operational and still hanging on. The rest of the farmland was lying fallow or was being run by corporations, and many of the people working them commuted to work from other towns. These days, the most lucrative 'commerce' in Signal Bend was crystal meth. As the Night Horde well knew.

A town like this, in the straits it was in, there wasn't much to do at night. Everything but No Place was closed by nine o'clock. No movie theater or video store anymore; nearest ones were twenty-five miles away, in the same strip center as the Walmart. No cable TV or internet, unless you ran a dish, which not many could afford. Three things: drink, fight, fuck. All three happened just about nightly, and usually in that order, at No Place. On Saturdays, when Tuck, owner of the bar and Rose's old man, brought in live music, you could add dancing to the list.

It wasn't Saturday tonight, though. The drinking had been going on for a few hours. Now it was time for the fighting.

Usually these fights were little more than good-natured scrapes, a lively but friendly disagreement turning physical. People cleared the furniture out of the way and tried to do minimal lasting damage to body or property. This one had a sharper vibe, though, Isaac noticed right away, when a flying bottle barely missed his head. Jimmy and Don were really fighting, and that had changed the attitude of the whole bar. Isaac spared a quick second to wonder what the fuck was up and then busted Ed Foss's nose for throwing a goddamn bottle at his goddamn head.

His brothers had noticed the difference in the scene as well, and most of them were going in hot. Isaac saw Dan, though, pulling two women out of the midst and sending them behind the bar. Leave it to Dan to remember his chivalry. As Isaac watched, amused, he took a punch to the lower back and turned to find Meg Sullivan glaring up at him, arm cocked for another go. He backhanded her and put her on the floor.

His chivalry wasn't dead, but if a bitch was throwing sucker punches, she got what she got.

Aside from ducking flying bottles and putting thug bitches in their place, Isaac's primary interest here was in minimizing the damage to the bar. Tuck paid the Horde to keep some semblance of order, so they were on the hook for damage done in these regular melees. Usually that wasn't a problem. Tonight it was. So he stayed out of the fray as best he could and surveyed, looking for the flashpoint—which was not, surprisingly, Jimmy and Don, who weren't fighting each other anymore. Showdown had Don on the floor, but Jimmy was engaged with Will Keller, and they were going at it with murder on their minds.

What the fuck was going on?

Then Jimmy got over on Will and put him against the wall, and Isaac caught a glint of metal in Jimmy's right hand. *Goddamn son of a bitch fuck.* Nothing worse than a twitchy asshole with a blade. No. Not gonna happen. There were at least three brawling bodies between Isaac and Jimmy, but Isaac plowed through them and grabbed hold of Jimmy's plaid shirt, yanking him back.

Not before his knife had found a home, though. Will went down quietly, sliding to sit on the floor against the wall, holding his side. Jimmy flailed with the switchblade still in his hand, now going for Isaac, but Isaac grabbed his wrist and broke it with one hard snap, and the blade fell from Jimmy's suddenly useless fingers to the floor, embedding in the rough wood.

Isaac was proud to be a man who kept his cool in a brawl, but now he was filled with a heady fury. He put Jimmy on the floor, his knee on the wrist he'd just broken, and laid in with abandon, pulping the murderous asshole's face.

A shot rang out, and the room went quiet. His knee still on Jimmy's wrist, and one hand around his throat, the other cocked back, Isaac turned toward the sound. Meg was behind the bar, with the new girl, whom Isaac was beginning to think of automatically as "Sport," in a chokehold, a little snub-nosed .22 at her temple. Sport's hands were on Meg's forearm.

"Back off him, Ike, or your new little friend gets a piercing." Meg grinned like she was proud of her turn of phrase.

The force of the chill he felt surprised him. Without breaking eye contact with Meg, Isaac released Jimmy's throat and started to back off, lifting up from his knees. He'd come up maybe two inches, when Meg was sailing over Sport's shoulder and landing on her back on the bar.

25

Isaac watched as Sport came in from the side with a hard punch to Meg's throat, leaving a visible gash where her big ring connected. Meg immediately began to choke desperately. And then Sport had the gun and was emptying the cylinder. She looked over at him and waved the now empty gun, in a *carry on* gesture.

Grinning, Isaac came to his feet, bringing Jimmy with him. "You and me, Jimmy—and your lovely missus—we'll be havin' a talk." He looked over at Show, who already had his burner open. Dan had taken Meg over from Isaac's *very* interesting new friend. Len, and now Rose, were tending to Will, who didn't look too bad off, thankfully. "Havoc'll be around with the van any minute. Comin' armed into Tuck's place—very bad idea, my man. Regrettable."

Jimmy was too messed up to speak. Isaac righted a chair, sat him down on it, and nodded for Dan to bring Meg over, too. Once Dan had charge of errant husband and wife, Isaac went to the bar. The rest of his brothers and the other patrons were setting the bar to rights. There was heavy damage this time, though. Dammit. The Horde coffers weren't empty, but they weren't so full they wouldn't feel the hit.

Tuck was leaning on the bar, considering the scene. Isaac leaned over and put his hand on Tuck's shoulder. "Sorry, man. We'll get it straight by tomorrow afternoon."

The old guy nodded. "I know. Thanks, Ike. Will okay?"

Isaac looked over and saw Will standing, his shirt open and a gauze bandage on his side. Rose had gotten her share of first aid practice over the years. "Seems to be." He turned back to Tuck. "You know what Jimmy and Will are beefin' about? That was no friendly disagreement."

Tuck shook his head slowly. "They came in together, looked normal to me."

Isaac considered that. Jimmy and his old lady had come in armed. That was a massive transgression, and they knew it. Something was up. He was looking forward to sitting down with the Sullivans tonight. Havoc had come in, and he and Dan were leading them out.

Now, though, the girl known as Sport was walking up to him, a wry smirk on her face and two beers in her hand. She held one out to him. "This is how you make your fun around here, huh?"

He took the beer and drank half down all at once. "Well, that was more fun than usual, but you know. Find it where you can." He cocked an eyebrow at her. "You handled yourself, though. Got a self-defense class in your back pocket?"

She was drinking as he talked, and he watched her throat move again, entranced. When she pulled the bottle away, she was wearing that wry, enigmatic smirk. "Something like that." She finished the beer and set the bottle on the bar. "Welp, I'm out. Interesting place you got here. Thanks for the Welcome Wagon." She turned and walked out.

Holy fuck. Her ass. How had he missed *that*? He drained his beer and went after her.

She was moving fast and almost at her car when he got outside. "Wait up, Sport!" he called. She reached her car before she turned, crossed her arms, and waited.

When he was standing in front of her, looking down into those sardonic eyes, he said, "Still don't know your name."

"I have an idea you will soon enough. Why spoil your fun?" She put her hand on the door handle. Isaac was amped up from the fight and seriously intrigued by this woman. Acting on animal instinct more than anything else,

27

he wrapped his hand around her slight wrist and pulled it away from the handle. She let him, still smirking.

With his other hand on her shoulder, he pushed her back against the Camaro. He leaned in close and murmured, "Something tells me you're a lot of fun, Sport." He kissed her.

Though she didn't kiss him back at first, she didn't resist, either. Her lips were warm, soft, and supple, and when he pushed his tongue against them, she opened her mouth and let him in. With a pleased growl, he released her wrist and shoulder so that he could cradle her face and kiss her properly.

Her tongue came alive then, undulating against his, and her arms snaked around his neck. He felt her wrapping his braid around her hand, and then she pulled it over his shoulder, bringing him even closer as she sucked his lower lip between her teeth, biting down. He was completely hard, his cock constricted in the leg of his jeans. When he dropped his hands to her hips and brought her tightly against him, she pulled away a bit. She licked her lips and looked up at him, her eyes contemplative.

He smiled. "Ah, Sport. I want to play with you. I got some business I need to take care of tonight, though. Pick this up later?"

"Won't rule it out." Damn, he was already growing to love that knowing smile. He kissed her quickly and put her in her car. As he watched her drive away, his smile became a snarl. He was extra pissed at the Sullivans now. They'd fucked up what would have been a really delightful night.

~oOo~

Isaac pulled up to the Night Horde clubhouse feeling agitated and angry. He glanced around the lot; looked like

28

he was the last one in. Good. That was how he liked it. He hated waiting for other people.

The Night Horde no longer ran a business per se, not a strictly legit one, anyway. In the town's heyday and for some time after that, they'd run a construction company, but there wasn't anything to build these days. By all appearances, they now were simply a recreational club. Wyatt and Victor had family farms. Havoc, Dan, and Bart worked at Keyes Implement Repair, fixing tractors, threshers, and the like. Showdown ran the feed store. Len owned the hardware store. CJ lived off his army pension. Isaac...well.

As a club, they earned three ways, the most lucrative of which by far was running protection and enforcement on the local meth pipeline from Crawford County, northeast to St. Louis and into Illinois, and southwest to Springfield, Joplin, and as far as Tulsa. They took a share from both sides of the line. No one in the club liked it, but meth was a way of life in mid-Missouri, and the only way to control it was to, in fact, control it. Help the local cookers get their product to a wider clientele. They ran it out of Signal Bend. All of it. Out. Let the cities deal with it.

Anyone who tried to keep it local had his mind changed.

The town had lost its police department in the early 1990s, when another national fiscal crisis had taken a toll. They were miles away from the nearest substation of the Crawford County Sheriff's Office. Isaac's father had led the club in those days, and, rather than watch the town and its environs descend into some kind of pioneer-days lawlessness, Big Ike had seen a way to keep order and make a buck. The Horde had become the town security, taking a monthly sum from local businesses for the promise of protection and a guarantee to fix the damage from what it could not prevent.

They were effective deterrents to crime. So effective, in fact, that Crawford County never saw a need to bring a substation within reasonable distance of Signal Bend, and the club maintained a cordial and very healthy relationship with Sheriff Keith Tyler, who took his cut of the meth profits and stayed out of the way.

The Horde also occasionally did custom bike work. That, though, earned, at best, a low five figures in a year.

The clubhouse showed its history as a rural construction company. The building was long, low, and serviceable, built mainly of cinderblock and surrounded by a large gravel lot that had once held heavy equipment. The property was ringed by an eight-foot, chain-link fence with privacy slats. Normally, though, the huge double gates were left open. There had been no need to lockdown for going on five years. They had beefs with crews in St. Louis and East St. Louis, but that trouble went down on the away field. It stayed out of Signal Bend.

Isaac was damn proud of that.

Which was why he was het up now. Something wrong was going down if Jimmy and Meg Sullivan, cookers extraordinaire, were walking around Signal Bend armed at all, much less bringing that shit into Tuck's. And the dynamics of the fight were puzzling: Jimmy and Don Keyes first. Don had nothing to do with the trade, though he had a deep connection with the Horde. But then the shift to Will, who was just a farmer—and Isaac's oldest friend. Good friends with Jimmy, too. Isaac had no fucking clue what that scene was all about. But he wasn't going home until he knew.

Neither were the Sullivans. He went into the clubhouse.

The Horde were lined up at the bar or sitting at tables nearby. Rover, their Prospect, was pouring whiskey. And there were girls. Always seemed to be girls around. The Horde was the only MC for miles, and lots of farmers' daughters managed to find the coin to tart themselves up and drive themselves out for a chance for a tumble with a biker. Hence the long row of dorm rooms at the back of the clubhouse. That, and space to entertain the occasional visiting brother. The Night Horde wasn't part of a large charter, but they were friendly with several and allied with one, The Scorpions, an international charter based in Florida.

Show looked up and saw Isaac striding in. "Hey, boss. Jimmy and Meg are waiting for you in the Room. Made 'em nice 'n comfy."

Isaac nodded. "You good to go, Victor?"

Victor stood on the rung of his barstool and reached over the bar. He grabbed a box of rubber gloves from the shelf underneath and tucked it under his arm. "You know it, Isaac. Born ready."

The Room was a former repair bay they now used to do their dirtier, wetter work. A room one could hose out and scrub down with bleach, if need be. Not much call for it usually—in fact, it held the booze back stock right now, serving as an overflow storage area as well as an interrogation space. Jimmy and Meg Sullivan were gagged and tied to metal chairs, their arms bound to the arms of the chairs, positioned side by side, about three feet between them. Isaac hadn't realized how much of a beating he'd laid down on Jimmy, but the skinny fuck looked pretty bad. His broken right wrist was swelling angrily, the hand attached to it livid.

Isaac looked at Victor, and gestured to Jimmy. Victor nodded and walked over to Meg. With a smile that should have turned her blood to ice, he ripped the duct tape off her mouth. She squealed as the tape took some skin with it.

31

Victor pulled a wheeled tool chest up alongside Jimmy, and Isaac grabbed a stool and sat in front of Meg. She was the weaker link.

Isaac leaned in a bit. Her throat was swollen, with a gash still leaking some blood, where Sport had landed her punch. Sport—that was were he should have been right now, dammit, his hands around her naked ass. That amazing ass. He tried to smile at Meg, but it came out a snarl. "Okay, Meg, sweetheart. This is how we play. I ask you questions. I don't like your answer, Vic takes something off your man. Do you understand the rules of the game?"

Meg took a big breath and began to blather. "Ike, man, you don't gotta do that. You and Jimmy's friends. I know you don't want to hurt him, that's crazy—NO!"

Isaac had nodded to Victor, who picked up a pliers and attached it to the nail of Jimmy's swollen right pinkie. Without so much as a pause for a breath, he yanked, pulling the nail straight out. Still gagged, Jimmy screamed like a 12-year-old girl at a boy band concert. His eyes bugged out. Victor dropped the bloody nail into a steel bucket at his feet. The bucket was not small.

Isaac turned back to Meg. "The question I asked was *Do you understand the rules of the game?* You didn't answer. Now I'm asking again. Do you understand?"

Weeping hard now, Meg nodded. "I understand."

"Good. Let's get to the real questions, then."

INTERLUDE: 1994

Johnny Accardo was up well before dawn on a mid-autumn Saturday, dressing quickly and lacing up his boots. He went to Lilli's room and knocked lightly. When he got no answer, he opened the door a couple of inches and peeked in.

Her bed was already made. No longer was there a long line of stuffed animals arrayed across the pillows; his daughter had boxed them up a few years ago, declaring that she was too old for them. All but one: a mangy, spotted dog. She'd had it her whole life. Its name was Dog. Johnny closed the door and continued down the hall.

He heard the sounds of breakfast. Somehow, he'd managed to be the last one up. He was impressed. His mother, who had moved in with them shortly after Lilli's mother's suicide, was pulling hard rolls off a baking sheet. Breakfast in this Italian home had almost always been coffee or hot chocolate and hard rolls with jam. Sometimes polenta in the winter. Neither Mena nor his mother had been able to adapt to the American way of cold cereal or eggs and meat. Johnny knew that one of the reasons Lilli enjoyed occasional sleepovers at her friends' houses was the chance to have brightly-colored, sugared cereal for breakfast.

When he came into the kitchen to pour himself some coffee, he saw Lilli packing up their lunch. She'd already filled their two big thermoses, too. She was dressed and ready. His girl. "Morning, Papa."

"Morning, *cara*. I think you're going to bag your first today. What do you think?"

She shrugged. "You always say that. I'll try, Papa."

"I know you will."

His mother pushed him to the table. "*Siediti. Gianni, mangi.*"

"*Inglese, Mamma.* In English." Natalia and Giovanni Accardo had immigrated to the United States with Johnny when he was three. They all became naturalized citizens, but she'd never assimilated well, and his father, enjoying the little piece of home in his home, had accommodated her refusal to learn English or any understanding of American culture. But his father had died ten years ago, and now his mother was Lilli's primary caregiver. Lilli was old beyond her fifteen years, but he needed his mother to be able to handle crises on her own. Without the language, she could not. Sometimes, he thought that he'd only made things harder for Lilli by bringing her grandmother in to live with them. But he traveled a lot for work, and he could not leave his daughter alone. Her mother had already done that.

Besides, Lilli and her nonna had bonded tightly. They adored each other. And Lilli spoke fluent Italian and, under the tutelage of his mother, could cook and bake like a pro. Between the two of them, they'd packed fifteen pounds on him.

His mother sighed, and, in heavily accented but intelligible English, said, "Sit. Eat. I bake you bread."

"Good, Mamma." He sat with his daughter and mother and ate breakfast. Then he and Lilli went off on their hunting adventure.

~oOo~

Johnny was impressed by Lilli's patience, her ability to be still for long periods. She took his instruction seriously, too. Though they enjoyed each other's company very much, spent the long drive into the woods engaged in lively debates, and chatted easily during their lunch break, they could sit side by side in perfect quiet for hours.

He was watching her, feeling mesmerized with love for her, when she shifted slightly and brought her Remington rifle to her shoulder. He turned his head slowly and saw that she was sighted on a pretty nice buck. Looked like an eight-pointer. This was the second season he'd been taking her out. She'd sighted deer twice before, but had missed both times. He resisted the urge to talk her through this chance. He'd taught her what she needed to know. Right now, she was still and focused and seemed to be waiting for her shot.

She fired just as the buck heard something from another direction, and his position shifted. Her bullet hit him in the shoulder, and he went down. But it wasn't a mortal hit. The buck was flailing and screaming, trying to get back on its feet. Lilli had to take the kill shot. He turned to her. She looked stricken, and he was afraid she'd lost her heart for this.

He started to raise his own rifle so that he could end the animal's suffering, when in his periphery he saw her sight her rifle again. The buck was down and flailing. Not an easy shot. When she took her stilling breath, he felt it rather than saw or heard it. She fired, and the buck's head dropped to the forest floor.

"Good, *cara*. Good." He put his hand on her back. She looked pale and upset.

They walked over to the buck. The kill shot had gone through his eye. A perfect shot. He watched as she dropped to her knees and stroked the buck's side. She was crying but trying not to.

He squatted at her side. "Good, Lilli. It's good to feel your kill. You have taken a life. Remember that. Guns are never toys. Never. When you point a gun at another living thing, you do it with purpose, and you do it to kill."

CHAPTER THREE

Lilli woke from the dream on full alert, on her feet and on the defensive before she was fully conscious. After a tense second, she realized where she was and concentrated on pushing the adrenaline surge down. She woke like this three or four mornings a week, sometimes in the middle of the night, too, so the process was routine.

Better than coffee, she supposed, for getting the day started quickly.

By the ambient light in the room, she guessed it wasn't long past dawn. She went to the dresser and fished her phone out of her pocket to check the time: 5:52am. Good morning, Signal Bend. She went into the shitty little bathroom.

Her stomach growled. She'd never had much of the burger she'd shared with Isaac last night, and it was pushing twenty-four hours since she'd eaten anything else. Plus, she might not strictly *need* coffee, but it was a nice start to the day nonetheless. Sadly, she had nothing in the house yet. Fuck.

Okay. Run first, then find that diner Mac Evans had recommended—Marie's, she remembered—for some breakfast. Then errands to stock the place up. She rummaged through one of her duffels and dug out a pair of spandex running shorts and a top. She combed her fingers through her hair and yanked it into a high ponytail. She found her trail running shoes in the other duffel. She intended to run through what served as residential areas, but there was a lot of gravel out here, and she didn't want to roll an ankle.

She hid her keys behind the garage. Signal Bend was probably one of those towns where nobody ever locked anything, but Lilli protected her shit. She had shit to protect.

Running through Signal Bend and the surrounding countryside gave Lilli a different insight from what she'd seen from the Camaro. The homes were widely spaced, even in town. A lot of them were obviously empty. Even banks seemed to have abandoned them. All that remained were swing sets rusting in yards, sometimes a car on blocks, weeds growing up through the engine. She passed one car with a tree growing through the back seat and out the empty rear window.

The occupied houses she passed were often lovely and quaint in their simplicity. Lilli saw lots of washing hung on lines, sheets catching the breeze and early morning sun. Just after six in the morning, and women were deep into their chores. Country life. It wasn't a world Lilli had grown up in.

She noticed that she was noticed as she ran. People— women and small children in their yards, men passing in trucks and tractors—gawked as she passed them. Isaac had told her that people didn't move to Signal Bend, so she was obviously a curiosity as a new person in their midst.

She ran for nearly an hour, judging by her pace that she'd gone about eight miles or so, when she was ready to head back. She wanted to loop rather than simply turn around, so that she could see more of the town, but she wasn't sure she had her bearings well enough to accomplish it.

Oh, well, one way to find out. She had her father's sense of direction. She'd figure it out.

It was coming up on eight o'clock, and she'd run about sixteen miles, when she turned onto the gravel road that would become the driveway to her little rental. She saw the bike pulled up in front of the garage as she crested the last hill. She'd only seen it a couple of times, never clearly or up close, but she guessed this was Isaac's Harley. He'd already gotten some intel on her, then.

And this was why she locked her shit.

She saw him sitting on the steps of the little wooden deck leading to the sliding glass back door. He was leaning back against the steps, his hands linked across his chest, his legs outstretched and crossed at the ankles. Damn, he was big. And not hard at all to look at. Well-worn black engineer boots. Dark straight-leg Levis. Black button-down shirt, folded back on his arms and open at the throat. Leather cuffs. Leather kutte. Black Ray-Bans. He looked like Mr. June in the Harley Biker Beefcake calendar.

She took all that in by the time she'd reached the garage. Without indicating that she'd also seen him, she paused at his bike, breathless from her run, and gave it a once-over. It was a nice bike, a huge black Dyna. Had some miles on it, but it was obviously well cared for.

"You like?" Isaac called over from the porch, where he was still sitting in the exact same position.

Lilli turned to him and shrugged. It pleased her to see him cock his head, as if he'd expected to startle her with his presence. "It's nice. I prefer something with a bit more speed."

She had to get her keys, which meant he was going to see that she'd hidden them. Letting him see *where* wasn't a problem—she could hide them elsewhere—but seeing *that she had* gave up a lot. Another new plan she needed. This biker was getting in her way. She went behind the garage and dug them out.

He was still sitting in the same position when she walked up to the deck. Even behind his sunglasses, his eyes were devouring her, she could tell.

"That bike is plenty fast, Sport. You ride?"

"I do."

"What d'you ride?"

"Last bike I had was a BMW—K 1300S."

He looked impressed, his eyebrow cocking up above his Ray-Bans. "Not much for the crotch rockets, but that's a lotta bike for a girl."

"Same thing you said about my car. Like I said, I like speed."

"Like *I* said, my bike's plenty fast. But it's about more than speed, Sport—or maybe you prefer *Lillian*."

She didn't miss a beat. As soon as she'd seen his bike in front of her garage, she'd known he had her name. "I don't, actually. I prefer Lilli. Three Ls, two Is. Got an early start this morning, I see."

He stood and took a long stride, so that he was standing right in front of her, looming over her. She was tall, but by her estimate, he had a good nine inches on her, at least. "Actually, haven't been to bed yet. It's still last night for me. My guy tells me you're Lillian Carson, from Austin, Texas." Brazenly, he slid his hand into the front of her running shorts, hooking his fingers over the waistband. He made a growling noise in the back of his throat. "Girl, these are the tiniest shorts I've ever seen. They distract a man from his work."

She liked his hand where it was. Her attraction to this man didn't surprise her; if she'd been asked to describe what she found sexiest, she'd pretty much describe him head to toe. And she was by no stretch of the imagination shy or prudish. Under normal circumstances, she'd have few qualms about putting him on the ground and mounting him right here. But he could be a danger to her. He had power—what she'd seen last night told her that he was *the* power in this scant little town and probably for some distance around it. It could be problematic if their needs crossed.

The question she asked herself, as her body responded enthusiastically to his touch, was whether she was better off keeping him close or keeping her distance.

She smiled up at him, seeing the sass of it reflected in the lenses of his sunglasses. "Work? That what you're here for?"

He turned his hand so that his palm was flat on her belly and then pushed it around, still partially under her shorts, until he hooked it over her left hip. She saw him notice the ink there and felt his thumb trace it. She managed to keep her heart steady and her breath even, but it was becoming a struggle. His palm was hot and rough on her bare skin.

"Well, work to start. See, my guy found something pretty interesting. I like to be forthright. I'm not much for poker. Chess is my game. Think it serves everybody best if things are laid out neat. So I thought I'd run it by you. He tells me he came up quick against a wall, looking into you. Not a lot of history. I find that…intriguing. You pop out of a pod a few months ago, all shiny and new?"

Okay. So he had a decent hacker in the club. Good to know. Not necessarily a crisis, though definitely a problem and a potential risk. At best, again, Isaac was changing the way she intended to do things. And her decision was made.

Keep him close. She couldn't say she was sorry about that.

Lilli shared Isaac's affection for forthrightness. As much of the truth as possible was always the best approach. Getting caught out in a lie always made everything more dangerous. Only as much subterfuge as was necessary.

"No, no pod. Don't suppose you'll just let that wall stand?"

He tossed his head back and laughed, a deep, mirthful sound that made Lilli's running shorts all the wetter. When he looked down at her again, his lopsided smile was broad and bright. "Sorry, no. You could make it easier on Bart and let me take a peek over it, tell me why it's there."

"Where would be the fun in that?" Her keys hooked on a finger, she reached up and undid a couple of buttons on his shirt. Around his neck, he wore a leather cord with a small silver medallion; it was nested in a moderate coverage of dark curls on his chest. She did love a hairy chest. She circled her fingers in it and felt his hand grip her hip hard.

He growled again, shaking his head. "I don't like secrets, Sport." His free hand gripped the back of her neck, and he came down close, not yet kissing her, though she could feel his beard tickling her chin.

She reached around his neck and brought his braid forward over his shoulder, pulling the elastic band loose from its end and running her finger through the middle to undo it. She wanted to see his hair. "Would you believe me if I told you it doesn't concern you?" She truly didn't know whether it did concern him, but the question she asked was not a lie.

"Everything that happens in this town concerns me." He tipped his head back and shook his hair loose. Then he pulled his sunglasses off and tossed them onto the deck. In the daylight, his eyes were even more intensely green, rimmed with dark emerald and changing gradually to peridot at the pupil. The thought occurred to her that a man like this might object to having his eyes described in terms of gemstones, and she was amused.

His hair was beautiful, thick and dark and wavy from the braid. She took a handful of it and pulled him down until his lips were heavy on hers.

He kissed her fiercely, his tongue thrusting immediately into her mouth, going deep. She matched his with her own, reveling in the scratch of his beard against her face. She hooked her arms around his neck and fed both hands into his hair, grabbing it tightly into her fists. He shifted his hands so that she was encompassed by his long, thick arms.

His chest was a broad rock wall crushing her breasts. Fuck, the man was all elemental sex. She moaned and tore her mouth free, tipping her head back to take a deep inhale. He shifted again, and she felt his hand on her throat, lightly, his thumb tracing a path down its length. She brought her head forward and met his intense gaze.

"I mean to fuck you, Sport, secrets or not. Now's the time to say you don't want it."

She grinned. She wanted it. But she'd play a little coy. "I have a pretty full day planned. Breakfast, errands. You weren't on my calendar. And I just ran a long way. I'm sweaty, and I stink."

"Yes, you do. I like it. I want you sweaty." He pulled her hips sharply against his thighs, pressing his erection to her belly. "How 'bout I buy you breakfast after?"

She released one of her hands from his hair and dragged it lightly around his neck, stopping when she got to the place where his shirt was open on his chest. She spread her fingers through the hair there, and he took in a breath and closed his eyes. "Can I eat my own, or are we sharing again?" she asked.

He opened his eyes and winked. He was enjoying the banter as much as she was. "You don't like sharing with me?"

"Barely got any of my burger last night."

"Hey—that wasn't my fault." He cocked his eyebrow at her. "I'm not hearin' you say no, Sport."

She pushed away from him, and disappointment passed over his face, but she grabbed his hand. "Gotta go in the front. I don't have a key for the slider."

He let her lead him around the house. As she unlocked the door, he said, "Nobody locks around here, you know. Folks trust each other. You want to blend in, you should pick up the customs."

She opened the door and stepped in, turning back with a welcoming gesture. "And yet you were skulking around while I was away. You'd have been inside if the door weren't locked, right?"

He came in and took the door from her to close it. "Hey, I was worried. Your cage was here, you weren't. Thought there was trouble. Who'd've thought you were running around town in your underwear. On purpose." Without even a pause, he grabbed her arm and turned her, pushing her front-first against the wall. He leaned down, and she felt his beard on the skin of her shoulder. Growling again, he licked from her shoulder to behind her right ear. "You taste great—salt and musk, and something sweet." His hands went around her hips and into her shorts, pushing between her legs. "Oh, yeah. Feel how wet you are."

The fingers of one hand probed her core; the others moved over her clit. The pads of his fingers were callused and hard, making her nerve endings catch fire. She moaned and put her hands on his, over her shorts, pressing him harder to her tender skin. Then, with a quick, forceful move, she shoved him back, gasping as his hands slid roughly out of and away from her. She turned and grabbed his kutte, yanking him back. Leaning in and going to her toes, she pressed her mouth to the base of his neck and bit down. He jerked and grabbed her ponytail, pulling her head back. She liked it rough, but she wanted to make it clear to him that she gave as good as she got.

He laughed, his eyes sparkling. "You like a tussle, do ya? Why doesn't that surprise me at all?" Grabbing her ass in his large hands, he lifted her up along his body, hooking her legs behind him, until they were crotch to crotch. He was hard against her core, and she could tell he had substantially more to offer than average. She draped her arms over his shoulders, looping his hair lightly around her fingers. He headed down the little hallway.

"Bedroom's to the—" she stopped when he automatically turned left, the correct direction. She furrowed her brow at him.

He winked. "It's a small town, Sport. Don't think there's a house I haven't been in. You're living in the Olsens' old place."

He went straight into the 'master' bedroom. When he saw the bed, though, he stopped and let her legs drop until she was on her feet. "Well, gotta say, I expected sheets and pillows."

There was nothing on the mattress but her sleeping bag. "Told you I had errands. I need to get some bedding. Are you saying you're too soft to fuck on a bare mattress?"

"Saucy wench." He put his hands around her waist and tossed her onto the bed. Before she could react, he snatched the sleeping bag out from under her, dropping it to the floor. Then he had her foot, yanking her running shoe off without untying it. Sock. The other shoe. The other sock. He took her bare feet in his hands and pressed his thumbs into her arches. He hit exactly the right spot to make her feet and legs—which had very recently run a long distance—relax exquisitely, and she moaned.

"Oh, I do like that sound." He loomed over her and grabbed the waistband of her shorts. She lifted her hips, and he tugged them down and away in one swift, determined move. He stood at the side of the bed and looked down at her greedily. Seemed like she had the kind of effect on him that he had on her. She sat up and scooted to sit on the bed in front on him.

When she put her hands on the big silver buckle of his belt, he growled again. *She* liked *that* sound, felt it right between her legs. As she opened his belt and began to unbutton his jeans, he bent over her and grabbed the hem of her snug running tank, his blunt nails grazing her back as he pulled it up. The tank served as bra, too, so it was tight. She stopped what she was doing and helped him pull it off. Now, she was nude.

"Fuck. You're gorgeous, Sport." The words were little more than a breath. When she looked up and met his eyes, his expression had changed to something intense and unreadable.

She opened his jeans. She was pleased to see that he wore boxer briefs—in this case, black. Considering the Johnny Cash vibe he had going generally, couture-wise, they were probably always black. As far as Lilli was concerned, there were only two ways for a man to wear underwear—boxer briefs or not at all. The lump of his erection was impressive and extended down his leg, even as it swelled and curved.

She slid her hands into his waistband and pulled his length free. Wow. Nice. Long and thick. And hard as steel. She wrapped her hands around him and squeezed. His hips rocked toward her as he growled again.

He shrugged his kutte off his shoulders and, while she held his cock in her hands, folded it and leaned over to lay it on the dresser. Lilli thought that said a lot about this man. She let go of him and raised her hands to unbutton the rest of the buttons of his shirt. He watched her, his hands on her shoulders. When she was done, he shrugged it off and let it drop to the floor in a pool.

Lilli took in the wide expanse of his chest. Jesus Christ, he was beautiful. Arms, chest, abs, all of it perfectly defined, dark curls covering his pecs and then tapering to a trail into the black nest around his cock. Both shoulders and his arms to his elbows were covered in intricate blackwork ink. His chest and belly were free of ink. He was standing before her, tall and broad and beautiful, his long, sable hair loose on his back. Without thinking at all, she grabbed his hips and leaned forward to press her lips to his hard, ridged belly. She ran her tongue through the hair around his navel. She couldn't recall the last time she'd been so viscerally attracted to another human being. It almost had to be a pheromone thing, their chemistry just perfectly in sync.

She felt his hand in her hair, curling her ponytail around his fist, forcing her to look up at him. "I want head. I want that fuckable, red mouth on me."

He did, did he? She smirked at him. "Yeah? What are you gonna do for me? Tit for tat, love."

He reached down and took her left nipple between his fingers, giving it sharp tug, making her gasp and moan. His mouth on her ear, making her heart race, he whispered, "Tit for tat, huh? How 'bout I make you scream until your throat cramps? You swallow, Sport, and I'll make it happen twice." He stood straight again, challenge in his eyes.

After a beat to steady her voice, she smiled at him. "You think you've got that kind of stamina?"

"You doubt me? By the time we leave for breakfast, you won't ever again."

Gauntlet thrown. She nodded and sucked his length into her mouth. "Ah, yeah. Yeah," he growled. It had been awhile, and he was big, but she was good at this. She relaxed her throat and took him all in. "Fuck!" he groaned, and then his hips were moving hard. His fist in her ponytail and his hips moving like that, he had control of the situation. She didn't want that. She gave head on her terms. She put her hand around his balls and squeezed, steadily increasing the pressure until she had his attention.

"Hey! What the fuck're you doin', Sport?"

Easing the pressure on his balls, she pulled him out of her mouth and licked her lips. Meeting his glare steadily, she said, "My rules. I set the rhythm. Hold still or let go of my hair." He stared for a few seconds and then nodded. Since he didn't let go of her hair, she figured he meant to hold still.

And he did. As she worked him, taking him deep, sucking, licking, nipping lightly, he kept his fist loosely in her ponytail but did not constrict or try to control her movements. As he got close, his hips began to flex gently, but he tried to stop. He was grunting rhythmically, in time with her movements, until he put his other hand on her head, his fingers gripping her scalp. "Now, now, yeah, fuck yeah." When he came, he held her head tightly to him, but she didn't care. He filled her mouth with hot, heavy liquid, and she swallowed around him. He tasted sweet and salty. Yep. Pheromones.

When he was finished, she pulled away and wiped her mouth with the back of her hand. He was staring at her, dazed, his eyes at half-mast. "That was fucking incredible." She pushed back on the bed and spread her legs wide. "Better not have worn you out."

He grinned impishly and stripped the rest of his clothes off. "No way. I'm tireless." As he tossed his jeans away, he caught his wallet chain and pulled the wallet up. He took two condoms out and dropped the wallet onto the pile that was his jeans. Then he crawled over her on the bed. Propped on his hands, he hovered. "You are a fuckin' sexy bitch, you know that?" He bent his arms and came down to kiss her.

She grabbed his hair in her fists and pulled him down to lie on her. Before he settled, she tried to flip them over, but he was quite heavy, and she only managed to rock him a bit. Laughing against her mouth, he pushed her shoulder flat on the mattress. "I don't think so. My rules now." His hands holding her shoulders down, he kissed along her jawline to her ear, sucking on the lobe for several intense seconds, then continued his journey, licking and sucking his way down her neck, over her collarbone, to her breast.

He was still soft; she could feel him on her leg, but when he drew her nipple between his teeth, sucking firmly and making her cry out and arch her back off the bed, she felt him lengthen and turn to steel. "Ah, yeah. That's it, baby. Your tits are so firm and sweet." He suckled her again, growling. The vibrations of sound against her flesh made her quiver. The tickle and scratch of his beard made her shiver. He released her shoulders to cup her breasts, and she wove her fingers into his hair. He kissed a trail across her chest and paid the same careful attention to the other breast. His hands moved down her sides. His mouth followed, kissing down her belly, his tongue laving her belly button, and then continuing downward.

It all felt great, but Lilli was too turned on for this sweet bullshit. She didn't want him to make love to her. She wanted him to fuck her. He was supposed to be making her scream. Twice. She yanked hard on his hair, and he pulled his head up, his brow wrinkled. "You yanked?"

"Are you gonna fuck me or not?"

She'd hurt his feelings. That surprised her. Isaac did not read like a guy who preferred satiny, sweet lovemaking. He read like a guy who liked a rough, leathery grapple. As she did.

He pulled himself back over her so that they were face to face. "You want to get fucked, Sport? You're gonna get fucked." He reached over to the corner of the mattress, where he'd laid the condoms. As soon as he'd rolled one on, he grabbed her leg and shoved it straight up in the air, pushing it back to her chest, spreading her wide. He gave her a look that said he'd expected that to be uncomfortable, and it was indeed a stretch, but she had years of yoga to prepare her to get fucked like this, and she just looked steadily back at him. He yanked her onto her side and shoved himself into her, letting go of her leg and pressing it down with his shoulder.

Propping himself on one hand, with the other he grabbed her nipple and pinched it hard. She cried out. Okay, this is more what she had in mind. He was thrusting into her deep and fast, pulling and twisting her nipple. The unfamiliar position gave her few options to participate; he had her fully under his control. So she went with it, savoring the deep intensity of his sideways entry, the sharp thrill of his fingers around her nipple. She was elevating quickly, heat pooling in her joints. She started moaning loudly every time he went deep. She was working her other breast as savagely as he was working the one he had; when he noticed, his eyes got dark, and he sped up his thrusts.

50

When she could remember to open her eyes, she watched him, saw him concentrating. Sweat ran down his temples into his beard. His chest was wet with it, dewy drops beading in the hair over his pecs. Knowing that he had to work so hard to keep his promise thrilled her endlessly.

Then he grabbed her leg and pulled out, flipping her to her belly with a growl. He was growling almost constantly now. He yanked her onto her knees, grabbing her ponytail and yanking her head back, and he was inside her again, pounding hard, the hair on his legs scratching at her thighs every time they slammed together. Okay, she was coming; he was so fucking deep, stretching her wide. She bucked against him, making as much noise as he was, her breath coming in something like shrieks now. "Fuck, Isaac. Fuck, it's good."

"Not enough," he rasped. "I want you screaming, baby."

He yanked her hair again, pulling her off her hands, bringing her back hard against his chest. With his other hand, he reached around and slapped her clit sharply. The sensation was like an electric bolt through her, and she cried out and arched hard. He did it again. And again. Then over and over, quick, sharp slaps, until she was coming so hard she could feel her juices running down her legs, even as his thrusts filled her, and she was screaming and screaming.

When it was over, he laid her down on the bed, and she relaxed, her muscles liquid, her brain muzzy. That was way up on the list of her best orgasms ever. Top three, anyway. Maybe higher. But he wasn't done. He was still moving inside her, still hard as granite. He hadn't come. "I owe you another one," he murmured behind her before biting down on her shoulder.

CHAPTER FOUR

Isaac was simultaneously exhausted, exhilarated, and so turned on he thought his cock might well explode inside her. Lilli. Beautiful name, beautiful woman.

Lilli. He'd have to get used to that. He'd known her only twelve hours, but 'Sport' had stuck in his head.

She was completely relaxed beneath him, breathing heavily, her strong, firm limbs pliable, giving easily to his touch as he moved inside her. She was tight, the lingering spasms of her climax still holding him firmly. Drenched with sweat, as he was, she smelled fantastic. He much preferred the natural scent of a woman to the acidic crap so many of them sprayed all over themselves, and Lilli's scent was intoxicating to him. Her taste, too. Damn, she made him hot.

"I owe you another one." He bit down on her shoulder, sucking her sweet sweat into his mouth. "You think you can take me again?" Her eyes still closed, she grinned.

He reared back and pulled out of her in one fast move. Then he grabbed her legs and flipped her to her back. She laughed, and what a sound it was, rich and full of pleasure. He didn't know what her story was—he'd damn sure find out—but she was something special, something to behold. Something dangerous.

Maybe it was just her newness. Living in a town like this, being single and wanting it that way, a man tended to cycle through a smallish number of willing women. Even the girls who came from other towns to hang out at the clubhouse were the same every week. Fucks got familiar pretty fast. The number of women not looking for more was even smaller. Isaac had been slowing down of late, wary of women looking for his ink. Not gonna happen.

But this wild thing writhing under him and looking up at him with bright, avid eyes—they were grey—she was something else entirely.

He hooked her legs over his shoulders and sank into her, pushing her thighs to her chest. She was strong and limber and hadn't yet balked at anything he'd done—no stretch, no force, no depth had been too much. In fact, she wanted more. She'd taken his cock without complaint. Usually he had to soften a woman up a bit first, get her ready, but Lilli had thrown that back in his face, wanting him to come at her hard.

He was at her hard now, thrusting with all the force he could muster, even feeling the intensity of it himself, his hips and thighs feeling bruised as they slammed against her. She was grunting and moaning, clawing at his arms. He was beginning to have trouble holding himself off. The amazing head she'd given him had bought him a lot of time for a fuck this strenuous, but she was a wild one, hot as hell, and they been going at it for awhile. He tried to distract himself with mundane thoughts, but he just didn't want to. He wanted to be present here, feeling her, hearing her, smelling her.

She brought her legs up even tighter to her chest, and then her feet were on his shoulders, and she was pushing against him hard. Confused at first, he looked down at her and saw in her eyes what she wanted. He knocked her feet off and gathered her up in his arms, coming up on his knees and lying backwards, putting her on top of him, her feet under his arms. He shifted to straighten his legs. "You want to ride me, that it?"

"Fuck yeah." She leaned back a little, her hands on his thighs, and did just that. He wrapped his arms around her legs and just held on. Jesus, the muscles in her legs rippled beautifully as she drove her hips down onto him, riding him every bit as hard as he'd ridden her. Her head was thrown back, and her ponytail brushed his legs. Somehow he thought that, that silky tickle across his knees, was the thing that was going to undo him. He'd promised to make her scream again.

He sat up and grabbed her arms, folding her whole body tightly to his chest. Staring deeply into his eyes, she stopped, panting, her breath leaving her body in sexy little moans. For several beats, they simply sat there, tangled together in a complex knot, sweaty and breathless, staring into each other's eyes.

In that look Isaac felt something shift into place between them; he felt it like a thrill up his spine. He had no idea what it meant. But he grabbed her ponytail and brought her mouth to his, sucking the sweat from her upper lip and then kissing her deeply. But softly. She went with it, kissing him back in kind, her hands moving into his wet hair and holding him close. Suddenly, she pulled back with a little gasp and stared at him, her brow furrowing. She'd felt it, too, he knew.

Something dangerous.

She yanked on his hair. "I thought you were gonna make me scream again. That was the deal, right?" She kissed him again, biting his lower lip hard at the end. He tasted blood.

"Fuck! Bloodthirsty bitch." He rolled abruptly, putting her on her back. Then he grabbed her ankles from behind him and held them out wide as he pounded into her, gaining more and more speed with every thrust. If this wasn't enough for her, then she was just too fucking much for him.

"Oh, fuck! Yeah! Yeah! Fuck! Harder!" Harder? Jesus Christ. He found something more to give her. And then, thank the blessed baby Jesus, she was screaming, her nails embedded in his forearms. She was tight, so tight, around his cock, and he finally, finally, finally let himself go with a long, loud, extremely relieved groan that came through his chest, his throat, his clenched teeth like it was being yanked out of his very cells. He came for fucking ever.

When it was done, he dropped in a heap on top of her, between her legs. He was still inside her. He was gratified to hear the strain in her breathing, so like his own. At least he'd worn her out, too.

She laughed. "Okay, fuck. That was fantastic. I won't doubt you again."

"See that you don't." He kissed her cheek. With a weary sigh—he was wondering about the logic of this kind of exertion, since he hadn't slept last night and wouldn't have the chance again until late tonight—he pulled out of her and sort of dropped off her to lie at her side. Normally, he'd be up and getting dressed right now. When he fucked, he did it at the clubhouse or at the chick's house, and he did not cuddle. Cuddling was where complications happened. But he didn't think he could move.

Plus, he wasn't done touching her yet.

She rolled to her side and grabbed her phone from the nightstand. "9:30. Does Marie's stop serving breakfast at some point? Because you owe me eggs and waffles." She put the phone down and started to roll onto her back again, but Isaac stopped her. Instead, he scooted closer as she lay on her side.

She had a line of text inked up her left side, from her hip to about even with her tits. It wasn't English. That and a very pretty, intricate black and grey butterfly, about the size of his fist, on her left shoulder blade were her only tattoos.

He traced the line of text up her side. "Marie's serves breakfast all day. What does this say?"

She looked back over her shoulder at him and didn't answer right away. Then she said, "It's Italian: *L'amor che muove il sole e l'altre stelle.*" The words in her voice were beautiful; she spoke as if she were fluent in the language.

"That's beautiful. What's it mean?" He spread his hand over her hip and rubbed a long oval over her thigh. He could not seem to stop touching her.

"The love which moves the sun and the other stars." He couldn't read her expression.

That sounded familiar to him, and he took a second and searched his head. "That's Dante, right?"

She turned fast, landing on her back. "Yeah. It's the last line of *The Divine Comedy*. You know Dante?" The look on her face was naked shock. That had rattled her. Not the fight last night, not a gun to her head, not him finding her and knowing her name, not the epic fuck. The fact that he knew Dante—that flattened her. He was offended.

"We hicks do go to school, you know."

Now her look was skeptical. "You went to a school where you read Dante?"

No, he hadn't. He grinned. "Well, we used to have a town library, too. I like to read. Always have. I told you, there's not a lot to do around here. So, why do you have Dante inked into your side?"

"My dad's favorite book." Instead of saying more, she got off the bed. "I'm starved. You owe me breakfast. I'm getting in the shower."

"Want company? I need one, too." He wiggle his eyebrows at her. "Always good to conserve water—we're on wells out here."

She shook her head. "That's okay. I'll go fast, leave you some." She walked into the bathroom and closed the door.

Isaac lay back, feeling like he'd done something wrong and not sure why he cared. But there was some insight there into the mystery that was Lilli. He'd need to work that out. He still had the condom on, now looking sad and deflated on his mostly-soft cock. He pulled it off and went hunting for a place to discard it. He ended up dropping it in the trash under the kitchen sink.

~oOo~

Lilli had refused to ride with him, saying she needed to have her car so that she could do errands after breakfast. So she followed him to Marie's. On the ride, Isaac thought about the events of the past half-day. Far more eventful than usual, they were.

Jimmy had sacrificed only three fingernails to the truth. Meg had tried a couple of dodges around the facts, but Isaac was nothing if not perceptive, and after Vic pulled the nail from the middle finger of his right hand, with its broken wrist, she'd caved completely, ignoring Jimmy's frantic head-shaking.

So now, Isaac knew that the St. Louis crew the Horde was beefing with, The Northside Knights, had some kind of new player backing them, and they were looking to annex the cookers down the I-44 corridor—which was, in its entirety, from Illinois to Oklahoma, Horde turf. They'd just about turned Jimmy and Meg, among the biggest cookers in Crawford County, but they were leaning hard on Jimmy to prime Will Keller for a buyout of his property—a family farm of a hundred-fifty acres, held by his bloodline for a century.

All of that for three fingernails. Well, he'd known she'd be the weak link. Meg didn't know why they wanted the property, but Isaac had a damn good idea. There was a lot of dense forest on that acreage—about half the property. The canopy was tight. Good obstruction from satellites. Built right, a fucking meth mass-production center could hide in there. Right smack in the middle of the pipeline.

Mass-produced crank on a scale like that was not going to happen on Isaac's watch. No enemy of the Horde was going to own property on Horde turf, period. A backer for the Northsiders with that kind of capital—someone who scared Jimmy Sullivan enough that he was willing to be tortured rather than name—was a very serious, very dangerous problem for the Horde, and for Signal Bend itself.

And then there was Ms. Lillian Carson, allegedly from Austin, Texas, but with no discernable Texas lilt in her voice. Bart had come up against the wall quickly, but he hadn't yet been able to breach it. He'd been perplexed, because she didn't seem to have worked hard to hide the fact that she was hiding. Her created history would pass the most cursory and rudimentary of checks, something typically businesslike—to rent a house, say, or get a job— but anyone who thought she might be up to something would quickly know she was. Conversely, the wall itself seemed strong. According to Bart, that was a very strange circumstance. He'd said it enthusiastically. Young Bartholomew liked himself a puzzle.

Interesting that she'd shown up the exact same day that Jimmy had gone off the rez. Isaac couldn't understand how those dots connected. Maybe they didn't; maybe it was pure coincidence that had brought trouble to town on two roads at the same time. But Isaac was paying attention.

He wasn't one normally to believe in coincidence, at least not without some deep inquiry first, but he found himself really hoping that whatever Lilli was hiding, it wasn't something that would get in his way. He liked her. He would hate to hurt her.

He would, if he had to. If she threatened his people or his town, he'd end her without hesitation. But he'd be unhappy about it.

Isaac felt sure her name was really Lilli. He caught that vibe right away. She seemed perfectly comfortable correcting his usage from Lillian to Lilli, as if it was a reflex born of long habit. He wasn't nearly so sure about "Carson." At least "Sport," he knew, was hers. He knew because he'd named her himself.

He pulled into Marie's, Lilli right behind him. Not too crowded—ten o'clock was late in the day for breakfast. The lunch crowd would be coming in soon. For now, there were only four other vehicles in the lot, including the Sullivans' pickup. That could be awkward. It wasn't until right then that Isaac realized what a stir he was about to cause, the President of the Night Horde walking into Marie's for a late breakfast with the new girl everyone was talking about. The smokin' hot new girl everyone was talking about. The one who'd been seen by the majority of the town this morning, running all over in what people were calling, variously, her underwear or a bathing suit.

Yeah, the tongues would be wagging this Sunday after church. And everywhere, every minute, from now until then. Oh, well. Been awhile since the gossips had something good to chew on.

He dismounted and put his helmet on the handlebars, then walked over and opened the Camaro's door for Lilli. She gave him a surprised smile and stepped out. Similar getup as yesterday: same low-heeled black boots, slim, low-waisted jeans, simple t-shirt—yellow today—that left just the slimmest bit of belly showing. An extremely distracting slimmest bit of firm, flat belly. No jacket; too hot for that. Aviator-style Ray-Ban sunglasses. She didn't seem to carry a purse. He added that simple fact to the growing list of fucking sexy things about her. Women with big purses freaked him out. What the fuck was so important they had to carry a damn suitcase with them everywhere they went?

Her hair was caught back in a ponytail again. It was long and thick, a rich dark brown, with just a hint of red in the sun. She did this fussy little thing with the ponytail, wrapping a lock of hair around it, tucking the end in. He'd watched her do it this morning. It was fussy, but he liked it. He didn't know why.

That was absolutely the only fussy thing she'd done. She wore no makeup or scent—and he would have protested if she'd gone to cover up the way she smelled naturally. Today, she wore no jewelry but the big silver rings, and he was beginning to think those, like his own rings, were more practical than ornamental. She'd done some real damage to Meg's throat last night.

He almost took her hand to escort her into Marie's but thought better of it, and instead put his hand on her back, bringing her gently forward to walk in front of him. When the bell over the door jingled to announce their entry, the ten other people in the diner—six customers, two waitresses (including Marie), and, peering over the service area from the kitchen, Dave (her husband and the cook) and Evan, the dishwasher—every one of them turned to see who it was and then stopped to gape. Gotta love the small town life.

Lilli, to her credit, seemed unfazed. She smiled and nodded at whomever met her eyes. He led her to his usual booth; they passed the Sullivans on the way. Jimmy's three nailless fingers were thickly bandaged, and his arm was in a cast. Havoc had driven them both to the urgent care center in Cuba and had seen to it that they told the right story about their injuries. From the look of Meg, though, her injuries hadn't really gotten started until Havoc got them back home. Jimmy was right handed, but he'd obviously overcome that to beat the shit out of his wife with his left. Isaac felt bad for her, and pissed at Jimmy, but it was hardly the first time Meg had walked around town with bruises on her face. Like a lot of women in this part of the world, she was well acquainted with the feel of her man's knuckles on her skin.

Besides, one of those bruises was Isaac's. She'd come by that one honestly, but he didn't relish hitting women. He didn't give them a pass when they came at him, but he took no pleasure in it, as he had breaking Ed Foss's nose last night. That had been satisfying. Backhanding Meg had been expedient.

Marie came over before their asses had fully settled on the seats. She turned the coffee cups over and poured for both of them.

"Hey, Ike." Fuck, he hated that. No matter how much influence he'd earned in this town, he'd not been able to get that name off people's lips. He supposed he should be glad they'd finally dropped the "Little," but that had taken his father's death, even though he'd dwarfed the old man by more than six inches and sixty pounds.

Lilli had pulled a menu from behind the napkin dispenser and was perusing the options. It wasn't often that people read the menu; almost everybody who ate here was a regular and had long ago memorized the offerings, which hadn't changed, except for the seasonal flavors of pies and fresh jams, since the day they'd opened.

"Hey, Marie. This is Lilli. Lilli, meet Marie, the best baker in five counties."

Lilli smiled at her, and Marie smiled warmly back. "Only five? Must be losin' my edge. What can I get ya, sugar?"

Reading the menu, Lilli ordered. "I'll have the waffles and eggs—sunny-side up."

Marie didn't bother to write the order down. "What meat you want—sausage links, bacon, or ham?"

"Bacon—oh, and can I get fruit instead of the hash browns?"

Isaac dropped his head to hide the smirk he couldn't control. Marie gave her a look. "Comes with hash browns, not fruit."

Lilli cocked her head. "Um, okay. Well, how about hold the hash browns and I'll have fruit extra?"

Okay, he should probably help her out, but he was enjoying it far too much. Marie put her hand on her hip. "It *comes*. With *hash browns*. And unless you want a piece of fruit pie or some orange juice, fruit's not on the menu."

Lilli blinked, and Isaac took pity on her. "You got the order, Marie. Thanks, hon."

Clearly vexed, Marie nodded at him and went back to the counter. Then Isaac laughed. He tossed his head back, put his hand on his belly and guffawed. Lilli was just as obviously annoyed as Marie.

"What the fuck was that?"

"You don't order off the menu at a place like this, Sport. You'd think a country girl from Texas would know that."

She didn't miss a beat. "Austin's not country. And I hate potatoes."

"Nobody hates potatoes."

"Just told you I did."

"You were eating French fries last night."

"French fries are different."

"Yeah, that's weird."

By way of response, she sat back, her arms crossed, and he conceded the point with a shrug. He watched as she poured three creamers and the sugar from three packets into her coffee. That was barely coffee anymore—why the hell even bother? He took a sip of his, black and strong. Then he just watched her. The sun was streaming in through the front window and slanting across her, giving her hair a reddish gleam and making her grey eyes sparkle. He shifted in the booth as his cock filled out a little and caught the seam in his jeans. He had half a mind to bail on the day and take her back to her bare mattress.

"How'd you know there wasn't trouble?"

Coming out of his increasingly sexual reverie, he shook his head. "Huh?"

She sipped that sweet confection in her cup and gave him a curious look. "You said you were worried there was trouble when you saw my car but not me. But you were all relaxed, leaning back on my deck steps when I got back from my run. How'd you know there wasn't trouble?"

Because he'd gotten a call from CJ that he'd ridden past her running down the road in her little top and littler shorts.

She'd attracted a great deal of attention this morning. She'd attracted attention last night, too. People were interested. And now they were eating together. Again, actually. He rolled his eyes. Town gossips would have them engaged by Saturday.

"Got a call from a brother who saw you on the road. Lots of people saw you, Sport. You might want to cover up some if you're gonna run all over town. You'll give the gossips tongue hernias or somethin'."

Marie brought their breakfasts—waffles, eggs up, and bacon for Lilli, and his usual order of steak, eggs over easy, and biscuits. Hash browns all around. He saw Lilli make a face at them on her plate. He hoped Marie hadn't seen as she refilled their coffees.

Isaac winked at Marie. "Thanks, hon. You mind leaving the pot?" He needed to fucking mainline the coffee today. His days of pulling all-nighters with impunity were behind him.

Marie set the pot on the table. "You bet, Ike. Let me know if you need anything else."

As soon as Marie walked away from their booth, Lilli started pushing the hash browns away from the rest of her breakfast, as if they were a contaminant. Isaac thought it was cute as hell, and he sat and watched her. She looked up, and he smiled and held her eyes for a second.

Dropping her gaze to his plate, she gestured with her fork. "I didn't think you ordered."

"Marie knows my order."

"You have the same thing every day?" She grinned at him like that was the craziest thing she'd heard today.

He just shrugged. A girl who didn't like potatoes didn't get to judge anybody's food quirks. "How's your breakfast?"

She had a mouthful of waffles. "Really good, 'cept for the hash browns."

He rolled his eyes at her. She was fucking cute.

~oOo~

By the time they'd finished their breakfast and were on their way out, the diner had filled just about full, and every eye on the damn place was on them. They had to run the gamut, greeting everyone. He introduced her as Lilli Carson, who'd just moved in to the Olsens' old place. Lilli was gracious and beautiful, but he could see that she was uncomfortable. So was he. They were being thrown together in a way he hadn't calculated, and they still hadn't known each other for even one day.

When they got out of the diner, Lilli turned to him, sliding her sunglasses back on, and said, "Thanks for breakfast. I'll see ya," and walked quickly to her car. He almost let her go—they had an audience. He didn't need to turn back to the diner to know he'd see a window full of faces. Anything he did to say goodbye to her in a way appropriate to the morning they'd spent together would further heat up fevered town fantasies.

But he didn't want to leave it that way. Besides, he needed to keep her close. There were things he needed to learn about her. Couldn't have her sneaking up on him. So let the town tongues wag. Fuck—give them something to wag about. He caught up with her in four long strides, just as she was reaching for the door handle. Déjà vu. He wrapped his hand around her wrist and, with his other hand on her shoulder, pushed her against the car.

"Where you goin' so fast?"

She nodded toward the diner. "We have an audience, and I have shit to do. But thanks, really. It's been a good time."

He slid his knee between her legs and moved his hand from her shoulder to her neck. "Told ya we'd have fun together. Don't think I'm done with you yet, Sport."

She smiled, just a little upturning at the corners of her sweet mouth. "Might be done with you."

"Are you?"

She looked up at him, that little smile still lifting the corners of her mouth. He pushed her sunglasses onto the top of her head so he could see her bright eyes. She hadn't answered. "So, are you?"

By way of reply, she hooked her hand in the open throat of his shirt and pulled him down. When his lips touched hers, she opened her mouth wide to him. She was so damn hot. Forgetting the audience, forgetting the secrets, even forgetting the bullshit he was going to have to spend the rest of his day dealing with, he leaned his weight into her, letting her feel how incredibly turned on she made him, and kissed her like he was ready to have her right there, standing in the gravel lot of Marie's, the cross on the steeple of St. John's Methodist Church making a shadow over them. Because he was. They made out much longer, and he might well do it.

With a frustrated growl, he pulled away. "You get to your errands. I'll see you. Soon, I think." He smiled and leaned down again, trying on the sound of her name as a whisper in her ear. "Lilli."

She cocked her head and gave him an appraising look. Then she pushed away from the car, got in, and drove away.

Isaac went to his bike without even bothering to look back at Marie's.

~oOo~

Bart was sitting at the bar with two laptops open. The clubhouse had a powerful satellite dish, so internet was not a problem there. Neither was TV. They had a huge set on the wall and threw open the doors to the town for sports events. The big fights and races. Football. Baseball. Hockey. A lot of people were fans of some or all of the St. Louis teams, and they came to the clubhouse to watch and to drink free booze. Just another public service of the Night Horde MC.

Isaac walked up and put his hand on Bart's shoulder. The youngest member, he was their intelligence officer. Very handy, scary smart, and a serious gadget geek. From what Isaac could tell—and he knew his way around a computer okay—Bart was a gifted hacker. He'd not yet encountered intel he couldn't get his hands on. So Isaac was concerned to see that he looked stressed out.

Part of that might be the six empty Red Bull cans on the bar. Bart was a big guy—nowhere near as big as Isaac, but six feet, probably 200 pounds, mostly muscle—but six Red Bulls was a shit ton of caffeine.

"Tell me, bro. What's the deal?"

Bart raked his hands over his dusky blond crew cut. He spoke quickly, his voice shaking. He was practically tweaking on caffeine. "This wall is military grade, Isaac. Fuck, it's practically weaponized. I'm worried that I'm gonna get tagged poking around too much more. I'm in full stealth mode, but I feel like I'm leaving a little bit more of my ass hanging out every time I go at that fucker. I don't get it. If she's got a secret that needs this kind of security, why did she put a fucking neon sign on top of it? Took me three minutes to find out her history is faked. I been at this wall fourteen hours straight, and I'm nowhere. No. Where. She just does not exist before three months ago."

That was certainly interesting news. Made Lilli a lot more dangerous. "It's okay, man. Pull back. Get some rest. I'll find what we need to know another way. No sense pushing our luck here. Who the fuck knows who's guarding her story."

"When I said military grade, boss, I didn't mean it metaphorically. Ten to one this is military protection. I don't know what the fuck that means she's hiding, but I'm sure that's who's helping her. Be careful."

"Noted. Now, I'm serious. Go back and crash. You did good, my brother."

Bart smiled gratefully and closed his laptops. He trudged to the hallway leading to the dorm rooms. Isaac watched him go, thinking.

With a wave of his hand, Isaac called over LaVonne, one of the regular girls, who gave especially good head. She'd been lolling on one of the couches, reading a magazine. When she saw Isaac call her over, she came right away, adjusting her skirt up and her knit top down.

"Yeah, Isaac?" Nobody attached to the club called him Ike. That, he could control.

"Do me a solid, sugar, and go back with Bart, help him relax."

She looked a little disappointed at first; Isaac figured she thought he was calling her over to service him. But she recovered quickly and smiled. Bart was a decent looking guy, not a bad hookup for a club girl. There were uglier patches, that was sure. "Sure thing!" LaVonne turned with a little shimmy in her hip and sashayed after him.

Isaac sighed and went behind the bar to pour himself a cup of what was clearly stale, sludgy coffee from much earlier in the morning. He was too tired to wait for a fresh pot, so he chewed on the black goo he'd oozed into his cup.

One problem addressed and not even remotely solved. On to the next. Maybe he'd have better luck there.

INTERLUDE: 1997

"Mr. Accardo, Lilli's on Line 3 for you."

"Thanks, Anne."

Johnny picked up the handset and pressed the blinking button for Line 3. "Hey, Lillibell. What can I do for my little girl?" Not so little any longer. She was graduating high school in two days, and in three months, she'd be headed off to college. He and his mother would be alone.

As soon as she spoke, he knew it was trouble. "Papa, I need you to come home. It's Nonna."

~oOo~

Johnny walked up the front walk with a leaden heart. This was the second time in his daughter's young life that he'd walked into this house when she'd been alone with the body of a woman she loved. Her mother, when she was ten. Now, eight years later, his mother. Her grandmother, her beloved Nonna, the woman who taken the place of mother in her life.

Lilli was sitting quietly on the living room sofa, still the red floral piece Mena had so carefully picked out when they'd bought the house. The living room was rarely in use, and it was strange to see Lilli, wearing jeans and a t-shirt from one of the concerts she'd been to, her hair loose and hanging mostly over her face, sitting in the center of that sofa, her face without affect. He came and sat next to her.

He picked up her hand, lying slack in her lap. "Lilli, talk to me."

She turned her head. He'd been wrong; her face was not without affect. Her eyes were stormy with feeling. "She's

70

still on the floor in the kitchen. I called 911, and they came, but when they decided she was dead, they just went away. I'm waiting for someone else to come to take her away."

Johnny could not even grieve for the loss of his mother, his beautiful, obstreperous, hovering mother, who had filled their lives with the brilliant aroma of Italian love. He would have to set that aside. His daughter was his only concern. He pulled her to his chest and held her tightly. "Tell me what happened, *cara*."

"She was in the kitchen, and I was watching TV in the den. She was singing at the top of her lungs. She sounded terrible, and I couldn't hear my show over her. I was thinking, 'shut the fuck up, Nonnie!' And then she did. I heard a crash, and when I came in, she was just lying on the floor. Her eyes were open. The last thing I thought about her was that I wanted her to shut up." She began to weep. Johnny was glad of it; the quiet calm had unsettled him. It had taken her weeks to come out of a fugue like that after Mena's death.

"Oh, *cara mia*. It's not the last thing you thought about her. You're thinking about her now. She was singing. She died happy. She died happy."

He knew it was true. It helped to know it was true.

CHAPTER FIVE

Lilli pulled into the garage of her rented house. She'd had to go all the way to the little shopping center on the far outskirts of the St. Louis suburbs to find everything she needed. Besides the 7 Eleven, there wasn't even a grocery in Signal Bend. But now, after spending several hours and several hundred dollars, she had a full stock of food and sundries. She had fresh linens for the bed and bath. She had the small appliances that the house had lacked— coffeemaker, toaster oven, things like that. And she had the supplies she needed adapt one of the small extra bedrooms to a room she could work in.

She opened the trunk and started hauling her purchases into the house. She supposed she could have parked on the grass, closer to the house, for the unloading, but she hadn't thought of it. She didn't really have a country mindset.

Once she had everything in the house, she spent an hour or so setting things up: getting the new linens in the wash (the rental thankfully had both washer and dryer), organizing the kitchen, trying to make the dreary little hut into something livable. Then she went into the smallest bedroom and started setting that up, too.

It was furnished with a twin-size bed and a small dresser. She pushed both of these to the side and built the small, cheap desk she'd bought. When it was together, she carried one of the chairs from the dinette set in; it would serve fine as a desk chair. She wasn't sure what to do with the trash she was making; she supposed she'd have to burn most of it, since it was unlikely the town had residential trash pickup. For now, though, she piled it all in the third bedroom. When the furniture was handled, she covered the windows with heavy black paper, then drew the drapes. She changed the doorknob to one that locked. It wasn't a great security solution; the door itself was only a typical interior door and thus wouldn't put up much resistance to someone determined to get in, but the lock would slow them down, anyway.

That room set up the way she wanted, she put the linens in the dryer, grabbed the carton that had held the toaster oven, and went back out to the garage. She'd chosen this property for its seclusion, so the precautions she was taking were probably more than she needed. But she was a cautious woman, and sometimes more really was more. She went in the side door of the garage, so that she could leave the overhead closed. With no windows in the building, the garage was near pitch black, only the dim light rimming the doors to ease the gloom. Lilli turned on the overhead fluorescents and opened the trunk of the Camaro.

It looked like the trunk was empty, but Lilli leaned in and pulled the vinyl backing away from the back seat. Instead of the innards of spring and padding one usually would find inside an upholstered seat, the Camaro held a small armory: An M16 assault rifle, an M25 sniper rifle, three semi-automatic handguns, and a small assortment of other types of weapons for melee and mayhem. There was also a satellite phone and a very special laptop hidden in the seat. Lilli collected the latter two items and put them in the toaster oven box. The weapons she left where they were; she had her favorite sidearm in the bedroom already, and she didn't expect to need the rest for some time yet. She closed up the back of the seat, shut the trunk, and left the garage, turning off the lights and locking it behind her.

When she got back into the house, she took the laptop and satellite phone into the office she'd just set up. She hooked the phone into the laptop, using the satellite connection to access the internet. It had been three days since she'd checked in. Her silence had been scheduled, but it still made her antsy to go so long.

When she got through the labyrinth of security and logged on, she found two new assignments, neither of which looked like it would take a great deal of time—a few hours each—but each with a hard deadline and high clearance. She knew what she'd be doing tonight. She replied, confirming the deadline for their completion. Then she logged out and came back in another way, so she could quietly check with her contact on what she was calling her side job. There was no new message, so she sent one of her own.

She wrote in code as if it were another language in which she was fluent, but the actual message she sent was: *In place. Need an update. Don't make me wait.*

~oOo~

She worked on her first assignment right away, finishing it and sending it back, newly encrypted, only breaking to make her bed and use the bathroom. She checked the time on her laptop: nearly eight pm. Her stomach rumbled, and she decided she'd pack it in for the night, make herself some supper, and spend the evening with a book.

She went into the kitchen and pulled out the fixings for a salad. She'd also bought a decent rib-eye; might as well have that as fresh as possible. She found a cast-iron skillet in one of the cabinets and put it on the stove.

While she cooked, she reflected on her first couple of days in Signal Bend. Things weren't going as she'd planned. She'd known that a new person in a small town would be noticed, so she wasn't trying to stay under the radar. She'd gone in conducting herself as if she were really moving to town for the long haul—hell, there was probably no reason that she couldn't stay long term if she wanted, assuming all went well, and if she didn't mind losing her real last name. She hadn't expected quite the notice she'd gotten for her car and her run, but those were totally controllable factors.

But with Isaac, she'd managed to make herself the talk of the town. That had been blazingly apparent at breakfast, but she'd gotten her first inkling of it when that bitch had gotten the drop on her at the bar. Setting aside her irritation at herself for not keeping an eye on her flank and letting some dumb broad put hands on her—put a damn gun to her head—she kicked herself for not recognizing immediately that just sitting with Isaac had pulled down a lot of attention on her head. She'd even remarked on the attention the other bikers were paying them, but she'd been so lulled by his presence that she'd thought no more of it.

Being connected with Isaac didn't kill her plans, though; it simply changed them. She had to factor him in. And there might be something useful in a connection to the most powerful man in town. It could give her decent cover. Hiding in plain sight was often excellent cover, because it confounded expectations. And she obviously could not be in plainer sight around these parts than when she was with Isaac.

He knew she was hiding something, but she felt fairly confident that it was beyond his ability to learn anything she didn't want him to know. She had to admit, too, that she enjoyed the little chess game—she'd liked his analogy a lot—they had going. It turned her on.

Which was, of course, the other thing. The thing that might actually be a complication. Isaac turned her on. A lot. She'd spent the better part of the day remembering the morning's romp. He was big, strong, gorgeous, had a great cock, and was really damn good in the sack. He had power—not just external power, influence, but inherent power. It came off him in almost visible waves. And he was smart. He'd shocked the shit out of her by recognizing where the quote on her side was from, but it was more than that. She could see his intelligence in his eyes.

He was, as far as Lilli was concerned, the complete package. So she wasn't sad at all that she needed to keep him close, keep an eye on him. But there was a danger, too, of getting attached. Lilli knew herself. She could get attached to a man like him. Wouldn't keep her from doing what she needed to do, but it could hurt, and that sucked.

Her steak was done. She made herself a plate and took it into the living room. The furniture there—or anywhere in the house, really—wasn't what Lilli would call "comfortable," but it was serviceable. She sat on the brown plaid couch and ate her dinner while she read.

Sometime after midnight, she headed to bed. She fell asleep thinking of Isaac, her hands between her thighs.

~oOo~

She woke up with a start in the morning, but at least she was still in bed. With the new linens, it was positively fluffy, and she lay for a few minutes and allowed herself the luxury of a slow waking. The mornings out here were surprisingly noisy. Lots of animal chatter. She checked her phone: She'd made it to half past six. Pretty good. And she had provisions, so she could have coffee.

First, though, a run. She went to the bathroom, then dressed to run—in her usual running clothes. If they were scandalous for the pious country folk of Signal Bend, well, they'd just have to deal.

She was going to have to figure out some kind of solution for her other training, though. There was no gym anywhere nearby. She guessed farmers worked their core by actually working, but these days her work only exercised her brain. For the most part.

She ran about half the route she'd run the day before, which she'd estimated to be about sixteen miles, give or take. She was fit, and an experienced long-distance runner, but sixteen miles was a lot two days in a row. She saw many of the same people, and got many of the same looks—some of them perhaps even more interested than they had been yesterday. Her breakfast with Isaac had made the rounds. This time, when she waved, several of them waved back. A little cachet came with Isaac, not surprisingly.

She started the coffee when she got back and jumped in for a quick shower while it brewed. Considering the decidedly rustic appointments of the house, the shower in this bath was halfway decent. A good size, with a good showerhead. The water pressure wasn't wonderful, and it took forever to get hot, but all in all, it more than got the job done.

She dressed in jeans and a t-shirt, then blow-dried her hair. She left it loose, for now. It would bug the crap out of her soon enough, so she pulled an elastic band over her wrist. A ponytail was her daily style. She wasn't much for spending a lot of time preening.

When she went back out to the kitchen, she stopped in the middle of the living room, staring out the sliding glass door. Isaac was leaning against the railing, looking in at her—assuming he could see that far into the room when he was standing in broad daylight. Jesus Christ. She had herself a stalker. An extremely hot, interesting stalker with a sexy, smoky voice, but a stalker nonetheless.

For a moment, she just took him in. He definitely had a look: same boots, jeans, dark button-up shirt, kutte, jewelry, sunglasses, hair in a braid. He was leaning against the railing, his arms crossed over his chest. Something in his stance indicated that he was irritated, as though she should have been expecting him. She went to the door and unlocked it.

When she slid it open, he pushed off the railing. "You lock the doors *when you're home*?"

She put her hands on her hips, still standing in the doorway, blocking the entry he obviously wanted. "Asking that question tells me that you know they were locked. Which means you tried them. Which means you would have come into my house while I was in the shower. So, yeah. I'll lock my doors, thanks."

He hooked his finger into the waistband of her jeans. "What do you think I would have done? You in the shower, all naked and wet. You sure you wouldn't have wanted me to find you in there?"

Her body responded to everything about him: his scent, which was all leather and man; his look; his touch on her bare skin; the deep rumble of his voice. She was sure her reflexes would have had a shower encounter such as he described going very badly for both of them, but right now, she couldn't say getting wet with him sounded like a bad thing.

She took a focusing breath. "What do you want, Isaac? I've got shit I need to do."

"For a woman without a job, you seem pretty fucking busy." He pulled a little on her waistband and slid another finger between her belly and the denim. It was an incredibly sensual move and had her nerves alight.

She wasn't remotely tempted to bite the hook he was dangling with his observation, however. She just kept looking him in the eye, her eyebrows raised.

Finally, he cleared his throat with a grin of surrender and removed his hand. "Okay, you win. May I please come in? I need to talk to you about a couple of things." She stepped back and let him in.

She turned to head to the kitchen and finally get her cup of coffee, but Isaac grabbed her wrist and pulled her back. His mouth was on hers before she had a chance to say anything. He fed his hands into her loose hair and held her head to his.

The kiss was deep, demanding, and…persuasive. Lilli gave into it for a few seconds, savoring his taste and the lush feel of his beard. Then she put her hands on his chest and pushed back. "Dude. That's not talking."

He growled and wiped his mouth, eyeing her thoughtfully. "Sorry. Couldn't help myself." With a grin, he added, "Didn't seem to mind much."

She rolled her eyes. "I think we've established the attraction. But that's not why you said you were here." Now she finally made it to the kitchen. "Want a cup? Fresh brewed."

"Thanks. But don't put any crap in it. What you drink isn't coffee. It's practically dessert." He leaned against the doorway of the galley kitchen.

She ignored his gibe and poured a cup for him, handing it to him hot and black. Hers, she fixed the way she liked it, creamy and sweet. Then she nodded to the little Formica dining table in the corner of the living room, and they sat down.

"So, what brings you lurking today?"

He grinned. "Lurking is such a sinister word. I prefer visiting."

"Uh-huh. Why the visit, then?"

"Thought I'd update you on my progress solving the mystery that is you." He already had her undivided attention, but her ears perked up a little more at that. He took a swallow of his coffee. "It's good. Strong." She waited, and he leaned forward, putting his hand on the table alongside hers.

"My guy tells me that what's between him and your info is military grade. The word he used was *weaponized*. Spent a long time poking at it, but he couldn't get through. He was worried about keepin' at it. I told him to back off. So I doubt we'll be poking at your story anymore. Not like that, anyway."

Lilli nodded and waited. There wasn't anything she had to say to that. She could tell him that backing off probably did save the club, and his hacker especially, a lot of grief, because eventually they would've tagged him. But she didn't. She just waited for him to continue his move. She knew he wasn't done. He wasn't conceding, not this quickly. She sipped her coffee.

He ran his fingers lightly along her forearm. "Question I have for you is what's the military—or the government, anyway—doing protecting the information of an unemployed chick living out here in the sticks? Gotta tell ya, Sport, that has me paying attention. I'm starting to think maybe your interests and mine are gonna complicate each other. I can't have that."

Lilli pushed her coffee cup aside and leaned toward him. They were nearly head to head. "That sounds on its way to a threat. Is that why you came today? To threaten me?"

He shook his head. "Just making sure all the pieces are on the board, baby. It's my job to protect this town, these people. There are things about you that make *you* seem like a threat. Can you ease my mind about that?"

Okay, it was time to make a move of her own. "Isaac, I tell you truly, I don't even know what it is you do that might make me a threat to you. I can tell you truly that I have no interest in your club. No professional interest, anyway. And

I can tell you I'm no kind of cop. Don't even like them. Really can't stand them, in fact. From what I've seen, you're more of a cop than I am. That's the best I can do."

For long seconds in which the silence was thick around them, Isaac regarded her, his eyes squinting slightly. Then he shook his head. "I don't know why, but I'm inclined to believe you. I'm not happy about it, and I want you to understand what I mean when I say I will protect my people no matter what. But we'll play a little longer, I think."

Lilli finished her coffee and took their cups to the kitchen. She didn't offer him a refill. Instead, she walked to the sliding door and opened it. "Well, thanks for the chat, Isaac. Have a great day." He sat where he was for a few seconds, watching her, then languorously stood and strolled over.

He leaned down and pressed a soft, sensuous kiss to her lips. "I'll see you soon, Sport."

CHAPTER SIX

Isaac's burner buzzed as he walked back to his bike. He yanked it out of his pocket and answered. "Yeah!"

It was Showdown. "Holding our friend here, thought you might want to drop in."

"On my way." He ended the call and mounted his bike.

He was having a shit week. Mountains of uncertainty and risk rising up out of fucking nowhere all of a sudden. He felt deeply conflicted about Lilli, and he was going out on a limb for reasons he couldn't explain. He needed to get inside his head some and understand whether he was making the right calls there.

But now he had to focus on the other trouble.

He was running point on a shipment into St. Louis today, so he would talk to Kenyon Berry, leader of the Underdawgs, the crew at the end of their pipeline. If the Northside Knights, whose interests had always been in crack, not crank, were making a run at the Missouri meth trade, Kenyon would know about it and have something to say.

Isaac had gone yesterday to check on Will, see how he was doing after being stabbed by a so-called friend, and get his take on his new beef with the Sullivans. Will had been abrupt and uncommunicative. Isaac had let it go, preferring to give him a chance to calm down and feel better, and then try again. He didn't want to go hard at a guy he'd been good friends with since grade school. Not unless he had to. For now, he had other avenues he could explore.

Like Mac Evans, for one thing. Slimy piece of shit. For the greater part, the residents of Signal Bend hung together.

The ones who'd stayed were committed to staying, and they felt a bond to the town and to each other. Even though there were some rank assholes among them, they were united by the common interest of keeping the town together. Not Evans, though. His only interest was himself. He'd helped banks evict and foreclose on dozens of families, getting a fee from the bank for his efforts. Profiting on the misery of his neighbors, people he'd known his whole life. He wouldn't get the kind of patience Isaac had for Will.

Mac had dodged Isaac all day yesterday, but Showdown had him pinned in his office this morning, so Isaac went straight there from his perplexing visit with Lilli. If the Knights' mysterious backer was looking for property in or around Signal Bend, then Mac knew about it. Fuck, he was probably in on it, or trying to be. The situation was about to change, though. Isaac was ready to make Mac an offer he couldn't refuse.

He pulled up in front of the realty office and went in. Show was sitting in front of Mac's large walnut desk, stroking his long, tawny beard, his big, booted feet resting on the heavy wooden inbox. Mac had a thing for the 1950s, so most of the décor in his office was of that era. Isaac figured Mac thought it looked vintage. Really, it just looked old. In Signal Bend, lots of old things stayed in use.

Mac was sitting in his roomy, 'vintage' leather chair, looking sweaty and uncomfortable. Lisa, his secretary, was not at her usual station by the door.

Isaac nodded a query toward her desk. Showdown answered, "Sent her home for the day. Mac here is giving her a paid day. Right, buddy?"

"Guess so." Of all the things to be unhappy about today, paying for Lisa's day off should have been low on Mac's list. But the asshole was all about the dollar signs.

Isaac turned the "Open" sign over, locked the door, and shut the blinds on the door and front window. Then he pulled up a chair and sat down next to Show, knocking his VP's legs off the desk. Mac was eyeing him nervously. As he should.

"Mac. Left a message for you yesterday, but I didn't hear back. So we thought we'd catch you early today. Got some questions."

"I'd have called back, Ike. I was tied up yesterday. You guys have no need to shut me down—I'm missing appointments here." Mac gave him a petulant look.

Isaac leaned forward, putting his elbows on Mac's desk. "See, buddy, that's the thing. That's what makes me wonder. How busy could a real estate guy be in Signal Bend? I feel like I'd know if there were more people behind on their mortgages for you to fuck out of their homes. So I'm wondering what could have you so busy that I don't know about."

From somewhere in the depths of his oily heart, Mac Evans must have found something he thought was courage. Or maybe he'd made a new friend he thought more dangerous than Isaac. Because he leaned forward, too, his palms flat on his desk, and said, "You ever think that you don't know everything that goes on? You ride around on your noisy-ass bike like you're the king of this town. Well, let me tell you, *Little Ike*, the world is a lot bigger than Signal Bend, and when it comes right down to it, you're just a small-time, small-town thug."

If Mac hadn't used that hated name, maybe Isaac would have reacted more calmly, spent more time trying to talk some sense into him. But Mac had chosen to heap scorn and disrespect, and he'd gone for the thing he knew would dig deepest.

Lightning-fast and without a word, Isaac grabbed a large pair of silver scissors off the desk and rammed it through Mac's hand, pinning him to the desk. Mac shrieked and instinctively tried to pull his hand back, worsening the wound but not freeing him from it.

He was making a huge ruckus. The realty building had some distance from other businesses, but not enough to be sure he couldn't be heard. As Isaac yanked the scissors out, Showdown clocked the squalling fuck upside his head with his old-fashioned Bakelite desk phone. He collapsed to the desk in a heap, unconscious and quiet.

Showdown gave Isaac a look. He was almost as tall as Isaac, and every bit as broad, and his steely blue eyes bored into Isaac's greens. "Brother, you can't take that bait."

Isaac glowered at him. "Fuck you. You know we were gonna have to do it hard anyway. Mac's an arrogant ass. But he's also a pussy. He'll fold." Show pulled his burner out; Isaac knew he was calling for the van.

They were going to have to fuck up another town resident this week. Putting hurt on Mac Evans wouldn't lose Isaac any sleep, but what the holy fuck was going on?

~oOo~

Isaac had to meet with Kenyon in St. Louis that afternoon, so he left Show and Vic to deal with Mac, and brought Len, Havoc, and Wyatt on the run. If all went well, it was a turnaround run, and they should be back before midnight. Not that any fucking thing was going well lately.

When they stopped for gas, Isaac called Show and checked in. Mac had caved, as Isaac had known he would, and, after

85

Bart took Mac's intel and dug deeper, they now had a name: Lawrence Ellis.

The ride into St. Louis was uneventful. As they rode into the more heavily populated areas, they spread out a bit, pulling away from the pickup with the camper top in which Darren Brown was hauling the actual product. Too tight a formation put them on law radar. Four men in kuttes got notice enough. And sure enough, five minutes after they crossed into St. Louis County, a county trooper pulled up in his cruiser, even with Isaac and Len, and sat there for a good three miles. Just making his presence known. Isaac waved when he pulled alongside, and again when he finally pulled away.

They met the Underdawgs at their usual location, behind a barbeque place on the northern edge of the city's Central West End. Darren and his brother George handled their business while the Horde looked on. When they were done, Isaac got two envelopes, one from each end of the transaction. That was the deal. The crews were friendly and had been for years, so it was their habit for everyone to sit down to some wings and beer before the Signal Bend group set back off for home. Today, Kenyon and Isaac sat apart from the rest.

Kenyon Berry was a tall, slim man with dark brown skin and darker brown eyes. He kept his head and face shaved smooth. He dressed like a businessman spending the day in the office—sharply pressed slacks, crisp button-down shirts, well-shined shoes, but no jacket. Isaac always felt a little scrubby sitting with him. He was also considerably older than Isaac, about the age his father would have been. Isaac was taller and heavier, and no less mean, but Kenyon had a sophistication that Isaac knew he lacked. He was just keyed into the world better. Maybe it was a city/country thing. Isaac had a great deal of respect for the man sitting across the dinged Formica table from him, and was honored that he got respect in return.

Kenyon finished a wing, wiped his hands clean, and took a long drink from his beer. "Tell me your concerns, Isaac, and I'll tell you what I know."

"The Northsiders have somebody new backing them, and it looks like they're trying to branch out into our turf—yours and mine. He's leaning on the cookers in Signal Bend, and now he's leaning on a farmer, trying to get his land. I'm thinking he's looking to mass-produce—take over the town, take over the corridor. Got a name today: Lawrence Ellis."

Kenyon abruptly sat back in his seat at the name. "This is news to me. But I know Ellis, and if he's the player, then things are about to get very interesting. He's Chicago, and he's connected all the way to DC."

Fuck. Now Isaac sat back. "What does that mean for us?"

"Nothing good. But like I said, this is new information. Let me think this through. I am not without friends, Isaac. That means you're not without them, either. But I need some time."

"I don't know how much time we've got, man. That kind of weight leaning on my town? These are not strong people anymore, Kenyon. They've taken all the lumps they can."

The older man stood and put his hand on Isaac's shoulder. "It's a strong town, Isaac. The ones that stay? They're the strong ones. And they've got you and your brothers. I'll know something in a few days."

~oOo~

Without illicit cargo to protect, they made good time back home, and they were at the clubhouse by 10:30. It was Friday night, and the place was pretty well packed with

Horde, hangarounds, and girls. The music was loud, the booze was flowing, and the bud was wafting. Len, Havoc, and Wyatt just about ran inside, girls already under their arms—Len had two, per his custom.

Gwen, one of Isaac's more regular fucks—and one not looking for anything more—came up. She had a voluptuous bod and fiery red hair, and tonight she looked especially good, if fancier than was really his taste: snug black skirt made out of some shimmery material, high, red strappy things on her feet, and a tight white top leaving just about nothing at all to the imagination. He could see the rosy tops of her areolae peeking above the neckline. He put an arm around her waist and kissed her hard.

He had business to attend to first, though. So he sent Gwen off with a pat and wink, knowing if he wanted her later she'd be there, and scanned the room for Show. He found him getting head in the hallway. Show was a family man, but his wife had had some kind of medical problem after their third kid, and that had killed their sex life. So he had permission for head. He was big and built—and, by biker metrics, a gentleman—and the girls loved him. Even so, he availed himself infrequently. Isaac caught his eye and nodded toward the office. Show eased the girl off his dick and followed his boss, closing his jeans as he walked.

Isaac closed the door behind his VP. "What's the deal with Mac?"

Show leaned against a tall metal filing cabinet. "Visibly, he's no worse for wear, other than the fancy new stigmata you gave him, but Vic had to go at him hard. He'll be uncomfortable for awhile."

Isaac saw no need for further details on that score. "Get anything more out of him?"

"Tough enough to get what we got—Mac's more scared of these guys than us, boss. Bart pulled the emails, and I had a look. There's nothing there but a few inquiries about the property. But the trail Bart found leads to Ellis. Who is this guy?"

"Bad news. Big player from Chicago. Kenyon's lookin' into it. Meantime, we pay attention."

Show stood straight and gave Isaac a concerned look. "Isaac."

"What?" Isaac knew he was about to get some advice. Usually he took counsel well from those he'd tasked with giving it—Showdown first and foremost. But he was off his game these past few days and already feeling pissed before he'd even heard what Show had to say.

"I know how you feel about Mac. I do, too. He's shit I scrape off my boot. But I think we need to bring him into the fold. If this Ellis guy is as big a player as you say, we can't have Mac Evans gettin' a friend like that. Goin' hard like we did today, that's the wrong play with him. We gotta work with him, make him *our* friend."

"Or we could just end him." Show huffed a laugh, but Isaac wasn't kidding.

When Show realized it, he shook his head. "Brother, you know that's not how we operate. That's last resort, and it's high profile. He's known beyond our scope. He's a simple little asshole, though; we can distract him with shiny things. Let's bring him into the fold."

Isaac knew Show was right. He was silent for a couple of minutes, brooding. Finally, he nodded.

When they went back out to the party, Gwen made her way right to him. But he didn't want Gwen. He knew what he wanted, and he'd had his fill today of not getting what he wanted.

He left the clubhouse and mounted his bike.

~oOo~

When he pulled up to Lilli's house, light was shining through the sliding glass door. She was awake, then. He'd expected as much; it wasn't even 11:30 yet, and she didn't strike him as an early sleeper. He dismounted and walked toward the deck. As he neared the steps, the door slid open, and Lilli was on the deck, wearing a pair of cotton boxers slung low across her hips and a little tank top. There was a lot of belly exposed between them. Isaac would have been distracted by all that firm, lovely skin, except that she was holding a handgun and pointing it at his head.

Shocked but calm, he stopped at the foot of the steps and raised his hands in front of his chest, palms out. "I've had warmer greetings, must say. From you, even."

Even though his hands were up, she kept the gun aimed. "What the *fuck* are you doing here now?"

Yeah, he was having a shit week, no doubt. He hadn't thought this through, apparently. He figured he'd drop in for a fuck. He couldn't get this woman out of his head. He was alert that she could be trouble, and he was working on the problem of her, yes, but it was more than that. She was in his head and his senses, like a phantom following him everywhere.

"Just came for a visit, Sport. I swear. Just bein' friendly."

She pulled the gun up, and he dropped his hands. "You come to my house this morning and threaten me, then you show up in full dark and want to be *friendly*? Are you drunk?"

He took one step up. When she didn't put the gun back on him, he came the rest of the way onto the deck. "I wish I was. You got no idea. I'm just here 'cuz I want to see you. And I didn't threaten you this morning. I just told you the score." He crossed the deck and stood before her. She decocked the gun—fuck, she'd really been ready to shoot that damn thing—and stepped back into the house. He followed and pulled the door closed.

"You hold that like you know what you're doing. That's no purse pistol." It was a Sig Sauer P220. Show and Havoc carried the same sidearm. Another piece to the Lilli puzzle: she knew her way around a handgun. Not exactly a mark in the "harmless" column.

She set the gun on the kitchen counter. Then she opened a cabinet and pulled a bottle of good tequila and two shot glasses down. As she was pouring, she asked, "Why are you here, Isaac?" She handed him a glass.

Maybe the night was taking a turn for the better. He took it from her, and they drank together. "You don't do the lime and salt thing, huh?"

"Not unless I'm looking for attention at a bar—and that hardly ever happens. You haven't answered my question." She poured two more shots.

"Yeah, I have. I'm really here just to see you." They tossed the next shots back. Lilli regarded him steadily, then turned to the fridge and pulled two bottles of beer out. She handed him one, and gestured with hers toward the living room.

She sat on the ugly brown couch, and he sat next to her. He stretched his arm across the back, his hand near her head. She gave it a suspicious glance but didn't make him move it.

Isaac finished his beer in three long swallows and set the bottle on the coffee table. He was feeling a little more mellow than he had for awhile. He needed a break from his busy head. There was a book open, face down, on the table. It wasn't in English. He picked it up: *La Nausée*, by Jean-Paul Sartre. He didn't know the book, but he knew the author.

"You read Sartre? In French? And Dante in Italian? How many languages do you speak?"

She considered him over her beer bottle as she drank. When she pulled the bottle from her lips, her eyes stayed locked on his. He didn't look away. Finally, she answered, "Including English? Eight."

That was a truth. He knew it. It just sounded true. He tried to decide whether she had a tell, or whether he was using some kind of intuition, or whether he was just fucking delusional and he had no idea when she was telling the truth.

He counted off on his fingers, thumb first: "English, Italian, and French. What are the other five?" She shook her head. He leaned toward her, vexed. She was gorgeous. He felt compelled by her somehow. He wanted her secrets out from between them. "Why is that a secret, Lilli? What is it you're hiding?" She turned to put her own bottle down, and he reached out and grabbed her ponytail, yanking her back. He wanted a fucking answer.

The look she turned on him was pure fire. Before he could put another coherent thought together, she'd knocked his hand free of her, and she was straddling him, one hand hooked around his neck, her thumb on his carotid artery, the heel of the other hand pressing his chin back. It hurt like a sumbitch, and he realized that she was very effectively cutting off blood flow to his brain. His vision was getting dark around the edges.

"Rough in the sack is one thing, asshole. Do *not* think you can knock me around." He put a hand around her wrist to pull her loose, but she increased the pressure on his neck. Finally, he put his hands up in surrender, and she released him. She stayed on his lap, though, her weight right on his cock. She had to know how turned on he was. When his vision cleared again, he saw her staring at him, her look still fiery, but the heat coming from some other place now.

Now he was sure Bart was right. Skill with a gun. Hand-to-hand self-defense. Military-grade internet security. She was ex-military. Had to be. Or current military. That made her both even more interesting and possibly less of a threat. He couldn't see his little enterprise pulling in that kind of attention when county law wasn't even interested. She must have some other, bigger fish on her hook.

He slid his hands up her arms and felt gooseflesh form beneath his palms. "What are you after, Sport?"

"I keep telling you it doesn't concern you."

"Give me a reason to trust you." He moved his hands to her head, threading his fingers into her hair. She leaned in as he pulled her close, and their mouths met roughly. He kissed her savagely, as if he were trying to find the truth in her that way, and she matched him, grabbing his braid in her fist. She pulled away first, unbuttoning his shirt and pushing her fingers through the hair on his chest and belly. When she bent down and sucked his nipple between her teeth, he grabbed her hips and thrust up against her with a wrenching groan.

Then her hands were at his crotch, fumbling with his belt and jeans. He tugged at her tank top, and she stopped and pulled it off. Jesus, her tits were great. Remembering that she responded to rough pressure, he took a nipple between the thumb and forefinger of each hand and pulled briskly.

She gasped and arched back, momentarily distracted from her efforts to free him from his denim. He did it again, and she ground on him with an earthy moan.

He needed a minute. Grabbing her hands and bringing them to his chest, he met her eyes and held them, getting control. The look she returned was heated and impatient at first, but then she settled, too. The thing that had passed between them the morning before, in her bed, was there again. He needed to think about what that was, but not now. Now she took her hands from him and reached into his jeans to pull him free. Then she stood and slid those red plaid boxers off her hips, letting them drop to the floor. She was perfectly, beautifully naked.

Before she could come back to his lap, he got out a condom and rolled it on. He grabbed his cock at the base with one hand, and reached out for her hand with the other. They linked fingers, and she straddled him, easing slowly down on him. He felt every millimeter of his rod slide into her, and she squeezed hard around him, holding him tight.

"Fuck, you have a great cock," she whispered.

"Yeah? You like that?" He held her hips down hard as he thrust up again and again, getting as deep as he could, making her moan. "You feel fucking awesome yourself, baby." A look crossed her face, and then she was flexing her hips hard and fast, driving him deep, really deep, and he didn't know if it was the overstimulation of the day, or the weird thread of hostility weaving through this fuck, or just the fact that she turned him on so goddamn much, but he knew this was going to be a quick one. She was working her muscles around him, milking him, and riding him in a frenzy.

He shifted, to sit up straighter and lessen the depth she was getting a little. Wrapping her tightly in his arms, loving the soft pressure of her tits on his chest, he kissed her, nibbling at her lip and then trailing over her jaw to her ear. "We're gonna have to go again, Sport. I don't have much longer in this fuck. You feel too damn good."

Pulling away a little, she smiled cockily. "Me first, though. Get me off." She lifted her breast, and he understood. He loved a woman with really sensitive tits. He was going to have to see if he could get her off that way alone. Maybe later tonight. For now, though, he loosened his hold on her and let her grind away while he suckled her, moving back and forth between her firm, lovely globes until her hands were knotted in his hair, and she was arched back, her ponytail dancing over his legs. She came with a strained, keening moan, and when he felt her spasms around his cock, he let go and joined her, pressing his face to her chest, surrounded by her tits.

She folded forward and relaxed on him, her head on his shoulder. There was something sweet in her position, and he rested his head on hers, hooking his arms around her. Her hair was slightly damp at her nape; the heady scent of her sweat and their sex overwhelmed him.

He wondered how close was too close.

INTERLUDE: 2001

Johnny sat alone among a sea of family members on the green grass of the wide university lawn. The wooden folding chairs, numbering thousands and arrayed in military-precise rows, were hardly luxurious, despite the pretty picture they made. For Johnny, his chair was a mini-torture device after the first two hours. But they were finally calling the graduates' names.

He'd hoped they'd go alphabetically. His Lilli had been first in line for every alphabetical arrangement her entire life, with the exception of third grade, when there had been a little boy in her class with the last name of Aarons. He was anxious to see his girl cross that stage. But the first name called was Riordan. Must be some other kind of order. Johnny was going to have to wait.

He tried to see her, but all he saw were the flat planes of mortarboards, many of them decorated gaudily. Lilli had done hers up, too, though hers was much plainer than the others. She'd simply done a wide bar of gold glitter. The rank insignia of a Second Lieutenant in the United States Army. His little girl was following his footsteps.

Johnny wasn't sure how he felt about that, to be honest. There were so many options that lay before her. She'd done so well in school: Dean's List, Phi Kappa Phi, Magna Cum Laude, the list went on. She could be anything, do anything. But what she wanted was to serve.

He was proud, yes. Busting his buttons with it. She'd been through a lot, his Lillibell. Already, at twenty-two, she'd lost more than most. But she was a strong, smart, brave girl, and she knew her mind. She would excel in the service as she'd excelled everywhere else. But he didn't want her to know war the way he had. He wanted her to have a bright, happy life of comfort, not the squalid privation of a soldier at war.

These were times of peace, though. Spring 2001. Perhaps she would know only adventure and not conflict.

Finally, he saw the glimmering gold bar, sparkling in the sunlight at it bobbed up the stairs to the wide stage. Her long chestnut hair flowed rich and loose under her cap. Even through four years of ROTC, she'd refused to cut it, preferring instead, while in uniform, to braid it and bind it to her head with pins. Lilli, beautiful as she was, had few vanities, but her hair was certainly one of them.

She was standing on the stage. Then he heard her name echo robustly over the sound system: "*Lillian Filomena Accardo, Bachelor of Arts in Renaissance History, Bachelor of Arts in Middle Eastern Studies.* His daughter, his only child, strode confidently across the stage, veritably buried under sashes and cords and medals for her accomplishments during her studies. She accepted the folder that would hold her diploma, shook hands with a short line of men and women, and then, before she descended the stairs at the other side of the stage, she turned and scanned the audience.

Johnny stood, alone in that sea of seated people, and waited for her to find him. She did, and, smiling brilliantly at him, she made their sign, the one she'd made every day before she entered her school building, the one he made every time he left for a business trip. Thumb, forefinger, and pinky extended in the sign language for "I love you," she laid her hand on her heart.

He did the same.

CHAPTER SEVEN

Lilli felt relaxed, resting against Isaac, her head on his shoulder. His cock was still mostly hard inside her, and she liked the full feeling of him there. She liked everything about this moment: the press of their bare chests together, still heaving from their exertion; the weight of his head lying on hers; the soothe of his hands on her back, his fingers combing through her ponytail. She felt…cozy.

She sat up. He looked like he'd been even more relaxed than she; his eyes were heavy as they met hers. "What's up?" he asked, his voice no more than a low rasp.

She'd been furious at his intrusion—he really was just about stalking her now—and more than half expecting him to have come on a dark errand. After his 'visit' in the morning, feeling threatened, she'd taken two handguns out of the Camaro and placed them, and the one she'd already had inside, strategically through the house.

She'd also sent a coded message asking for intel on the Night Horde and its leader. She hadn't been especially interested before, but his acute interest in her meant her own security needed offense as well as defense.

When he'd rolled up at nearly midnight, she'd been ready to kill him. But then he was standing on her porch, and the threat she felt dissipated. She didn't understand it. She was attracted to him, sure. Very much. But it was more than that. Her reading of him rested on the thin blade between danger and appeal, and it perplexed her.

Now, straddling him like this after another bout of hot and unexpected sex, she shook her head. "You have to stop dropping in unannounced, Isaac. It's not cool."

"It's the country way, Sport." He traced a lazy circle around her nipple. "And it seems to turn out pretty well here, more times than not."

She rolled her eyes. "I don't care what way it is. It's not my way. Next time, I'll just put a bullet through your eye and be done with it."

He tightened his arms around her with a force a couple of steps beyond friendly. "Now who's making threats? You want to be careful, Sport." The balance between danger and appeal tipping decidedly toward the former, Lilli pushed to get off him, but he held her in place.

She gave him a look that meant she'd dance if that was what he wanted, and he smiled and relaxed his hold. "Tell you what. Give me your number, and I'll call first—when I can."

She considered him. There was a twinkle in his eye, and his expression could best be described as an amused smirk. He was still inside her, his cock beginning to harden again. He was enjoying himself. Rather than make her angrier, though, his mood relaxed her.

"Your *guy*'s not good enough to find that out for you?"

"Sure he is. Better if you just give it to me, though, don't you think?" He winked.

With another roll of her eyes, she nodded and pushed again to get up. This time he didn't obstruct her, though they both groaned when he slid out of her.

She gave him her cell and her landline, writing them out on the back of her grocery receipt. When she turned around, Isaac was standing right behind her, his jeans closed again, but his kutte and shirt off. Jesus, he was hot—huge and muscular, with beautiful ink, those leather cuffs around his wrists, the medallion around his neck. It looked something like an upside-down cross, but not exactly.

Lilli handed him the paper, and he took it with a lift of his eyebrow. As he put it in his wallet, she reached out her hand and lifted the medallion. "What is this?"

"It's Mjölnir." Lilli didn't recognize the word, and she wrinkled her forehead at him. He laughed. "Thor's Hammer. You know Thor, right?"

"Yeah, I know Thor. I just wasn't expecting you to say a word like that."

"You really think I'm an idiot bumpkin, don't ya?"

She didn't. She knew he was smart. But he was more worldly and well read than she'd given him credit for, that was true. "No, I don't. It's just—"

He cut her off. "It's fine. Underestimate me all you want. Just makes my job easier, figuring you out. A lot of us around here, me included, have Norwegian heritage. I like mythology, and, well, Norse god of thunder, Harleys, seemed like a fit to me. So, Mjölnir."

She smiled. "Viking stock, huh? Explains your size."

Grinning, he put his hands on her hips, and she realized she was standing there naked. "Like my size, do ya?"

She shrugged. "It'll do."

He reached back with one hand and tugged on the band holding her ponytail. "Take this out. I like it loose."

She did as he asked, nodding toward him. "You, too, then. I like yours loose, too." He did as she asked.

He combed his fingers through her hair, fluffing it around her shoulders, laying it over her breasts. "You got sheets on that bed now?"

"I do."

Trailing a finger down the middle of her chest, he murmured, "I want to take you back there and fuck you in your bed. Take my time. What d'ya think?"

Lilli shook her head. "I'm not much for a sweet fuck, love."

"I said I wanted to take my time. Didn't say I wanted to be sweet." The gleam in his eyes was feral.

"Then I'm in."

~oOo~

Lilli woke with a start and got oriented quickly. The room was bright with sunlight. Crap. What time was it? She reached over and grabbed her phone: 9:38. Jesus. She had no idea when she'd last slept so late. She lay back and let herself wake fully up.

Then she noticed the bed was full. She looked to her left and saw a broad wall of back and a mane of sable hair. Isaac. He'd spent the night. How the fuck had *that* happened?

No, she knew exactly how it happened. She and Isaac had essentially fucked each other unconscious. Holy shit, that had been one for the books. She was realizing that she was sore virtually everywhere now.

He was sleeping on his stomach, the pillow gathered under his head and chest. The sheet and light blanket were pushed down low, only covering his legs and the bottom of his ass. She reached to shake him awake and then stopped. She

101

wanted to look for a minute. She'd not seen his bare back until now. That seemed strange; they'd been naked and enthusiastically intimate two of the four days they'd known each other, and he'd showered in her bathroom, but somehow she'd missed this view.

Inked across his muscular shoulders, one side to the other, starting just below the pieces that ran from his shoulders down his upper arms, was the word HORDE in thick, black letters six inches tall. He had no other ink on his back. The only other marks were several—maybe as many as a dozen—long, livid scratches. She looked at her hands and saw blood under her fairly short nails. She also noticed bruises forming on her breasts and belly. Arms, too.

It had been a wild night, definitely. She sat up, groaning at the sharp soreness between her legs. She'd grown accustomed to wanting more than the man she was with could or would give her. She'd had some encounters that had gone quite badly when the guy couldn't find the line between rough and brutal. It looked, though, like she'd met her match. It also looked like they'd perhaps lost that line together.

She remembered every second of it, of course. She just hadn't been aware they'd crossed a line. What she remembered was wild, unrestrained, enduring passion. Her throat was sore from her screaming. Remembering, she felt herself getting wet. She was far too sore to do anything about that, but she indulged a stray whim and stroked the beautiful, broad planes of Isaac's back.

He flinched at her touch and rolled quickly to his back. She watched his face move from alarm to confusion to understanding and back to confusion. He took a deep breath and blinked several times.

"Damn. Sorry—I didn't mean—I don't—sorry." He sat up, wincing.

Enjoying that he was at a loss—and that he, too, was sore—she let him swing for a few seconds. Then she smiled. "If you're trying to apologize for still being here, don't. It's fine."

He reached out and lightly stroked her upper arm, where a large bruise in the shape of his hand and fingers was flowering. "Anything else I need to apologize for?"

She reached out and grazed her hand over the open bite marks on his neck and shoulder. "Seems to me we're even."

"Damn, Sport. I don't want to sound all flowery, but I don't think I've ever had a fuck like that before. You're somethin' else."

She grinned and stood, making sure not to react to the discomfort throughout her body. She thought today would be a good day to skip a workout, though. She combed her hair back with her fingers and pulled the elastic band from her wrist to make a ponytail. "You want breakfast? I've got eggs and bacon. You like over easy, right?" She hunted around for her boxers and tank, then remembered they were in the living room.

Isaac leaned back against the headboard and gave her a look that she didn't feel like interpreting. "That'd be great. Thanks—and yeah. I like my eggs over. You mind if I take a shower?"

"My well water is your well water." She turned and walked naked out of the room.

~oOo~

He walked up behind her as she was frying the bacon. "Was kinda hopin' to find you in here naked," he growled.

103

She laughed. "That's how very unfortunate cooking accidents happen." She'd dressed in last night's boxers and tank when she'd found them in the living room.

Wrapping her ponytail around his hand, he gently pulled her head to the side and kissed her neck. The gesture was sweet and possessive, and she turned a quizzical eye on him. He only smiled and stepped to the side to pour himself a cup of coffee.

Dressed again completely but for his kutte, his wet hair braided, he stood looking out the sliding glass door, coffee in hand, while she finished breakfast. When she set the plates on the table, he turned and joined her.

They ate in silence for most of the meal. As Isaac was sopping up the leavings from his eggs with a piece of toast, he said, "You should come with me to Tuck's place tonight. Saturday—there's live music. You dance?"

She was surprised. "Do you?"

He clucked. "There you go, underestimating me again. Yes, I dance. But I asked if you did."

"Are you asking me on a *date*? Won't the town gossips have a field day?"

"Baby, they started hearing wedding bells when they saw us at Marie's. I'm not known to feed my fucks. There's nothing we could do to stir them up more—unless I knock you up, which I have no intention of doin'."

The conversation was taking a turn Lilli had not expected at all. The whole morning was way off script. "So, what, then—we're a couple because you bought me breakfast?"

"How about this: we're a couple because we fuck like freight trains, and there ain't nobody else around can handle us." He pushed his plate away and leaned forward. "Look, Sport. It's a small town. Staying away from each other wouldn't be easy. And I like you. I damn sure like gettin' you naked. I'd love it if I could come by without getting a gun pointed at my head. Here's somethin' else: I haven't had breakfast with a woman I've fucked in fifteen years or more. I don't sleep over. But here I am, and I'm not in a rush to go."

"And that's supposed to mean what to me, exactly? I'm supposed to be honored, or something?" She hadn't woken up with a guy in years, either—and fuck, she'd *made* him breakfast. This was new territory for her, too. She hadn't been in what could be called a relationship since college.

"Jesus, you're prickly. No. It means I know I like you more than just a fuck. I think there's something happening here. I think you feel it, too. I want to play that out a little."

She shook her head. There had been a wide swath of hostility running through their sex last night—they had the wounds to prove it. She liked rough sex, but she wasn't in the habit of needing first aid afterward. "We don't trust each other. Not a great place to start something."

He grinned as if what she'd said had given him an opening. She supposed it had—she hadn't refused outright. "Didn't ask you to marry me, Sport. Just sayin' we play it out. Least I know for sure you're hiding somethin'. You're not hiding that." He picked up her hand and linked his fingers with hers. "Unless you're entertaining other offers?"

She was quiet, thinking. Something in her resisted the direction he was leading them simply because she hadn't seen the path. It had not at all been part of her plan to get involved with anyone in Signal Bend. But she did like him. She couldn't say she exactly enjoyed his company, because their conversations had so far been mainly adversarial. But she enjoyed his presence, she did enjoy the verbal sparring, and she was definitely attracted. Dangerously so. And it remained a good idea to keep him close, despite the entanglement.

She'd been quiet too long. He squeezed her hand and said her name. "Lilli?"

Something about the way he said her actual name resounded in her. The entanglement could indeed become a problem, but she wanted it. "Okay. I still want you to call before you come over."

He smiled broadly. His teeth were even and white. Lilli realized that she'd never really gotten around to noticing that—she usually focused on his beard and his lips. "Noted. You never did answer my question, so I guess you don't dance?"

"I dance. Country's not my genre, though." She got up to clear the table.

He grabbed her hand before she could pick up his plate. "From Texas my ass. Have you ever even *been* to Texas?" She didn't answer; there wasn't any point. He pulled her onto his lap, and she raised her eyebrows at the macho gesture. He only smiled back. "If you can move, baby, I can teach you the steps."

~oOo~

Isaac got a call about half an hour later, after helping her clean up the breakfast dishes. Saying he'd be back for her at eight o'clock, he'd kissed her and headed out. Lilli was glad. She had things to do, and she needed some distance from him to do some thinking, too. She took a quick shower, then got on her laptop and logged on.

She didn't have a new assignment, but she did have notification of deposits made to her accounts to compensate her for those she'd just completed. One thing about working this kind of contract work, with so much security, nothing got bogged down in "channels." Deadlines were short, but payments came quickly.

She also had two messages from her side contact. One of them was simply coordinates. It was the update she'd been waiting for, so the rest of her day was now planned. Looked like she was going to get a workout after all. She memorized the numbers and moved to the other message: Intel on the Night Horde MC and on Isaac, whose last name was Lunden—probably good to know that if they were a "couple" somehow, so she should make a point to ask him. She scanned the attachments, printed them off, and made a file. Interesting. Definitely material that could give her some extra security with him, if she needed it.

She wasn't surprised that the town was kept going by the meth trade—that was the sad state of rural towns across the Midwest. She was impressed, though, to see how Isaac and his biker brothers had managed to keep the town above it even as they were in the thick of it. He moved it straight through town without stopping.

Also interesting to see that there seemed to be virtually no crime in or around Signal Bend. Nothing—not even DUIs, another thing that tended to trouble towns like this. First hand, in the few days she'd been here, Lilli had seen vandalism, assault and battery, public drunkenness, among other things—hell, even attempted murder. But none of that had been reported or investigated. Looked like the MC was the only law that mattered. Lilli admired his commitment to keeping his town alive and safe.

Isaac was careful, but Rick, Lilli's hacker contact and, well, accomplice on her little side project, was extremely good—among the best in the world. In one day, he'd connected some dots and found some trails. There was stuff here that could hurt the Horde badly—or at least look like it could. None of it would stand up, unless she got something first-hand, but it would give her leverage, if she needed it. She wasn't interested in hurting them—him—at all, except in self-defense.

Her own feelings about things like laws were ambivalent. She saw law and morality as nothing more than human beings' silly attempts to order a world made of chaos. In her experience, outlaws were no better or worse than any other person. Often, in fact, they were braver, more honorable.

Once she was done with her messages and had sent back the appropriate replies, she changed into hiking gear, filled a backpack with a packed lunch, water, a camera with a long-range telephoto lens, her sat phone, the GPS, and her Sig with a couple of extra mags. Just to be sure. If the day went well, she shouldn't need the firepower. But she always went prepared.

~oOo~

The day went as planned. When she got back to her little rented house around six o'clock, she downloaded the photos to her hard drive, then uploaded key images into a message to Rick. Hopefully, he'd be able to get confirmation to her soon. Her eyes told her that the confirmation was a formality. She had her guy.

She took another shower and got ready for her 'date' with Isaac. She rarely wore makeup, but tonight she did—just a little; she didn't have much. She didn't have sexy clothes per se, that wasn't really her thing, but she chose a pair of slim, low-waisted, straight-leg jeans and wore her tall Docs with the buckles up the side. She wore a fitted white button-up shirt and left a couple of buttons undone at the top and bottom. She was far too used to her hair being pulled back to be able to tolerate it loose and in her face for long, but she compromised and pulled a bit back from her face, braiding that part down the back of her head and leaving the rest loose on her back. Her silver hoops and rings—the only jewelry she had with her. She didn't really know why she was making an effort to dress for a date, but it entertained her to do so.

When she heard his bike roaring up the road, she grabbed her leather jacket and locked up the house, going round the front to meet him.

CHAPTER EIGHT

Lilli was walking across the yard toward him as Isaac pulled up. Damn, she looked good. The sun hadn't yet set, and as she walked, he could see flashes of belly where her shirt was open. Her hair was pulled off her face but still long and loose, and she looked fucking perfect. Pair of badass biker chick boots around her calves, too. She was going to look amazing riding bitch with him tonight. The thought made his balls twitch.

They had some shit to talk about, but it could wait. For now, he just wanted to take this woman out and let the town do with that what it would.

"Hey, Sport. You look damn good."

She smiled and walked up to his bike. "Thanks. You look exactly the same."

"Well, I'd've gotten pretty for you if I'd known you were dressing up. Nice boots." He handed her a helmet, but before she could put it on, he hooked his arm around her waist and pulled her against him. With his other hand on the back of her neck, he drew her head down for a lingering kiss. "Mmmm. Nice. I assume you know how to ride bitch?" She gave him a look that said it was a stupid question. "Okay, let's give the people a thrill." He swatted her ass and released her, and she mounted the bike behind him.

~oOo~

Isaac didn't often ride with a passenger. It was an intimate thing, riding with a woman wrapped around him—more intimate, in his mind, than sex. Lilli rode well, moving with him smoothly, instinctually. They seemed to be physically

110

in sync in all sorts of ways. He was well on his way to a boner by the time they approached No Place.

As usual on a Saturday night, Tuck's was packed. The music blared through the walls and out into the parking lot. There were a few clumps of people drinking around their trucks, not having yet made it into the bar. Isaac pulled up in front, noting that most of the Horde were already inside. He liked the club to keep a strong presence here, especially on Saturday. Live music and a larger number of women tended to make the men extra scrappy.

They dismounted, and Lilli handed him the helmet he'd lent her. She passed a careless hand over her hair, and that seemed to be the extent of her concern about it. Damn, he loved that, a woman who just was who she was, looked like she looked. He'd noticed that she'd primped some tonight, but he couldn't even tell for sure what she'd done. Her beautiful grey eyes stood out more, and he liked that just fine, but they weren't buried under black crap, like a raccoon. Whatever fuss she'd gone to tonight, it was working.

He took her hand—she flinched a little, but didn't pull away—and he led her inside.

Didn't take long for them to have the attention of the room, despite the dim lighting and the live band. It was too early yet for the dancing to get really started, so people were arrayed at the tables, which had been pushed along the walls to make more room for the dancing that would come. The wags had had a couple of days now to get the word out. Isaac nodded and smiled as he led Lilli through the room, shaking the hands that were extended, but not stopping to introduce her. He wanted to get to the bar and have her meet his brothers first. They all had opinions about her and about his interest in her. They would be her toughest audience.

Looked like almost all of the Horde was lined up at the bar. Before they'd arrived at the bar side of the room, the band—Jesse's Wild Bunch, one of the regular acts that cycled through, playing shit-kicking country with a little bit of blues mixed into the third set—announced its first break, and the sound of the room shifted down to conversation level, at least until somebody got around to feeding the juke.

With his hand at the small of her back, Isaac gently pushed Lilli to step in front of him. Then he just went down the row. "Lilli, I'd like you to meet my MC brothers: Showdown, Bart, Havoc, Dan, Len, and CJ. Down there at the end is Rover, he's prospecting for the club." Each man nodded cordially when his name was called. Lilli stood in place while he named them. Then, when he was done, she walked down the line with her hand out, shaking each man's hand. She smiled prettily and said something low to each; they leaned down to hear and then came back up with a smile.

Holy fuck. She was flirting. She hadn't even flirted with *him*. By the time she got down to Rover, who was fucking *blushing* when she was finished with him, she'd won the whole crew of idiots right over. She walked back toward Isaac with a little pop in her sway. Minx.

She turned back to his brothers. "You boys fancy doing a couple of shots of tequila with me?"

Havoc piped up from his seat halfway down the bar. "Never leave a lady drinkin' alone. My daddy taught me that."

Lilli leaned over and caught Rose's attention—actually, she'd had Rose's attention for that whole show, but now the bartender came over with a dry smile and a wink. "That's shooters for the line, then?"

Lilli winked back. "Yes, ma'am. The good stuff. And we'll probably go a few times."

Rose nodded. "The whole show?"

"Absolutely."

Isaac stared at Lilli in bemused awe while Rose lined up nine shot glasses and expertly filled them with Patrón and set them in front of the Horde and Lilli. She dealt cocktail napkins like playing cards and put a wedge of lime on each one. Then she handed Lilli a shaker of salt.

"There you go, sugar. You get it started."

Lilli grinned at Rose and then at Isaac, who had not picked up his glass. He couldn't believe what he was seeing. This was a different, vastly less guarded version of the woman he'd been spending time with. His brothers, all of them, stared at her hand as she licked the space between her thumb and forefinger. She did it slowly, her tongue extended just enough and sharpened to a firm point, fully aware of her audience. Then she shook salt over the wet spot.

Isaac's cock pulsed and swelled.

She offered him the salt shaker, but he shook his head. Shrugging, she slid the shaker to Showdown. Every man salted his hand. Isaac couldn't believe that, either. These were men who drank their booze straight. Fuck, they hardly bothered with glasses. And here they all were, salting their hands, with little lime wedges on napkins in front of them.

Their hands salted, Lilli raised her shot glass, and they all did the same. Isaac took his, now, too. They all watched as Lilli licked the salt off her hand—doing that sensual little thing again—and tossed the tequila back. She picked up her lime, and the men watched as she slid it into her mouth and sucked it. When she set it back on her napkin, the meat was almost entirely gone. She'd sucked it clean.

He wasn't surprised. Lilli had an extremely talented mouth. But his men were transfixed. None of them had drunk but him. When Lilli slammed her glass back on the bar, it shook them out of their pornographic fugue, and they did their shots.

Isaac knew what she was doing. It was brilliant; he simply hadn't expected it. As beautiful and feminine as she was, she was so *not* girly, she confounded his expectations of women in so many ways, that he hadn't even considered that she could play the sex kitten. But she'd read the situation, caught the vibe of mistrust his men were sending her way, and she'd played their expectations against them. She'd made herself a hot piece of ass.

Well, she couldn't help but be that. But now that was all his men saw. They were disarmed.

They ran that line three times, her treat. She looked no worse for doing three quick, generously poured shots of top shelf tequila, but Isaac wanted a long, pleasant evening, so he thought it best to get some food into her before she got it in her head to make any more friends. He stepped behind her, pressing his body to hers, and whispered low in her ear, "Share another burger with me?"

She turned her head slowly, tucking into his neck a little. "How do you make a boring sentence like that sound so hot?" Maybe she was feeling the shots a little, after all. He grinned and kissed her nose.

"That a yes, then?" She nodded, and he caught Rose and ordered.

They took their food to a table that emptied as Isaac led Lilli to it. Soon enough, they had two more tables pushed to theirs, and all of the Horde were sitting with them, stealing fries until Isaac ordered three more baskets of them. The Horde didn't, as a rule, pick up women at Tuck's. They drank and they kept the peace, in their way. They usually headed back to the clubhouse, where women were primed and waiting and didn't need sweet talk. So Lilli had their full attention.

They had a few beers with the food, and Isaac—who drank daily, was big, and thus had a very high threshold for drunkenness, so high that he rarely breached it—watched Lilli mellow, her focus soften. There was something underneath her buzz, though, that he couldn't quite read. He'd caught her giving him sly, almost greedy looks, and when he touched her, she reacted strongly. Not enough for the dolts sitting around them to notice, but he definitely did.

Then he got it. She was horny. Here in the middle of the bar. Well, wasn't that interesting.

The band started its second set while they were eating, Isaac and Lilli sharing the burger with each other, the fries with everyone. People all over the bar started getting up this time to dance, and Isaac saw Lilli paying attention.

The second song came up, and the dancers immediately lined up. The band was covering Trace Adkins' 'Ladies Love Country Boys.' Oh, Isaac couldn't pass that up.

He brushed her hair from her shoulder and leaned in close. "C'mon, Sport. Let me show you how to dance."

"I know how t'dance, asshole. Tol' you that already."

Was that a little slur he heard in her speech? Nice. Lilli off her guard. He was looking forward to that, but he wanted to play it slow, so he needed to make sure she paced herself. Plus, she had to ride back with him. "Well, let me show you how we dance around here, then." He stood, bringing her up with him. She let him lead her to the dance floor, and Isaac taught Lilli the Electric Slide.

She was right. She could really move. Even tipsy, she picked up the steps quickly—not that they were all that hard—and she was loose right off the bat, her body instinctively, fluidly moving with the beat. He watched her hips sway. That ass. Damn. Just…*damn.*

He was glad when the dancing shifted into pairs and he get could get his hands on her. He taught her the two-step, another easy dance, and she took to it immediately. He was surprised to find that she willingly let him lead. He put her in a spin, and she came back beautifully. He did it again, though, and she looked a little woozy. Drunk Lilli. Isaac was charmed.

With a saucy smile, she went up to her tiptoes and leaned close. Reading that she had something to say, he bent toward her, and she said in his ear, "Your music sucks, but you're a great dancer. It's really hot." He laughed and brought her even closer.

But being so close to her, her hips moving against him, was driving him crazy. And it was increasingly apparent that drunk Lilli was extremely horny Lilli, because she was all up on him, making the most she could of the closeness and movement while they danced. She was working up a sweat, too, and he found the way tendrils of her hair clung to her face and neck, and the way her *white!* blouse was dampening, and the way she smelled—all of it, everything about her—was just too fucking much.

He danced her to the edge of the floor and growled in her ear, "We need to sit down and get a drink, or I'm gonna drag your amazing ass to the restroom and bend you over the sink."

She tipped her head back and grinned at him, her bright grey eyes hooded. "You see me stoppin' you?"

Jesus Christ.

"I'm not jokin', Sport."

She only raised her eyebrows, challenging him. Knowing full well the show they were putting on and not giving a starving rat's ass, he leaned down and kissed her ravenously, exulting in the eager movement of her tongue with his. Her arms looped snugly around his neck as she opened her mouth wide and let him have his way. He grabbed her thighs and pulled her up, hooking her legs around his hips. And then he walked them back toward the restrooms, ignoring the hoots of his brothers at their table.

He got her into the ladies' and locked the door before he released her legs and let her slide them back to the floor. Still kissing her, he walked her backward until she bumped against the sink, and then he spun her around. She put her hands on either side of the old-fashioned porcelain bowl and looked at him in the mirror. He met her reflected gaze in the glass and brought his hands around her waist to undo her jeans. He moved quickly, yanking them and her –oh, *nice*—sheer white lace thong to her knees. He pushed gently but steadily between her shoulder blades until she bent forward. Then he snagged a condom from his wallet, opened his belt and jeans, and rolled it on.

"Come on, come on, come on," she whispered.

"Easy, baby. Gimme a sec to get dressed. Told you I don't intend to knock you up." Condom on, he grabbed her hip in his left hand and slid his right down her ass and between her legs. God, she felt good, silky and so damn wet. "Fuck, Sport. No wonder you're impatient. You're so wet I could drink you." He flicked his drenched fingers roughly over her clit until her hips bucked and twitched, then he positioned himself and slid easily into her.

"Oh, fuck yeah. Go hard."

He was deep in her, and she was tight and hot. He was already panting with the need to move. And this had to be a quickie. But they'd had really rough sex less than twenty-four hours earlier—blood-in-the-bed rough sex. "You sure? After last night?"

She looked up and caught his eyes in the mirror. "Go!"

He took her at her word, starting off hard, slamming into her as hard and fast as he could. She bucked against him, her hands clutching the sides of the sink, her knuckles white. "Fuck, yeah! Yeah! Fuck, make me come! Harder, God, harder!"

Holy shit, this woman. He folded over her, bringing his hands from her hips to take her clit and a nipple, sliding into her top and pinching her through the soft lace of her bra. He was rough and moved fast, pinching and pulling as he drummed into her. She made no effort whatsoever to be quiet, but the band was still playing, so people would have to be clustered around the restroom door to hear. Not that that wasn't likely.

As worked up as she was, he was at least as much, though he was keeping comparatively quiet, biting his lip viciously to do so. He was worried he was going to come before her. He was alarmed at how often he had trouble holding off with her. It was not usually a problem.

But then she was coming, shouting wordlessly, her muscles clamping down around his throbbing, hypersensitive cock. He grabbed her hips again and held off until she was finished and then, with just a couple more deep, powerful thrusts, he came, too, grunting, his fingers digging into the flesh of her hips, until he thought he'd collapse.

He rested his forehead on her back for a second, but then she stood straight and pushed back from the sink, making him slide quickly out of her and take an awkward step to keep his footing. She pulled a couple of paper towels from the dispenser and wiped herself. Pulling up her jeans and thong, she looked at him in the mirror and said, "Probably should get back out there." She washed her hands and waited by the door for him to pull himself together.

An abrupt end to an intense fuck. He was spun.

~oOo~

They closed the bar. Aside from a few parking lot scrapes, easily dispensed with, and one rowdily inebriated Darren Brown to contain and find a ride home for, the night was easy. They drank, they danced. And they'd fucked. They'd done another couple of rounds of shots between the band's second and third sets, and Lilli was on the edge of being too drunk to keep her seat on his bike. From that point, Isaac's mission became keeping her at that level of drunkenness and no more.

Lilli danced with all of the Horde who asked her. Isaac was pleased to see that she kept more distance from them than she had with him, but he also noticed the way all the men's—all of them, not just his brothers—eyes tended to focus on her ass while she moved. It pissed him off. He understood it—Lilli had the kind of ass you saw in ads for sexy underwear. Or on biker pinup calendars. Impossible not to appreciate. But he was feeling more and more territorial about her with each passing day. Fuck, with each passing *hour*. And he knew the town already considered her his, so he would have to respond to any challenge to that. So he glowered at his brothers dancing with her until he couldn't take it anymore. He swallowed back the rest of his beer and stood up.

She was dancing alone, suddenly. Dan, her most recent partner, was headed off to the john. Isaac started making his way to her, around the tables and chairs, and the weaving bodies of drunk dancers, when he saw Steve Bohler grab her and spin her around, trying to dance with her. She pulled away sharply, but Bohler grabbed her again and put his hand square on her ass.

Oh, that asshole was going to lose that hand.

Isaac charged forward, plowing through the people on the dance floor, but when he got to Lilli, he stopped short. He didn't see what she'd done, but Bohler was on the floor, clutching his throat and not breathing much at all. She must have punched him, she and her big silver rings.

Isaac touched Lilli's arm, and she spun on him, backing off instantly when she saw it was him. "Asshole got fresh. Frien' a yours?"

He brushed her cheek, while Bohler continued to writhe unattended. "You okay?"

"Sure. Room's a little spinny, but I'm good."

"You mind if I take it from here?"

"He's all yours. I'm gonna sit." She wandered unsteadily back to their table, and Isaac grabbed Bohler by his shirt, got him to his feet, and dragged him outside. He met Havoc, Len, and Show coming in, looking like they'd just been scrapping, too.

Show got a look at Isaac and Bohler, and asked simply, "Need help?"

"Nope. Somebody stay with Lilli. I'll be back."

"He hurt her?"

"She hurt him. But he took liberties. Needs a lesson."

As he dragged Bohler out and to the back of the building, he heard Len tell Show, "I got his back."

When he was done with Steve Bohler, he was well certain that there was no amount of drunk that would cause that cooker to forget his manners again around any woman, much less Isaac's. He shouted a reminder as he was mashing Bohler into jelly.

His woman. Fuck. He had a woman. Hell, it had been his idea. He wanted her. She was not whom she claimed to be, and he needed to give a shit about that. She could be a threat to the club, and that made her a potential threat to his town. But he wanted her anyway.

He turned, shaking the blood off his be-ringed hands, and saw Len leaning against the corner of the building, regarding him curiously. Isaac walked past him without a word and went back in to find Lilli.

~oOo~

They left when Tuck and Rose closed up. Lilli had sobered up a little, but Isaac was still concerned about her ability to sit the bike. When she'd made the turn from buzzed to drunk, it had happened quickly. Something for him to keep in mind. Still, she'd managed to disable Bohler handily. Isaac wondered what she was truly capable of sober.

He pulled her close. "You good to ride, Sport?"

She smiled up at him, and in the sodium glare of the parking lot lights, he could tell that her eyes weren't quite

121

as focused as he'd like. "Abso-tive-ly. Let's ride." She grabbed her helmet and fumbled it.

Alrighty. He made a snap decision. For this woman, he was doing lots of things he'd made a point not to do. Why not keep it up? His place was half the distance hers was. He was bringing her home.

He mounted, and she climbed on behind him—a bit awkwardly, but not so bad that he thought they'd have to hoof it down to the 7 Eleven for a giant coffee.

"Hold on tight, Sport, okay? Don't want to lose you."

She laughed. "You're just tryin'a get felt up." But she did—she held him tight, and he felt her breasts on his back, her thighs squeezing his.

He took it slow, but they still pulled up to his house within fifteen minutes. She dismounted and took a quick extra step, finding her footing. "Hey. Where are we?"

He'd purposely neglected to tell her where he was taking her, figuring she'd fight him, and it was much harder for her to do anything about it from here. "My place. C'mon, I'll show you around."

She glared at him, standing akimbo. "Did I say I'd stay at your place?"

"You didn't say no." It wasn't a lie—he hadn't asked, so she hadn't refused. His assertion confused her, and diffused the fight in her. He held out his hand, and she took it. He led her into his house, which was unlocked, for the most part. There was a room in the house, as well as two outbuildings, he always kept locked. Otherwise, he only locked up if he was leaving overnight.

As soon as he got her into his front hall, she yanked on his arm, pulling him back to her. She reached up and pulled the band loose from his braid, unwinding his hair. Then she fed her fingers into it and brought his face down to hers. Before she kissed him, she asked, "Got sheets on your bed?"

Fuck it. He'd show her around in the morning. They'd talk in the morning, too. Getting her to talk might be easier when she was like this, but he could get it done when she was sober. What Bart found out was best discussed in the light of the day, anyway. His hands under her shirt, on the satiny, firm skin of her belly, and then on her back, unhooking her bra, he kissed her.

"I do. Wanna mess 'em up?"

INTERLUDE: 2002

Lilli wondered if it always rained at funerals. She knew that couldn't possibly be true, but she'd now been to three funerals, and it had rained at every one.

Her mother.

Her nonna.

Now, her father.

She was alone in the world now. And she'd left him to die alone.

She'd been on a training exercise at aviation school when he'd fallen ill, and it had taken a day for the message to reach her. It took another two days to work out the logistics to get home. By the time she got to the hospital, he was gone. He'd had a massive coronary. The doctors told her he'd never been conscious since 'the event'—that was what they called it, the event, like it was a fucking prom or something—so he hadn't known he was dying alone.

She knew, though. She knew.

He was buried with full military honors at the veteran's cemetery. The place had a haunting beauty, a stillness and symmetry, every stone the same—white, narrow, and precisely aligned. The 'mourners'—she guessed they were called mourners even if they would leave the cemetery, grab tacos at the drive-thru and go on about their damn lives—were all his former Army buddies or his business associates. Her father socialized a lot; as a high-level executive, it was part of his job. But he didn't have many friends. He was naturally a loner, a family man who preferred the quiet of his home and his family. He was not quick to trust people. Except his old war buddies. They were far flung, though, and only met annually for a big fishing trip. Or when one of them died.

No, her father kept to himself. Since his wife and mother had died, Lilli was the only person he confided in, the only one to whom he felt close.

And she'd gone away and left him alone in that big house full of ghosts. At least 'the event' hadn't happened at home. Who knew how long he would have lain there if it had. But it happened on the golf course, while he was entertaining a client.

Her father hated golf.

When the military honors were over and the priest had completed the service, the rain pounding on the green canopy that protected him, the casket and the seated family—which was only Lilli—she stood and let the so-called mourners come to her to offer their condolences. The rain discouraged any lingerers. She stood there, holding a folded American flag, as every car pulled away, everyone heading back to regularly scheduled lives. Finally, she was alone at the graveside, her father's casket still propped above the hole someone had dug for him. It was fitting that she was alone.

She didn't know how long she'd stood there, but eventually, a man in a tidy black suit, holding a discreet black umbrella, came up beside her. "I'm very sorry, miss, but we need to inter…"

Her father. They needed to inter her father. She looked up and saw two men in work clothes standing at a respectful distance, getting wet and clearly waiting for her to move along. She did. She went home.

She had a regularly scheduled life to get back to, as well. She had one week's leave. One week in which to figure out what to do about the leavings of her father's life—and her own. The house she'd grown up in, full of the curios of a lifetime. Family photos. Her childhood keepsakes. Her grandmother's pottery. Her father's den, full of plaques and trophies and mysterious papers. Her father's car—his beautiful, black 1968 Barracuda fastback. He'd loved that car like a son. Her mother's…no, there was almost nothing left of her mother. Her father had gone through the house in a purifying rage shortly after they'd buried her.

She wanted almost none of it. She packed up the family photos, the books, her grandmother's pottery, a few pieces of jewelry, and a couple of mementos and put it all in storage. Then she contacted her father's lawyer and set to him the task of selling everything else, taking his percentage, and sending her a check for the rest.

She threw her duffel into the back of the 'Cuda and drove back to Fort Rucker, Alabama from Stockton, California, which was her home no longer.

CHAPTER NINE

Lilli knew she was drunk—too drunk. She'd had too many shots, too many beers, and not nearly enough to eat during the day. She'd screwed up. But she could not make herself care. She felt good. She felt loose. She'd had fun. And she felt really, incredibly, epically fucking horny. She was standing against Isaac, pressed snugly to the hard wall of his huge body, feeling the rough, thick skin of his palms and fingertips on her back, unhooking her bra.

(She was in his house, though; this was a problem. She didn't even know where his house was. She needed to focus on that.)

She was standing there, feeling his hands on her, his mouth on her, his big, hard cock bound in his jeans but still digging into her belly. And then his hands were on her breasts, cupping and caressing under her buttoned shirt and loose bra. Too many clothes. There were far too many clothes in this scenario. She fumbled at the buttons of her shirt, needing to free his hands and her breasts.

His mouth still hard on hers, he chuckled and turned his hands, grabbing the placket of her top from the inside and ripping it open. The buttons that had still been closed must have held, because Lilli heard a clear sound of rending fabric as her shirt fell open wide.

As she shrugged it off her shoulders, she backed away from his beautiful mouth enough to say, "Tha' sucks, dude. I don' have many clothes with me."

(Something told her that she'd said a wrong thing in that sentence, but she didn't bother figuring it out.)

"I'll buy ya a new one," Isaac growled and he yanked her bra off her arms and took full possession of her breasts.

"Fuck, you feel good." Surprising her completely, he dropped to his knees, pressing his mouth to her belly. His beard tickled and scratched as he sucked her skin. She felt his hands at her jeans, opening them roughly, and she canted her hips closer to him, grabbing fistfuls of his hair to keep him as close to her as possible.

"God, God, God," she moaned, wanting to be naked, wanting him to be naked. But his hands were on her ass now; he wasn't pulling her jeans down, though he was biting at her thong, plucking it with his teeth. She moaned, feeling a need for his rough hands on her bare skin.

"You smell so *goddamn* good." He took a deep breath and growled it out; she felt the rumble of it against her pubic bone. His hands gripped the backs of her thighs and slid firmly down until he reached her boots. "These are badass, Sport. Sexy as fuck." He pulled down the zipper on one, then the other, and held her hips as she kicked her feet free of them.

Then he reached up and grabbed the loose waistband of her open jeans and yanked hard, bringing them down, her thong tangled up in them, until she could pull her feet and legs finally free.

And again, she was naked while he was fully clothed. But his hands were on her, finally. He pushed her roughly against the door—Jesus, they were still standing in his front hall—and lifted her right leg to hook it over his shoulder, spreading her wide. He ran his fingers back and forth through her folds, over her clit, and she couldn't shut up, she couldn't hold still. She had her hands yet knotted in his hair, and she pulled, trying to bring his mouth back to suck on her. With a low, unbelievably sexy chortle, he obliged, his hands wrapping around her hips until his fingers hooked in the cleft of her ass. He pressed his mouth to her clit and sucked it hard into his mouth, dragging it over his teeth.

"Oh, fuck!" Her hips were spasming so hard she didn't think she could keep standing, especially not with her right leg over his shoulder. But he pushed harder on her, holding her up on the door, his hands clutching her ass. She felt his fingers at her anus then, and she arched hard, pulling away from the door. "Oh, yeah! Oh, do it!" God, she wanted that. She needed it.

Isaac stilled and pulled away. Whimpering with the loss of the beautiful sensations he'd been making all through her, dizzy with drink and desire, she opened her eyes and looked down at him, kneeling at her feet.

He was looking up at her, panting, his beard glistening with her wet. She still had his hair in her fists; she let go now, and brushed her hand through his beard. He turned his head and kissed her palm. The simple gesture made her loins cramp. As they looked into each other's eyes, Isaac brought a hand around to her front and pushed it between her legs, sliding his fingers slowly between her folds. He rubbed hard circles on her clit until she whimpered, then moved to probe inside her until she moaned. Then he drew his fingers back farther and pushed against the taut seal of her anus. Her hips flexed involuntarily, and she nodded. "Yeah. Please. Please."

He pushed his finger in, and when she cried out, he stilled again. "Don't stop. I want more." He pulled that finger out and went back in with two this time. And this time, he flexed them inside her, back and forth—and he leaned forward again and sucked her clit.

Ecstasy exploded through her body, and her knee gave, which drove her body down farther onto his fingers. She came immediately, screaming his name and writhing on his face and hand until she was flailing. He stopped and stood, holding her up as her body twitched the end of its release.

"Jesus motherfucking Christ, woman," he growled. He swung her, still woozy from the crushing intensity of her climax, into his arms and carried her down a hall. She had no idea where he was taking her, and she didn't care a whit.

He laid her on a bed, a huge king-size bed with lush cream-colored sheets and a fluffy black comforter. Comfy. Feeling liquid and loose, she opened her eyes and watched him stripping his clothes off in a clumsy rush. It was cute to see her huge, macho biker man hopping around on one leg, trying to yank his boot off. She squirmed, nesting deeper into his soft, lovely linens.

(*Her* biker man? Was he *her* biker man? Should she stop and think about that?)

He was naked now—so fucking gorgeously naked, with that amazing, beautiful cock standing right up for her—and her crawled over her with a fistful of condoms. When he was looming over her, grinning at her like a wolf, his long hair hanging around them, she rolled to her stomach. "I want more of that."

He groaned, and she felt him shift; then his hand was moving from her neck down her spine to her ass. He pushed his fingers between her cheeks and massaged her. "You want me up your ass?"

"God, yes." She knew he was big, but she didn't care. She wanted it. Nothing else would give her what she needed.

"Lilli—are you sure? I don't have lube."

She rolled to her back as he still hovered over her, framing her with his arms and legs. Taking the hand that had been on her back, she pushed it between her legs, grunting a little at the sweet pleasure of his touch. "Does it feel like you need lube? Use me."

He looked hesitant, confused. Shaking off her tipsy haze a little, she asked, "Don't you want to?"

He laughed. "Do I want to have your ass? Your spectacular ass? Uh, yeah, I do. But, baby, I can honestly say that never once in all my years of fucking women has one ever *asked* for that before."

She shrugged, unsure whether he was criticizing her or praising her or what. She didn't really care, unless it got in the way of what she wanted. Because she was just about vibrating with need. "That a problem?"

He shifted down to his elbows, and she felt him feeding his fingers into her hair. His cock was pressed uncomfortably into her belly. She could think of a much, much better place for it. But he was staring into her eyes, and she settled, letting him have the moment he apparently needed. "You astound me," he whispered, then kissed her.

The kiss was deep and passionate—meaningful, somehow—and when he sucked her tongue into his mouth, she moaned and arched, loving the coarseness of his body covering hers, but wanting so much more. "Please, please, please," she whispered against his lips.

With a wild grin, almost a snarl, he came up on his knees and flipped her over. He dragged her hips up until she was on her knees. Then he pushed a hand between her legs, fingered her clit roughly, and then plunged three fingers into her core. She cried out and arched, loving his intensity. He pulled his fingers back, wetting her cleft, circling her anus.

Then he stopped. "You want me to cover up?"

Her head and chest on the bed, Lilli lifted up a little and looked at him under her arm, upside down. The room tipped back and forth a bit. "Not for this, no."

He growled and shoved himself into her core. She tried to care that he wasn't wearing a condom, to remind him not to come inside her that way, but he felt so fucking good. And then he withdrew, and she felt him pressing steadily against her anus. She could feel his girth already. But she wanted it. This was not something she liked all the time, but now, yes. Oh, yes.

He entered her, moving slowly. God, he made her so full. Already she felt stretched and full to bursting. She could feel the muscles around him and around her clit pulsing, and she moaned.

"Fuck, baby, fuck. This is so good it might well kill me." He was still moving slowly, and she could feel a tremor in his hands where they held her hips. She pushed back toward him, bringing him into her, to the hilt. They both cried out at that. And then he started to move, rocking in and out, slowly at first, but speeding up with every firm thrust. She could feel his whole body shaking.

God, it felt good. She moved with him, moaning, feeling the tight, slick slide everywhere, in her joints, in her core, in her head. She could hear the high-pitched sounds she was making, like a whine, and she grabbed handfuls of his comforter and buried her face in it.

He stopped and pulled out, and she gasped as the head of his cock left her. Looking over her shoulder at him, she asked, "Why'd you stop? That was great."

"I love your ass, baby, but I can't get to enough of you." He turned and lay on his back, then guided her over to straddle him. "Legs forward, feet on the bed." Once she figured out what he meant, she did it. And then he guided her down, holding his cock. He pressed against her anus and filled her the way she wanted again, and she dropped her head back and moaned.

"You set the pace, Sport. And I can get to all your excellent parts." As if to demonstrate, he grabbed her nipples and gave them just the right pinch. Her whole body clenched as she cried out.

He arched back as she clamped hard around him. "Fuck! Easy, easy. To be in you bare, Jesus."

She set the pace, moving on him just right to feel full and stretched but not torn. He worked her breasts, her clit, and her core, taking his time as he moved from one to the other to the other until she was in a frenzy, bouncing on him, no longer caring if he made her too full. Then he slid his fingers into her, pressing his thumb to her clit, his other hand tweaking her nipple, and she thought she'd die. He was everywhere, exciting every part of her.

Her climax was on her, she came forward, shifting to her knees and bucking on him, her hands on his pecs. Isaac grabbed her hips in a death grip; she could feel the bruises happening, and she could not have cared any less. He was sweating and grimacing as if in pain. "Baby, come on come on," he chanted.

Another minute or so, and it was there. She somehow felt the need to announce it, "Oh, God, I'm coming. I'm coming, I'm coming. Oh, fuck. Fuck, it's big."

He grabbed her ass in his hands and rolled, putting her on her back. The shift of his cock in her tight shaft made her scream. His hands on the backs of her thighs, he pushed her legs to her chest and slammed into her until she screamed again, coming so hard she saw stars. He shouted, "Oh, fuck, oh, fuck, oh, *God*!" and then he held, twitching, for a long moment, his neck corded with effort.

He pulled gently out of her as soon as he was done and flopped to the bed at her side. They lay together, panting.

133

Lilli felt sated and dizzy. She was also quite sore. She needed a bathroom. As she started to scoot off the bed in search of one, she felt Isaac's hand clamp around her wrist. "Don't go."

She turned and regarded him. There was something in the way he said that, in his choice of words, that seemed important. She couldn't figure out what, though. She also needed water; she could feel the hangover on its way. Fucking tequila.

"Just need the bathroom."

He smiled and released her wrist. "First door on the left." She stood, swayed, found her feet and moved gingerly to the bathroom.

Yep. Quite sore. She peed, carefully cleaned herself, and then looked for a glass so that she could get a drink. Nothing. So she put her mouth to the stream from the faucet and drank that way.

When she came back to his bedroom, he was sitting up in bed, his legs under the covers. His bed was gorgeous. A dark, reddish wood, polished to a high gleam, it was a four-poster bed with heavy, elaborate posts. He'd neatened the linens and turned the other side down for her. A bit suspicious of what was going on, she eased her sore self into the bed and looked at him, waiting for…something.

He handed her a tall glass of ice water. "Thought you might need some hydration." Smiling, she took the glass and nodded her thanks.

His expression was concerned. "You okay, Sport?"

She drank the water in long, loud gulps, draining the large glass. "Yeah. Just…sobering up.

"Should I be sorry about what we just did? Did I take advantage?" He handed her his half-full glass of water, and she drank that, too.

"No. Just—I usually know a guy better before I do that." She was feeling really guarded as the giddy tequila haze ebbed away. Jesus Christ. She was in his house. She had no idea where he lived. She was naked and had no idea where her clothes were—oh, wait. By his front door. He'd ruined her top. She had no weapon. She was completely vulnerable to him. She'd let him—no, she'd *begged* him to—go up her ass. Without a condom. This was a ton of trust she'd inadvertently given him, this man at whom she'd been aiming a kill shot not much more than a day ago.

He took the second empty glass from her and set it on the nightstand before he scooted closer, picking up her hand in his. "I think we're getting to know each other in the important ways first." He lifted her hand to his mouth for a kiss. His lips still brushing the back of her hand, he said. "You amaze me, Lilli. I'm not afraid to say I'm gettin' caught up here."

So was she; she knew it. She shook her head. This was all a bad, bad idea. She had no business getting involved with him. "Isaac, I"—she was overtaken by a huge yawn. Embarrassed, she stuttered, "God. I-I'm-I'm sorry."

He laughed. "It's cool. Let's sleep. We can talk tomorrow." He shifted to lay his head on the pillow, and he stretched out his arm to invite her close. He wanted her to lie on him and sleep. No. That was another bad, bad idea.

He obviously sensed her hesitation, because he smiled and said, "Lilli, I don't bite—well, only when you ask me to. I just want to feel you. There hasn't been a woman in this bed in a very, very long time.

Every time he said her name, she felt like he was pulling her closer to some point of no return. She relented, and lay down in the warm curl of his arm, her head pillowed on his firm, gorgeous chest. He kissed her head and turned out the light.

~oOo~

"Lilli! Fuck—Lilli!"

She came awake with a start. She was straddling Isaac, and he was holding her hands—curled into claws—away from his head. She relaxed immediately and leapt away from him and off the bed. Her head felt like elephants were doing the merengue on her cerebellum.

"Sorry. Sorry. Fuck." She backed toward the door. Goddamn it, she wished she knew how to get back to her place.

He got up and came toward her. "It's okay. You just freaked me out. Are you okay?"

"Yeah. Just a dream."

"Helluva dream, Sport."

"Yeah. I'm okay—it's gone now. I'll just—you have a couch or something I can sleep on?" It was still too early to be light.

He reached her and took her hands. "Nope. No couch for sleeping. Come back. I'm cool. You're cool. We'll just go back to sleep."

She didn't want to, but *fuck* her head hurt. "Okay. Got any aspirin?"

He grinned. "You bet. Here, just get back in bed"—he helped her in and covered her up—"and I'll be right back."

He brought her aspirin with another big glass of water. She took the pills and drank all the water. When he got back into bed, he pulled her down, her back to his chest. Tired, hurting, and freaking out, Lilli didn't resist. They spent the rest of the night, quietly, sleeping like spoons.

~oOo~

When she woke again, the room was bright with morning sun, and Isaac was sitting, fully clothed in his usual Johnny Cash ensemble, on the side of the bed, his hand on her leg.

"Morning, hellcat. You feelin' okay?"

She was, actually. Some residual headache, and some soreness in her nethers, but she felt okay. "Yeah. Hungry. Do you have breakfast things here?"

He winked and patted her thigh. "I'm not much in the kitchen, but there's coffee, and a bunch of different kinds of cereal, hot or cold." He dangled a black t-shirt on his finger. "I owe you a new top, and I'm good for it, but you can have this for now. The rest of your clothes are on that chair in the corner." He nodded toward a really nice wood and leather chair, on which she could see her jeans and underwear. "I put out a fresh towel if you want a shower. Sorry I don't have an extra toothbrush, but the paste is on the counter.

She felt awkward and shy. She hadn't been in this position in…she'd never been in this position before. "Thanks, Isaac." She sat up.

He moved closer to the head of the bed and leaned over her, his hands on either side of her hips. He kissed her gently, running his tongue softly over her lips. "Mmmm.

Don't mention it, Sport. You and I need to talk, though, I think."

She agreed, so she nodded.

"Okay. I'll meet you in the kitchen. Down the hall, to your right, through the living room." He gave her another quick kiss and left the room.

~oOo~

She felt fresher, less sore, and nearly at full power when she found him in his kitchen. She'd taken a mini-tour on the way, not snooping, but paying attention to what she saw. There was a lot—a *lot*—of beautiful wood furniture throughout his house. Must have been worth a fortune. What décor he had was mostly wood, too, some amazing sculpted pieces made of different colors and types of wood. Even the picture frames were lovely. There was a wall of photos in the main hallway, and she'd lingered over those. Isaac seemed to have come from a family of four—mom, dad, older sister, and Isaac. The photos seemed to stop when Isaac was in his early teens. As she went on through the living room, she noted with pleasure a full wall of gorgeous bookcases, nearly overflowing with books.

The kitchen was a very basic country kitchen which didn't seem to have been updated since the 1940s. Even the appliances were old—a monstrous white double gas range, and a refrigerator that long predated the "frost-free" era. The sink was a huge porcelain thing with drainboards on both sides. The cabinets were wood, painted white, with fabric front panels. Lilli thought there were tiny, faded strawberries on the fabric. The floor was an old fashioned sheet linoleum in a faded red color with little gilt flakes in it.

There was a long, narrow table, with beautifully turned legs, under a big window. On it sat a coffeemaker, a pop-up toaster, and a microwave.

Lilli was starting to get the idea that Isaac lived in his childhood home. He lived alone in his childhood home.

In the center of the room was an oblong table made of cherry or mahogany. It had a lustrous finish, like all of the wood she'd seen as she'd found her way into this room. He was sitting at the table with a cup of coffee. When she'd come around the corner, he seemed to be simply staring into space. He turned now and smiled broadly as she entered. "You look good, Sport. I'm thinking there's nothing you look bad in."

She liked wearing his t-shirt. She swam in it, but she still felt sexy wearing it. "Well, orange is very much not my color. For future reference."

He winked. "Better stay out of trouble, then." She didn't catch the joke at first, then—*oh, orange jumpsuits, got it*—she rolled her eyes.

"Cereal's in the left cabinet, bowls and cups in the right. There's milk in the fridge and coffee under the window. Help yourself."

She could feel him watching her as she crossed the room and got out a bowl and a cup. She put them on the table and then turned for some cereal. When she opened the cabinet, she squealed.

Isaac jumped in his seat behind her. "Fuck! What?"

"Oh. My. *God*. You have Cookie Crisp? Chocolate Chip Cookie Crisp? I *love* Cookie Crisp! I haven't had any in *years*."

He laughed. "I have a thing for cereal. I don't cook, and if I'm too busy to hit the diner, I'll just have cereal. I like the sweet shit for when I'm stoned."

"I like the sweet shit for when I'm *breathing*. Oh, this just makes my day!" She brought the box to the table and filled her bowl until it mounded above the rim.

"How are you gonna get milk in there?"

"Watch and learn, watch and learn." She went to the fridge and pulled out a glass bottle of milk. Then, in the system she and her girlfriends in middle school had perfected, she slowly poured milk into the cracks and crevices left by the little cookie wafers. She got plenty of milk in the bowl without displacing a wafer.

Isaac nodded. "Impressive. If you love that shit so much, why don't you just buy yourself some?"

Lilli sat at his beautiful table and tucked into her bowl of delicious decadence, feeling relaxed and happy. With her mouth full of cereal, she shrugged and answered. "Don't know. Wasn't breakfast at our house, and I never think of cereal when I'm at the store." She swallowed and filled her mouth with more scrumptious morsels.

He laughed. "You're fuckin' cute, you know that?" He stood and got himself a bowl, then reached for the Cookie Crisp and milk. Lilli resisted the urge to bat his hand away from the box. It was his, after all.

As they ate, Isaac watched her, his sideways smile planted on his face. Then, when they were done, and, still grinning, he'd watched her drink the milk from the bowl, he put the dishes in the sink and said. "Okay, Sport. Time to talk."

Suddenly, Lilli felt a great deal less relaxed and happy. She waited for him to sit back down, and then she started, "Isaac, about what you said—"

He held up his hand to stop her. "We shouldn't start there. We should start someplace else." He stood again and left the room. When he came back, he was holding a small sheaf of white printer paper. "Let's start here." He laid the sheets in front of her and sat back down.

Lilli looked down at a printout of an article from the online edition of *The Stars and Stripes*, the newspaper of the US Armed Forces. The first page showed the headline: ON THE FAST TRACK: BLACK HAWK PILOT, YOUNGEST WOMAN TO REACH O-4 RANK. There was a photo of Lilli, in her flight gear, her helmet under her arm, standing next to her copter. The caption read, simply, *Maj. Lillian Accardo*.

Fuck.

CHAPTER TEN

Isaac watched Lilli read the headline of the article about her and waited for her reaction.

He'd had some time to process the information he had. He'd been shocked at first, then a good deal more suspicious. As he thought about it, though, he couldn't see the threat. What he'd learned of Lilli over the past several days didn't jive with some military intrigue focused on his club or his town. What had happened between them the night before had only strengthened that understanding. So now he was simply impressed.

Bart, genius geek that he was, had managed to find a crack along the sides of that wall. He still couldn't get through it, so Isaac had no idea what the fuck Lilli was doing in Signal Bend, but he had this, and so he had her name. Bart was working on getting more of her history, but Isaac hoped that he would now hear it from Lilli herself.

She turned and said, "How long have you had this?"

Understanding why it was an important question, he answered, "Yesterday. After I left your place. That call I got? Was Bart."

"What else do you know?"

"For now, that's it. Bart found that article. He'll be looking for more, of course, but not till tomorrow. I'm hoping he won't need to bother. Will he?"

For a full minute or more, Lilli just stared at him. He could almost see the gears turning; he just didn't know where they were headed. Finally, she cleared her throat and shifted sideways in her chair. "You have plans today? That phone going to go off and interrupt us?"

"No plans. Shit shuts down on Sundays, for the most part. That phone rings, it's an emergency. My other phone rings, I'll ignore it. We talkin'?"

Her expression was flat and stony. This was not the woman squealing over kid cereal fifteen minutes ago. "We're talking. First thing I'm saying, before I give you anything, is my guy is better than your guy. I know more about you than you know about me. You want to hurt me, I take you and your club down, too."

His stomach coiled into a knot instantly. Christ. Had he misread her that badly? Had he put his club at risk for a good fuck? He leaned forward, his forearms on the table, and snarled, "You here to hurt me and mine?"

She shook her head. "No, Isaac. I knew nothing about your club until a couple of days ago. When you threatened me that morning, I got myself some security. That's all it is. I'm not here for you, and I have no wish to hurt you. I'm protecting myself."

"But your guy knows what you know." Fuck. *Fuck*. He'd misplayed every turn.

"He does. He won't hurt you, either."

"So now I'm trusting someone I've never even seen?"

"Looks that way."

Isaac shoved his chair back and stood up, nearly tipping it over. He stalked around the kitchen for a minute and then came back and leaned on the table, facing her. "If my club or my town gets hurt because—because of—this"—he gestured wildly between them—"I will rain unholy fire, I swear to God."

143

"It's called Mutually Assured Destruction. I can't hurt you because you can hurt me, and vice versa. I'm going to tell you what's behind the wall that Bart won't breach—not for weeks, anyway. He's really good, though, to have found this"—she pushed at the pages in front of her—"I could get him a contract if he wanted it."

Isaac snorted. "He's a convicted felon, Sport. Government won't want him."

"You'd be surprised who the government wants for certain kinds of jobs. All the hackers I know have records. But that's beside the point. I know about the meth. I know your contacts. I have interesting details that you think you protected. I don't care about any of it, unless you're coming for me. It's not why I'm here." She crossed her leg over her knee. "So the question is, are you coming for me?"

She had completely blindsided him. He'd been prepared— or he'd told himself he was, anyway—for her to be working against the club somehow. He'd hoped—and expected, truthfully—that she had no interest in the club at all. It seemed he'd been right, until he'd made her feel threatened. Fuck. Now, she was primly telling him that she could fuck him, his club, and his town hard whenever she felt like it. And he had nothing on her but an apparently glorious military record. He slammed his fist into the table. "FUCK!"

Very calmly, she said, "Isaac, sit. I don't want to hurt you. If we're being straight, then let's be straight. I will tell you some things, but it cannot—*cannot*—leave this house. And there are some things I just can't tell you. In fact, I can't tell you a lot that has to do with the reason I'm here under an assumed name."

He sat. "What the fuck? That's what I need to know."

"I'm not in the Army any longer. Now I do very highly classified contract work. My identity is concealed because there aren't many who do what I do. It's also why we don't work from DC. We're spread out in out-of-the-way places. I'm out of bounds to tell you that much. I won't tell you what it is I do."

"Why is the wall so obvious?"

"So that they know as soon as someone starts looking. Well-concealed security has a blind spot; it takes time to see that anyone's poking around. A hacker who hits a wall like this, though, is known right away. Bart is tagged, I'm sure. No matter how good he is, if he probed hard enough to come up with that article, then they know he's looking. He needs to wipe his slate and start fresh. You should probably use that only-for-emergencies phone and tell him that now, in case he's putting in some off-the-clock time. The biggest threat I posed to you before I did my own digging was you digging into me."

Isaac nodded, stood and pulled his burner out. Fuck, fuck, fuck. He was so angry his hands were shaking. But who was he angry at? Her? He felt betrayed, but had she betrayed him? How? No—he was angry at himself. He'd been sloppy. And he was in deep with this woman. He'd spent most of the hours after her nightmare watching her sleep, fucking *guarding* her, feeling protective and—and—FUCK.

Bart answered, clearly from a deep sleep. Good; he hadn't been working. "Yeah."

"Stay off the Lilli thing, Bart. Do NOT fuck with it again. She says she's sure you're tagged. Do you know what that means?" Because Isaac didn't, not really.

"Fuck. Yeah. I'm on it." He sounded fully awake now.

Isaac ended the call and came back to the table. "Is this talk gonna have any satisfaction for me, or are you just going to keep ruining my fucking day?" Jesus, he needed to punch something.

"You know my name is Lilli Accardo. You know I was an officer and a pilot in the Army. I'm not from Texas. I'm from California. The rest of it is just normal stuff that people share in the process of getting to know each other. It's protected because it's identifying, nothing more. So if you still want to get to know me, then we should maybe spend the day doing that. Both of us. But I'm still Lilli Carson in this town. Anyone who doesn't know differently right now should never know differently. I assume your club knows how to keep quiet."

He nodded. But there was too much missing. The moves weren't clear. "You haven't told me shit I didn't know. Why here? Why Signal Bend? Nothing you've told me should have put you in need of protection from us. You have something else to hide, something that can hurt you."

Again, she simply looked at him, thinking. Then: "If I tell you the rest, it stays between you and me. *Only* you and me. The risk I take to tell you is huge."

No, it wasn't. She'd seen to that. "That's why you got intel on us, right? So there wouldn't be that risk? You seem pretty fucking safe." She was like a completely different person. Not the prickly, bantering woman he'd met, not the wild bedmate, not the free and delightful drunk. Not the kid eating cookie cereal. This version was calculating and eerily calm.

"I'm here to kill someone."

Stunned, he sat there with his mouth open, unable to think what to say. Finally, words happened. "Are you telling me you're a government *assassin*?"

But she shook her head. "No, this is a personal project. Someone who hurt me and mine very badly in Afghanistan and got away with it. I consider it an assassination, as do the people helping me. But legally speaking, I plan to murder him." She smiled. "And now you can hurt me, too."

Oh, shit. Isaac's mind raced, trying to fit this new information into his understanding of her. And now he had a whole new set of problems related to Lilli. "Who? Someone in Signal Bend? In my town?"

"No, but someone fairly close. I wouldn't move into the same small town as my target. There's some modest distance between us."

He tried to think. He knew everybody in town and virtually everybody in a radius ten miles or more around the town. Who'd been in Afghanistan? He could think of a few people, but no one he'd peg for doing something that would warrant that kind of retaliation. He took a calming breath. Stepping back from this a little, he ordered his thoughts. His club and his town were safe from her. He believed that. She had nothing to fear from him, so he had nothing to fear from her. And if what this guy did was as bad as all that, then he'd help her take the fucker down. "You gotta tell me who he is, baby, and what he did."

But she shook her head. "No, Isaac. You need to stay out of it. Knowing any more than what I've told you puts you at risk if I go down. And that puts your club and town at risk."

"And if I want to help?"

"The people with the most vested interest are involved. There's a plan in place, and we're working it." She leaned forward. "Is that enough to trust me?"

She was sitting at his table, wearing his t-shirt, her beautiful hair long and loose, lying over her shoulder. He was falling in love with her; he'd understood that last night, watching her sleep. He wondered if the dream she'd had—the nightmare—had to do with this guy she was after. If someone had hurt her, Isaac wanted him dead.

He trusted her. From what he could tell, she played it straight or said why she wasn't. And he wanted her. He wanted to be able to trust her, and he wanted her to trust him. "Yeah. I trust you. I get any of that back?"

"I trust you, Isaac. I wouldn't have told you any of this if I didn't. I'd have just used what I know and gotten you out of my way."

"Jesus, Lilli. That's cold."

"No. It's smart. Getting involved with you is not. But here I am."

Isaac got up from his chair and went to squat next to hers. They had an opportunity to turn this conversation, this day, this thing between them around. He put his hands on her thigh. "Are you involved with me, Sport?"

She slid her hand under his, and he folded his fingers around it. "Yeah. Way too deep." She leaned down and kissed him.

With a sigh, Isaac laid his forehead on her leg. "What are we gonna do about that?"

She laughed. "Why don't you show me around your house?"

"Good idea." He stood and held out his hand.

~oOo~

He showed her around the house, told her that his family had lived in it for generations. He was the first to live in it alone, in fact. The family farm had been large, but all of the arable land had been sold off, and now only the homestead, on seven acres, was left. His grandfather had been the last to work any farmland; Isaac's father had been the last to sell it.

Lilli made several comments about the beauty of the wood pieces throughout the house, and he was glad to hear it. He was looking forward to taking her outside. But first, she wanted to look at the wall of photos. That gallery had grown for generations. Isaac was the only one not to have added a single photo. He'd changed the frames but had not added any new pictures.

He pointed out grandparents and great-grandparents, aunts, uncles, cousins, and people so far removed generationally they could rightly be called ancestors. She pointed to pictures from his life, and he identified his parents and his sister. "That's my mom. She died when I was twelve."

"She was beautiful."

"Yeah, she was. She hanged herself."

Lilli turned fast, her eyes wide. He never talked about his mother—hell, his family—at all. There were patches who only knew what happened through rumor and gossip. She put her hand on his arm, and he muscled away the urge to shake her off.

"Isaac, I'm sorry." He shook his head, ready to move on, but she moved to stand in front of him. "Isaac. My mother cut her wrists and bled out in her bathtub. I found her. I was ten."

He looked down at her with a start. "God." Something came over him in a jolt that he could not possibly define, and he grabbed her face and kissed her, fervently, his tongue probing deeply into her mouth. He felt her hands clutching his shirt as she kissed him back. When he pulled away, he searched her face for some kind of clue that she thought making out over their mothers' suicides was inappropriate, but she simply looked well-kissed. Still, he muttered, "Sorry."

"Don't be. I get it." She traced the length of the scar on his face.

He closed his eyes at the tender contact. "Never known anybody who does before. Nobody gets it."

"I know. Why'd she do it?"

He shook his head again, hating to go to that place. Then he shrugged. "My father was a mean bastard. Best answer I got. She didn't leave a note. Yours?"

"No note from her, either. I don't know much. My dad did a purge after she died. But from what I remember, and what I know now, I think she was bipolar. My most vivid memory of her is her body in the bathtub, and sitting in there with it waiting for somebody to find me, but I also remember that she used to take me 'adventuring,'"—Lilli made the air quotes around the word—"her word for it was *avventurandosi,* and we'd end up in these crazy places with her freaking out because she didn't speak very good English, and I had to talk to strangers to try to get back home. I'm guessing that was mania. It wasn't a great time." She stopped and furrowed her brow. "Wow. I've literally never told that story to another human being, ever."

Isaac felt the urge to kiss her again, but he tamped it down. "Jesus, Lilli. That's intense."

She laughed sadly. "Yeah. Just to get it out of the way, I'm an only child, and my dad died when I was twenty-three. He was awesome."

"Can I ask how old you are now?" He knew that was a question a lot of women hated.

She didn't hesitate. "Thirty-three. You?"

"Thirty-nine."

She grinned. He loved her smile; her mouth was rosy and lovely, and her eyes lit up. "See, look at how much we're learning. You said 'was' when you mentioned your dad. We both orphans?"

"Yeah. He died twelve years ago. Dropped his bike on an icy road and went under a truck. He was the MC president before me. He was Big Ike, and I was Little Ike until he died. That's why I hate that fucking name."

"Did you live here with him?"

"Not since I was eighteen. I stayed at the clubhouse. Moved back in here after he died."

"What about your sister?"

"Martha. Don't know. She's four years older than me. She left in the dark one night not long after my mom died, and no one's heard from her since. I get why she left. My old man was already turning his meanness on her. But she left me behind."

"Did he..." She didn't finish, but she didn't need to.

Isaac shrugged. "Some. Not so unusual in these parts. Got better when I grew to be a lot bigger than him. Stopped, for the most part, when I started prospecting." He shook off the melancholy gloom that was beginning to settle on his shoulders. "Anyway, that's the past. You said your mom's English wasn't good?"

Lilli smiled. "So *my* past is still in the present, I see. My mom was born and raised in Italy. My dad was born there, too, but he came over really young. They met when he was stationed in Europe—he was in the Army, too. Special Forces."

"He was a badass, then. I see where you get it." That pleased her, and Isaac was glad of it. But she'd made him curious. "Lilli, what languages do you speak?"

The pleased smiled he'd brought out disappeared, and she looked guarded again, as she contemplated him. Then, she sighed, as if resigned to her fate. She counted them off on her fingers. "English, Italian, French, Spanish, German, Arabic, Farsi, and Hebrew."

He laughed, loudly, and she looked at him like he was both crazy and rude. "Sorry. It's just—I don't get intimidated often, but that did it. How fucking smart are you?"

"Pretty fucking smart, but that's beside the point. I was raised bilingual. It makes picking up new languages ridiculously easy. No need to be intimidated." Now she wore a sly grin. "Not by that, anyway."

Okay, now he needed to show her that there was something he could do, too. He took her hand. "Come with me. Get your boots on. I want to show you something."

When she was appropriately shod, he led her out to the largest outbuilding and unlocked the door. She practically shrieked.

"Hah! You locked it!"

Laughing, he said, "Easy, there, Sport. This I lock. The house, I don't." He opened the door, and the strong aroma of wood shavings billowed out on the late morning breeze. It was his favorite smell. Well, second favorite now, supplanted by the natural scent of the woman standing with him. He let her go in first, and she stood just inside the doorway and gaped.

"Isaac, what?" She was taking in what he'd spent most of his life building up. Saws and planes and a massive lathe, chisels and files and rasps, stain and varnish and brushes and wood. A huge work table in the center of the room. All of it neatly organized. He thought this big room was beautiful. He could live in it.

"It's my woodshop. The furniture and doodads in the house that you like—I made them."

She turned her gaping face toward him and gaped some more. She went over to his row of shelving units, where he stored the pieces he intended to sell at art shows and craft fairs around the state. She picked up a burled vase that was part of a run he'd turned from some beautiful walnut he'd found near Kansas City. The turnings were his most artistic work.

"You *made* this?" He nodded, feeling suddenly self-conscious. She carefully set the vase down and ran her fingers lightly over the whole shelf of turnings. Then she went to his stock of carved pieces and spun to face him. She was holding a hummingbird at a lily, the bird no bigger than her palm. Her eyes were damp. "Jesus, Isaac. This is—it's beautiful. I'm—in awe."

The hummingbird was no big deal. He'd price it for twenty bucks, dicker down to fifteen, at a craft fair. He could carve a couple of those in an afternoon. There were a dozen on the shelf right now. But Lilli was carrying that one around with her as she looked at everything in the room. He went to her. "You want that?"

"What? Oh, I'm sorry—I didn't mean—" She blushed. "My nonna loved hummingbirds." She moved to take it back to the shelf, but he caught her arm and held her.

"Nonna?"

"Grandma. Italian."

"Keep it."

"No, Isaac. I'm sorry, you should sell it. It's so beautiful."

"Keep it. If you like it, you should keep it. It's not a big deal to me. Look—there are a bunch on the same shelf you got that one."

"But this one is the prettiest." She smiled up at him, her eyes still shimmery. "Thank you." He was blown away by how much this revelation had affected her.

Now she pushed her hand up his chest and hooked it around his neck, pulling him toward her. Before she kissed him, she whispered, "You astound me," and brought his lips to hers.

Isaac was experiencing an acute case of emotional vertigo this morning. He still felt a little unsteady. But he was getting to know this woman, and he was letting her know him. Since the difficult discussion in the kitchen, there was a different atmosphere between them. They weren't trying to figure each other out. They were relaxed, and he recognized that this was the first time they'd been relaxed together, at least when Lilli was sober.

He wrapped his arms around her waist and deepened their kiss, lifting her off her feet. She hooked her arm, that hand still holding the carved hummingbird, around his back. He set her on the worktable, then reached back and took the carving out of her hand, setting it on the table, off to the side.

He'd built the table to suit his size, so its surface was right at the level of his hips. With Lilli sitting in front of him, they were crotch to crotch. She moaned and looped her legs around him, crossing her ankles on his ass.

The feel of her tongue moving on his, the taste of her, the way he could feel the muscles and tendons in her thighs squeezing him—fuck, everything about this woman made him hard. When she whimpered sweetly and flexed on him, he tore his mouth away from hers with a gasp.

"I want to be inside your sweet pussy right the fuck now. Too sore?"

Her eyes hooded with lust, she smiled and pulled at his belt. "Not for that."

Isaac growled and set about getting his woman naked.

INTERLUDE: 2009

Captain Lillian Accardo climbed down from her Black Hawk helicopter, call sign Big Donna. Her squad was waiting for her—fist bumps, high fives, and hugs all around. Another mission completed; objective secured, all troops back at base. Aside from a black eye Okada got when he came up too quickly behind Miller, no casualties at all.

Chief Pettijohn came toward her, heading to her ride to do the post-mission check. "All well, Cap?" he asked as he approached.

Lilli stopped and turned back to consider her ride. "She's still got that little shimmy in the swash."

"That's because she's such a sexy beast," he winked and moved on past, toward the copter.

Lilli liked Chief. He was old-school Army, iron-grey crew cut and stub cigar included, but even so, he didn't have trouble with a chick pilot. More did than didn't, but she was making her way. It had taken her almost a year to get her own squad fully on board, but she had them now. She was fairly certain most of them had forgotten she had tits, or had just stopped caring. She took pains not to make them especially obvious—not because she feared the men would make inappropriate contact, which she could handle, but because she liked that the only difference they now saw in her was the insignia on her uniform. She wasn't a piece of ass; she was their superior. She had their respect.

"Hey Cap, we're in for cards. You in?" That was Okada. Lilli smiled but shook her head. "Tempting, but I'll pass tonight." This close to the front, fraternization rules were looser; camaraderie, trust, and morale were paramount. So she could certainly go hang with the enlisted men of her squad if she wanted. But tonight, she wanted some quiet. She nodded to Mendez, her co-pilot, indicating that she had the debrief, and he was off the clock.

She reported in to Col. Corbett, the battalion Commanding Officer. Corbett had been one she'd had to work to win over. But after scores of successful missions and few casualties—and no troop losses—and after comporting herself solidly in her supervisory position, and proving physically capable, as well—even equal to, if not more capable than, many men in camp—ol' Corby had warmed up to her.

It didn't hurt that she was on her third straight long rotation in camp; with nothing and no one in the States to draw her interest, and loving her job like a calling, she was perfectly content to stay put where she was useful and needed. When she'd requested a third rotation, sitting across from Corby at his insufficient camp desk, he'd contemplated her closely for a long, uncomfortable time, his eyebrows raised. Then, he'd nodded. Since that day, he'd been in her pocket. She was going for a below-zone promotion to Major in a few months; she was fairly certain Corby would do what he could to see that she got it.

She'd earned it. She worked hard, she led well, she was smart, and she didn't back down. But below-zone promotions were rare. She knew her shot was better because she was a female in combat, and there would be good press if she got another early promotion. She wasn't averse to accepting an advantage. Her sex worked against her 99.99% of the time in her chosen career. If there was a chance for that scale to tip slightly in the other direction, she'd take it.

When she was done with her debrief with Corby, she came out of the command tent and ran headlong into Captain Ray Hobson. He shoved her off and sneered at her. Hobson had a massive pole up his ass over Lilli. He hated women in camp, he hated women in command, and he damn sure hated a woman several years his junior, in the same rank and doing the same job as he. He hated her with a bitter fire she'd at first found bewildering. Now she hated him right back with an even hotter fire. He was a misogynistic asshole who found every opportunity to try to make her feel small and threatened. Time was, he'd succeeded. Now, Lilli was just waiting for him to touch her. Just once, so she could put the bastard on the ground.

"Sucking up again, Hot Lips? You were in there awhile. Musta been sucking something. I'm up for nexts." He grabbed his crotch.

Lilli's gorge rose at her inability to take him down for that. But she couldn't go at him physically, not first. And she wouldn't report him. With one piece of paper, she'd undo all her hard work. No matter how unjust it was, reporting harassment would lose her the respect of just about everyone in camp. Hell, just about everyone in the Army. She would not give this amoeba the satisfaction.

Instead, she sneered right back at him and said, "That's comedy gold, Hobs. You must've kept the boys in the frat house howling. One way or another."

His voice low, he hissed, "You're nothin' but a cunt, Accardo. Never be more than that."

She brushed past him and crossed the dusty camp to the mess. She needed to get out of her flight suit, which was blazing hot in the 120F heat, but she was starving. And frankly, right at that moment, she wasn't feeling like stripping down to take a shower. Privacy was at a premium on a Forward Operating Base, and she felt exposed. It burned her that Hobson could still do that to her, but he could. So she went into the mess, got herself a tasteless chicken sandwich, some chips, and a soda, and sat alone, sweltering and fuming.

She was about halfway through her meal, such as it was, when Lopez, her crew chief, sat down across from her. She looked up, chewing.

"Permission to speak plainly, Cap?"

Lilli nodded.

He leaned in close. "There's some guys around here, their dicks shrink right up around a woman like you. Some, they just about turn inside out. Gives 'em a second asshole where their dick should be."

Well, that was colorful. And he must have seen her confrontation with Hobson, which sucked. Bad enough she had to deal with it; she didn't relish anyone knowing about it. "Your point?"

"Just don't let the assholes get you down, Cap. We got your back. You should come play cards. Sitting here alone is just… sad. Miller's wifey sent everybody a personal fan, so it's only, like, a hundred in our hut." He lowered his voice even more. "There's local beer, too. Okada scraped it up."

"You know I can't drink with you, Sarge." Alcohol was supposed to be banned on base, but Corby didn't enforce that rule, as long as the troops maintained some control over themselves. These troops saw a lot of action, and he reasoned they needed some ease. Grateful for the privilege, few got drunk. Still, Lilli didn't want to end up in a bad position. It was entirely possible that she could get called upon to fly unexpectedly, and she wouldn't risk her men. Plus, she was in charge. Wouldn't do to get loose and flirty around these guys. She'd worked hard to get them to see her otherwise.

"I know. But we'll be extra entertaining tonight. C'mon. What else are you gonna do?"

With a sigh and a smile she said, "Gimme fifteen for a shower and a change."

"Excellent! Bring lots of cash for us to take from you!" He put up his fist, and she bumped it.

"Dream on, Lopez. I'll try to leave you milk money when I'm done."

After her shower, wearing desert fatigue pants and a loose t-shirt, her hair braided and coiled again on the back of her head, Lilli joined the poker game. As soon as she came into the hut, the guys made way for her. They dealt her in on the next hand. Several guys had bottles of beer, a kind Lilli didn't recognize. Others had what would look to a layperson like bottles of regular Listerine. Except the mouthwash had been replaced with whiskey, scotch, or gold tequila and sent over in care packages from home. Contraband, but everybody looked the other way.

Okada waved a brown bottle in her direction and said, "Wanna brewski, Cap? It's warm and tastes like cat piss, but it gets the job done."

Seriously. He said *brewski*. He talked like that all the time, like he was an extra in *Animal House* or something. Lilli thought it was charmingly dorky. "As delightful as that sounds, Okada, I'm gonna let you boys enjoy that on your own."

Lopez tossed her a bottled water, and they got back to the game, which was competitive as hell but not serious at all. The guys trash talked and made sophomoric jokes. They also gossiped like they were at a quilting bee. Always remembering her role, Lilli still found a way to be in the mix with the rest of them.

This is what Lilli loved. She loved flying, she loved the adrenaline, the challenge of her job. She loved being good at it. Her job fulfilled her. But this, these guys, this bond—she didn't need any family but this. She would die for any one of them; she'd do it without a second thought.

CHAPTER ELEVEN

Lilli hiked back the seven miles to the Camaro. She threw her pack in the trunk and got in behind the wheel. She sat there, not noticing the heat in the black interior on this sweltering mid-July day, trying not to despair.

She hadn't seen her target in almost two weeks. She was beginning to think her window had slammed shut on her while she wasn't looking. Rick had no new intel for her, either. By the time he'd had confirmation for her, the target seemed to have disappeared.

Fuck, fuck, fuck!

Now Rick was in heavy search mode, trying to get a read on the new location—which meant that Lilli might be leaving Signal Bend. If things worked out according to plan, she would stay put for months, minimally, to avoid suspicious movements around the time of the kill—if, in fact, there was an investigation. But if the target had moved far, then she would have to follow.

She didn't want to go. With every passing day, she and Isaac were getting more wrapped up together. If things worked according to plan, there was no reason Lilli would have to leave Signal Bend at all if she didn't want to. She could do her actual job from anywhere, and a remote location was preferred. Although she'd only known Isaac a few weeks, Lilli understood that she'd stay if she could. She felt a bond with him that she had not felt before, not with someone who wasn't blood.

Lilli had a fairly extensive sexual past, but she didn't have a lot of experience with matters of the heart. She'd had a couple of steady boyfriends in high school, and she'd ended her virginity with the second, but she'd never thought she was in love with either. Living the cliché, she'd gotten experimental and adventurous in college and had slept with rather a lot of people for a while, until she'd met Peter, a grad student. They'd been serious. She'd thought she loved Peter. But when he'd gotten a job at a college in New Mexico and moved away, she hadn't even considered continuing the relationship long-distance. Within a couple of months, she'd more or less stopped thinking of him. So she'd been wrong—not love. Once she joined the service, her opportunities for romance had dwindled markedly. She'd had a couple of entirely physical arrangements with other officers while she was in Afghanistan, meeting for righteous, rowdy fucks when they could get R&R time together. But she'd never truly bonded with anyone.

What she felt with Isaac was something different. It reached a different place in her. She'd thought it was just something elementally physical, like their bodies were somehow more in sync than others, because she was drawn to him in ways that freaked her out a little. If they were in any kind of physical proximity, she found it very difficult not to be touching him. And maybe that was a lot of it, especially at first. But in these last couple of weeks they'd talked—not banter, but real talking—and she'd told him things she'd never told anyone. Things about her family, her mom. About her love for her father and how she missed him. Even some things about the Army.

She'd never talked about any of that with anyone, because she'd never had anyone to talk to before, no one she trusted to have that kind of power over her. But she did trust Isaac. She didn't know what he'd done to earn trust she'd never given before, but he had it.

She hadn't given him any more information about her target or why she meant to kill him, but she'd been tempted once or twice. She hadn't because to disclose would be to extend the risk to him. And to his credit, he'd only asked one more time, and when she'd refused, he'd let it drop. He trusted her, too.

She was in love with him. She hadn't said it; she didn't know if she could say it, but she was coming to understand the truth of it nonetheless. For the first time in the ten years since her father had died, Lilli felt like she could have a home.

Leaving Signal Bend would hurt.

Finally becoming aware of the heat in the car, her hair soaked and her t-shirt plastered to her dripping body, Lilli started the engine and drove back to Signal Bend, a despondent weight heavy in her chest.

~oOo~

She showered when she got home and dressed in black spandex shorts and a running top. She'd hiked 14 miles already so had no plans to run, but it was too hot for more clothes than these. Plus, she thought she might get in some yoga toward evening. One of the biggest challenges she'd faced being out in the country was the lack of a good gym. She was using yoga for all her muscle work. She'd found she enjoyed going outside with her mat as the sun was slanting low in the west, just as the cicadas were starting to sing, and finding some focus. She needed focus.

But at the moment, she needed to get online. She had three projects on deck, one of which was a very big deal, and she wanted to see if Rick had anything new on her target.

No, he didn't. They were both puzzled—no gas receipts, no hotel, no airfare, no credit card purchases of any kind, and no withdrawals from his bank accounts in eleven days—and that last was only a hundred dollars. It was like the man had been sucked up into the sky—or, more likely, down into hell. It was like he knew someone was after him. If you wanted to disappear in the twenty-first century, you went off the grid. That was what her target had done.

Reading over Rick's coded message, Lilli realized she was feeling something like relief. If the target couldn't be found, she wouldn't have to go. That was bad. People had put their necks on the line to get her into a position to deal with this. She couldn't lose sight of the objective because she'd found Isaac. She needed to keep her priorities straight.

She hadn't told him yet that she might be leaving. She wasn't sure she was. Until she had more information, she couldn't plan one way or the other. And things with him were good. She didn't want that to change, not yet, not unless it had to. It felt wrong to let what was happening between them deepen, but she couldn't let it not. She was letting herself get caught up, too, even knowing what she knew. Every day they spent together would make a separation all the harder, and she didn't care. She'd never had this before, and she wanted it.

She finished the two smaller projects that afternoon, encrypted them, and sent them back. She had a new message regarding the larger, more important project, shortening the deadline. Great. This one was so sensitive they'd broken it into decontextualized segments and passed them out among a few contractors like her, because they didn't want the whole content known to any of them. That was great, very secure, but what she did was translation and decryption, which made context highly important. Doing what she did out of context was like solving a random section of a 10,000 piece jigsaw puzzle without edge pieces or the picture on the box for reference. And now they wanted her segment in three days. Lovely.

She worked on it for the rest of the afternoon. Around dusk, she shut everything down and locked up. She was experiencing a jolly case of 'tech neck.' She had excellent posture naturally, but tended to shrug when she worked on a computer. Rolling her neck, she went out to the living room, grabbed her mat, and headed outside.

The evening was muggy and still, but much cooler than it had been earlier, and she did love the sounds of night animals beginning to stir. Her favorites, when they came out after dark, were the whippoorwills. Even on a warm, thick night, she'd leave a window open so that birdsong could lull her to sleep. She went down to a nice, level grassy spot in her yard and rolled out her mat.

Well into the asanas, she heard a bike coming up the road. She wasn't expecting to see Isaac today; he'd had some kind of club business in Joplin and expected to be back late. She didn't pry into any of that. She had her secrets, so she left him to his. He knew she was interested in whatever he wanted to tell her.

The landline hadn't rung, so she assumed she'd find a missed call on her cell. Since she'd asked, he'd made a habit of calling first, but he had not bothered with the detail of getting her okay to come over. He called. As far as he was concerned, if she didn't pick up, that was her problem, not his. Since things had changed between them, she didn't actually mind as much his coming by unexpectedly, so she'd let him slide. Now, she unwound herself from Ashtavakrasana and rolled up her mat as he parked the bike and swung off. She slid her little flip flops on and walked toward him.

Even through his sunglasses, Lilli could see his eyes sparkle with the intent to say something smartass. She stopped at her deck and waited for him to reach her. She knew she was a sweaty mess; she also knew that was how he liked her.

"Hey, Sport. What the hell were you over there doin?" He hooked his sunglasses into his kutte pocket and pulled her close.

"Yoga. Gotta do something to stay strong. Not exactly a Gold's Gym on every corner around here."

"Well, that thing you were doing just now, that was fuckin' sexy. No wonder we can do what we do. But we have a weight room and some other shit at the clubhouse. Might be time to bring you into the inner sanctum." With a wink, he leaned down and kissed her.

That was Lilli's one reserve. She didn't want to go to the clubhouse, because she wasn't sure she was staying, and she thought Isaac would feel even more betrayed if he let her all the way in and then she left. If he knew she might be leaving soon, she didn't think he'd want her at the clubhouse.

A voice in her head told her that he had to know she hadn't been planning to be here permanently. They hadn't talked about it at all, but he knew she came with almost nothing. He knew she'd rented a furnished house. He knew why she was here. He *had* to know she might not stay. She wasn't being dishonest by not talking about it now. Was she?

"Lilli? You just went far away. What's up?" He put his fist under her chin and raised her head a little.

She refocused and smiled. "Sorry. Just thinking about getting naked with you. How was Joplin?"

He chuckled. "Those two sentences right next to each other just had a wreck in my head. Joplin was complicated. Let's get naked. You're all sweaty and hot, and I want to peel those tiny little clothes off you." He slid his hand into the back of her shorts and squeezed her ass.

"Sounds like a plan." She started up the deck steps, his hand still in her shorts, but he grabbed the spandex and pulled her back.

"Uh-uh. Out here. Let's put that little mat thing you got there to some good use."

She turned back to see that mischievous gleam in his green eyes. The benefit of living out in the country: everywhere was private. She backed down the steps, and he pulled the mat out from under her arm. Taking her hand, he walked down the length of the house back to a large elm tree. In the few weeks she'd lived here, Lilli had not been back this far. The property she'd rented was on almost ten acres, but she didn't think in terms of acres. She'd been raised in a subdivision, in a smallish city. She'd gone to college in a big city. She'd spent years in the desert. She understood blocks, and she understood miles. Kilometers, too. But acres meant little to her. She'd done a lot of hiking while she worked, but had never explored this little corner that was ostensibly hers.

It was lovely. The land sloped down a little beyond the elm tree, and Lilli could see random sparkles that were the sodium arc lamps around other houses. Along the horizon, she thought she could see the black ribbon of the interstate, white and red lights moving over its length in pairs. It was twilight.

"Wow. It's beautiful back here."

"What—you've never seen this? Lilli, you live here!"

But she didn't, not really. She didn't live anywhere. She shrugged. "Busy, I guess. Never looked around back this way."

Shaking his head, he stooped and rolled her yoga mat out under the tree. He came back to her and slid his fingers under the skin-tight hem of her top, which just grazed the bottom of her rib cage. She raised her arms and let him pull it off. As he did, he said, "We should walk the property. It's

168

not much, but it's got some of the prettiest views around here. You should know what you have."

Lilli didn't saying anything. When he'd freed her from her top, he snaked his arms around her and pulled her close, his mouth coming down hard on hers, his tongue in her mouth right away. She adored the feeling of being bare against his rough clothing, all leather, denim, and metal. He hooked his fingers over her shoulders, and she felt his leather cuffs pressing into the skin of her back. He pulled her backward and kissed along her jaw, down her throat, and over her collarbone, a low rumble in his chest. He beard was rough and soft all at once, and she arched farther back, trusting him to hold her, wanting to feel the silk and scratch of his mouth on her breast.

He obliged, growling more loudly now, sucking her deeply and rhythmically into his mouth. She gasped, "God!" and laced her fingers into his hair. He'd been wearing it differently lately, catching half of it back in a ponytail and leaving the rest to lie on his back. She loved it. He looked wild and unbelievably sexy with that dark mane over his shoulders.

He brought her back to stand straight and pushed his hands down her sides, into her shorts at her hips, sliding the slight piece of spandex with him as he continued down her legs, kneeling as he went. She put her hands on his head as he helped her step out of the snug shorts, losing her flimsy sandals.

He slid a hand between her legs and teased at her folds. His fingers were instantly slick with her, and he groaned. "Fuck, I'll never get over how beautiful you are," he murmured, kissing her belly, before he stood and swept her off her feet. He laid her on the mat and started taking his own clothes off. He laid his kutte down under the tree and tossed his t-shirt on it. He started to toe his boots off, but Lilli sat up and stopped him.

"Don't. Leave your boots and jeans."

He cocked an eyebrow at her. "Yeah?"

"I like the way your clothes feel on my skin. Hot and rough." She really, really did. She could feel the wet trickling along her folds as she anticipated it.

He gave her an absolutely lecherous grin and grabbed a condom from his wallet. Standing just outside the canopy of the big elm, he opened his jeans, pulled his steel rod of a cock out, and rolled it on. When he joined her on the mat, he lifted her onto his lap and onto his cock without hesitation. Lilli gasped as he filled her so quickly. Oh, God, it was good. He always felt so damn good. Like he was die-cut just for her. She wrapped her arms and legs as tightly around him as she could, wanting the press of his chest against hers, the short, softly coarse curls rasping over her nipples.

She rocked on him, driving him deeper, and he wrapped his hands around her ass with a wrenching groan. His face in the crook of her shoulder, his lips against her neck, he rumbled, "Ah, Christ. Do you know how fucking good you feel on me? So damn tight and soft, holding me in. I love the way you smell, the way you taste. I love the sounds you make. Fuck, baby, I love you."

She froze. A beat later, he lifted his head and met her eyes. He shifted and held her closer, got deeper, making her gasp despite her turmoil. "That wasn't sex talk, Lilli. I'm tellin' you I love you. Don't make a fuss. Just sayin' what I feel."

She loved him, too. She was lightheaded with it. But everything was complicated. "Isaac…"

He shook his head. "Only thing I want to hear out of you right now is screaming, cuz I'm gonna make you come so hard your eyes cross." He rolled up onto his knees and put her on the mat, kissing her deeply.

He was as good as his word.

CHAPTER TWELVE

It was still dark when Isaac woke in Lilli's bed. That was becoming routine for him; when Lilli dreamt badly, she usually did so in the predawn. They'd spent most nights together over the past few weeks, and he estimated that she woke violently at least as many nights as she slept peacefully. Sometimes she woke repeatedly. Mostly, the excitement happened between three and five am. So he was beginning to wake before her.

Only twice had she actually come at him while she dreamt. Usually, she simply started awake, sitting up as if alarmed. Other times she jumped out of the bed, ready to fight. Always, as soon as she woke, she shook it off and settled back in bed with him. She would not tell him what was going on. She'd say only that it was over.

Aside from the two times he'd had to fend her off, he'd intervened only once, and that had gotten him punched in the face before she was fully awake. So he sat and watched, waiting for her to wake. He always asked, but she never told him. He assumed it had something to do with her time in Afghanistan. He knew a couple of vets, and they had twitches, too. Lilli was extremely level in every other way. Whatever was tormenting her seemed to be relegated to the shadows of her sleep.

Isaac was frustrated, though. He felt protective of her and wanted to do something that would help her. The best he could offer was comfort when she settled back under the covers. She always curled snugly into him, and he held her while she eased back to sleep.

This morning, though, there was more on his mind than waiting to see if Lilli would dream. He could feel that there was something going on with her, something she was keeping from him that was more than the secrets he knew she had. They'd gotten close over these weeks, and despite the rapidity with which they were growing together, he knew it was real. His father had been alive the last time he'd been any kind of serious with a woman. It wasn't something he wanted or needed, at least not until now. What was happening with Lilli was something different, and he wanted it.

But the last few days, he could feel her putting a wall up. After he'd shown her the article Bart had found, and they'd talked, Lilli had been as easy and open with him as he'd been with her. Now, though, she was pulling back. It was subtle, and he couldn't put his finger on how he knew, but he did. He could feel it. It was in the way she'd drift off sometimes, just for a second or two, while they were talking. It was more clear in the way she was avoiding going to the clubhouse. He hadn't realized it until last night, because she'd been dodging it so deftly, always sending the conversation somewhere else, but she was dodging it.

It didn't make sense. He knew she wouldn't be intimidated by the men, as some women were. She'd met most of them and utterly won them over—and, anyway, she was plenty used to a roughhouse crowd. She was pretty damn roughhouse herself. He couldn't imagine she'd have trouble with the women there, or with what went on with the women there. But there was something. He just didn't know what it was. Not yet.

He wanted her there. Bringing her to the clubhouse made her more his. Now, in the minds of his club, she was his latest little bit of tail. Bringing her into the club changed that, made her his woman. With the shit that looked like it was about to come down on the Horde and on Signal Bend, getting her under the protection of the club was important, no matter how badass she might be.

Putting his ink on her would make it stick, but they were a goodly ways from that. That was not a thing Isaac took lightly. He'd never before had any thought of ever marking a woman, taking an old lady. He could see it happening someday with Lilli, but the secrets—all of them—needed to get cleared out first.

He'd told her the truth last night under the elm—he loved her. That much he knew. He trusted her. But she was holding something back. He knew it meant she didn't feel like he did; she didn't trust him completely. She was keeping a guard up. It didn't change how he felt, and he wasn't sorry he'd told her. Isaac liked to be straight. Lies and dodges made nothing better. And that was why he was awake now, wondering what new thing Lilli was hiding.

About fifteen minutes or so later, she came awake with a gasp. It was still mostly dark, and he whispered, "Hey," so she'd know he was awake.

She turned to him and scooted closer. "Hey. Did you sleep at all?"

"Enough." He pulled her in and kissed her head. "Lilli, talk to me."

"Isaac, I told you, they're nothing. They turn to mist as soon as I wake up. I barely remember."

He didn't believe her, but it was a lie he understood. He'd let her have that one. There was a small lamp on the dresser next to the bed. He turned it on and shifted her so they were face to face. "No, Sport. Not the dreams. Tell me what's going on. There's something new. Something you're avoiding."

"I don't—"

"No. No lies. The secrets you have I understand. This is different. Lies I won't deal with."

He waited, holding her gaze, while she thought through whatever it was she needed to think through. Eventually, she sat up and really faced him. "I love you, Isaac."

"Lilli, you don't have to say it because I did. I'm more secure than that." He smiled and took her hand.

"Then you know that's not why I'm saying it. I've only said it to one other man, and I realized later that I'd been wrong. I made a promise to myself that I'd never mistake companionship for love again, that I'd never say those words again unless I was sure they were true. I need you to know that, because I'm saying them to you."

"Well, that's good, then. But what's the catch? That's not what you're dodging, Sport. If you love me, don't lie to me."

The breath she took was shaky. He heard it, and he felt a thin catch of something like anxiety. "I lost my target. He's just disappeared, fell right off the grid. My guy is looking. When he finds him, wherever he finds him, I have to go. It means I might have to start over somewhere else. Maybe far away. Maybe very soon." She took another shaky breath. "I'm sorry, Isaac. I should have said, but I didn't want you to pull away. That was selfish and shitty, and I'm sorry."

Isaac was not an idiot, not by a long stretch. He was aware that Lilli had not exactly *moved in* to this little house in the country. Aside from the hummingbird carving he'd given her, there was virtually nothing in it that had any personality at all, and Lilli was chock full of personality. She hadn't even been interested enough in the place to get to know her own yard. So what she was saying now didn't blindside him. It swiped at him, because he'd been coming to hope—maybe even to expect—that once she took care of her business, *then* she'd settle. Whatever it was she did for a living, she could obviously do it here.

"Lilli. Can't you come back when you're done?"

"This isn't the kind of thing where I can just sneak in and then right back out. I have to stay put for awhile wherever he is, to cast off suspicion. I'd rather not get caught."

"Can you let him go?" He knew the answer, but he still had to ask.

"No. Part of me wishes I could. A month ago I would have flattened anyone who suggested that might be true, but it is. Part of me wants to let it go and just stay here. But people put themselves at risk to help with this, and I can't let them down."

"Baby, you have to tell me who you're after. What he did. You're telling me that you're part of a fuckin' conspiracy to kill a guy, and it might take you away. You have to tell me more than that."

She shook her head. "I've told you why I can't. I can't extend the risk any further. And you can't take that risk. There's more than yourself you need to consider."

"What if your guy doesn't find him?"

"Then we fail. And I stay. And that asshole gets away with a lot."

He was rooting against her, then, but he wasn't going to say it. He wrapped his hands around her arms to pull her close, but she held back.

"You're okay with this?"

He pulled harder and dragged her into his arms; she put up only a token resistance. "There's a lot about that whole thing I'm not okay with. I'm not okay with you putting yourself in that kind of risk regardless. I'm not okay with the thought of you leaving and not coming back. But it's not like I can put what I feel for you on hold while you work your shit out. So I say we deal with what comes as it comes."

He'd pulled her to his chest; now, she sat up, her hands on his shoulders, and looked into his eyes. Her eyes glimmered with unshed tears. That was new; he hadn't seen Lilli cry—or even come near it. He put his hand on her cheek, tracing his thumb over her cheekbone. "You okay, Sport?"

She smiled, and a tear fell onto his thumb. "Yeah. Just...I love you."

"I love you. I don't say that lightly, either. No lies, Lilli. If you can't tell me something, at least tell me that. But no lies."

She nodded, and he kissed her. Then he pulled her down to lie on his chest, and they slept until the sun was bright.

~oOo~

Lilli was off running in her tiny little stretchy clothes when the burner went off. Isaac answered. "Yeah."

"Isaac, it's Kenyon."

That could only be bad news. Kenyon had called twice in the past week or so, bearing nothing but bad news. Lawrence Ellis was indeed looking to buy Will out—by one kind of incentive or another. Ellis was indeed looking to annex the meth trade as a complement to his robust cocaine and heroin enterprises. Get the junkies all up and down the socio-economic and cultural spectra. The Northside Knights, Ellis's point men for crack in St. Louis, seeing an opportunity for an up in their own beef with the Horde, had set Ellis on the Horde's heels. And Ellis was putting muscle and money on the ground.

Seeing dark clouds on the eastern horizon, Isaac had turned west, meeting in Joplin with crew heads from there and Tulsa. So far, things were quiet in that direction, but they were much smaller and more remote from the power centers. St. Louis, with its proximity to Chicago, looked to catch fire. Becker, from Tulsa, and Dandy, from Joplin, were mostly interested in not getting singed. So Isaac left that meet knowing he'd need to sweeten the pot before he could hope for their backup. What looked to be brewing was big enough that decades-long alliances weren't strong enough on their own.

And here was Isaac, trying to hold together his little town of a few hundred souls. Damn, he hoped Kenyon was right, that it was the strong ones who stayed. Because these poor saps must have been tough as jerky by now, all they'd been through.

"Kenyon. What's the word?"

"Not good, I'm afraid, brother. Not good. I'm thinking I'm in need of some fresh air, maybe a ride into the country. I'm wondering whether I might pay you a visit tomorrow."

Kenyon had never come out before. There was no need. The Horde escorted the product to him. Isaac's brain kicked into gear, working out the implications of this request. "Of course. You want me to set you a place at our table?"

"No need, Isaac. I'd just like a chat with you."

"I'll see you tomorrow, then." They ended the call. Then he called Show and had him gather the troops. They were all working their day jobs, but they'd need to take a few hours off. Isaac had an idea that the shitstorm was threatening to become a tsunami.

He took a quick shower before he left; he wanted to give everyone time to get there. When he was dressed and ready to go, Lilli still wasn't back yet. She ran a fucking long time—which probably accounted for the brilliance of her ass. He left a note on the counter, explaining that he needed to get to the clubhouse but he'd see her later.

~oOo~

Isaac walked into the clubhouse and scanned the room. As he walked through the main hall toward the Keep, his brothers fell in line behind him. Showdown came from his right, from the office, and joined Isaac at his side.

"Where's Wyatt?" He was the only member Isaac hadn't seen as he moved through the clubhouse.

Show gave him a look as he stepped back, so Isaac could go through the door into their club meeting room first. "Out of touch. You know—he takes his brother out and they do their Wild Man thing every year, camping and fishing and, fuck, howling at the moon for all I know. Left over a week ago. They'll be off the grid another two weeks."

Off the grid. Isaac took another couple of steps toward his leather chair at the head of the gleaming ebony table—his own design and creation—and stopped in his tracks as a whole slew of pieces he'd had no idea connected suddenly fell into place.

Wyatt and his younger brother, Ray, were off the grid and had been for more than a week. Ray was an Army vet. Jesus, now that Isaac thought about it, he was pretty sure Ray had been a pilot. He'd done a couple of tours in

Afghanistan, and he'd come back pissed and deeply weird. Mostly, these days, he was a hermit and a drunk.

Motherfuck. Was Lilli gunning for Wyatt's brother? Isaac couldn't believe he hadn't made the connection before. He'd spent no small amount of time trying to work out who Lilli was chasing, and Ray had never even fucking entered his consideration. But Ray was club family. When Lilli told him she wasn't interested in the club, and he'd believed her, he guessed he just stopped thinking about anyone having to do with the Horde.

Oh, Christ. *Christ.* How could he let her kill a brother's brother? How could she let him stop her? Had she known all this time that he had a connection to the Horde?

No. No way. He refused to believe she'd known. No.

"Boss?" Show put his hand on Isaac's shoulder, and Isaac looked around to see everyone sitting, looking at him with varying expressions of curiosity and concern. He cleared his throat and sat down. He was going to need to go back to Lilli as soon as this meeting was over. They needed to fucking *talk*. But for now, he had to set that aside and focus his attention on the problem of Lawrence Ellis and the coming visit of Kenyon Berry.

They hadn't met as a full table in a couple of weeks. In quiet times, they only had a scheduled business meeting once a month. The brothers knew their roles and had their schedules, and Isaac and Show dealt with adjustments on a case-by-case basis. But the quiet times were ending, and it was time to clue everybody in officially to what they'd all come to learn informally.

He explained about Ellis's pressure on Will Keller to sell, and he described Will's new hostility to Isaac. Everybody knew that Isaac and Will were friends from way back, so they understood that Will shutting Isaac down was a very bad sign.

Len spoke up. He was only a couple of years older than Isaac and Will, and he and Will had played on the church baseball team together for years. They were friends, too. "I'll give him a run. Been awhile since I had the boat out. I'll see if he wants to take a cooler and a couple of poles."

Isaac nodded. "Len, it's crucial, brother, that Will holds out. He needs to know we got his back. And he needs to know there's more at stake here than money. He needs to be *sure* of that." Len nodded.

Isaac looked around the room, the faces of his brothers reflected in the gleaming, dark surface of the table he'd made with his own two hands. The wood was a special import and had been expensive. He was proud of the work—lustrous wood pieced precisely together, the seams all but invisible, with a turned braid forming an oblong center. The table was surrounded by red leather chairs. The rest of the room was typical biker bullshit—plaques and trophies, framed photographs and carved platitudes. But the table was class.

He faced his brothers around that table and cleared his throat. "Look. The hard truth here is we're getting dragged into a war. Hell, we're the main enemy, looks like. This is more than the Northsiders gettin' chippy. This is about big time money. I am doing what I can to get backup, bringing Dandy and Becker on board, meeting with Kenyon tomorrow. Dandy and Becker are gonna want something from us, cuz they're not keen on bringing this down on them. I explained that if we fall they're next, but I'm thinking we're gonna need to break off some of our piece, share it with them. Show and I are working those details out, and we'll bring it to you when we have a plan. For now, we need to focus on the town. Ellis is making some noise already. With Kenyon coming to us, my bet is things are about to get a lot louder. We need to keep everybody here steady."

CJ spoke up. The oldest active member, he had a long club memory. "Sounds like you're thinking this is gonna be like '87 again."

Isaac had been fourteen in 1987. He knew it mainly from stories, but he knew that what was about to happen was nothing like it. "No, man. '87 was nothin' but a turf war. Horde took the Dusty Riders down. Bloody, but brief. What's coming is big money, connected money, on a bulldozer. Ellis is looking to turn Signal Bend into his company town, cooking meth on a mass scale. And he's looking to flatten the Horde to do it. This won't be a turf war. It'll be a fucking extermination."

The room was thick with quiet as the Horde contemplated the weight of Isaac's words. He'd sounded hopeless. He was feeling hopeless. But he had to give them hope. "Let's focus on what we know, what we can do. If we stand strong, we can fight this back. We just need the town behind us. Everything as normal, but we up our presence. You're in town, you're in your kutte. And you're carrying. No exceptions. We protect our people."

Havoc shook his head. "Can't while we're workin', boss." A club with day jobs outside had its complications, definitely.

"Keep 'em close, then. And I'll talk to Don. Any other concerns?" The table was quiet. "Okay, I'll know more after the sit-down with Kenyon tomorrow." Isaac graveled the meeting to a close and stood.

Show asked, "You want to talk about tomorrow's meet?"

"Later. I have something I need to deal with first." Isaac slapped Show on the arm and left the clubhouse. He needed to see Lilli *now*.

~oOo~

When he got to her place, she was walking toward the garage, apparently on her way somewhere. She looked surprised to see him pulling up, and not what one might call thrilled. She pulled her phone out and looked at it; no, he hadn't called first.

She stayed where she stood as he parked the bike and dismounted. "Baby, we have to talk."

"You didn't call."

"No. Lilli, are you after Ray Hobson?"

INTERLUDE: 2010

"Alright boys, don't make me pull over."

Goldman snorted. "Hey, he started it, Major."

Lilli shook her head and amped the tunes. She liked some Rancid when she flew a mission. This was a big one, bringing her squad into a firefight, already engaged. Lilli was flying in a backup squad, called in when the estimates for enemy combatants on the scene had turned out to be grossly miscalculated. The mission was serious and deadly, but the atmosphere in the cabin was not. Everybody knew they were headed into fire and might not come back. The adrenaline in the cabin was so thick it had smell and taste. The troops were giddy with it and acting goofy. That was just how things worked. When danger was looming, soldiers often got rowdy. They'd be plenty serious when they were in the thick of it. Now, though, the gunners, pilots, and crew chief were the only ones fully down to business.

It wasn't her squad, not entirely—or at least not completely, not the way she thought of it; injuries on another squad and a couple of troops rotating out recently had shuffled the squad rosters. Three of the men she thought of as hers were on the ground now, engaged in the firefight already: Miller, Okada, and Scarpone.

Actually, she thought of them all as hers, her family, almost everyone on base. But she had become very close with the men who flew with her consistently, and things had felt fractured since the roster shift.

She had a brand new co-pilot, too. Captain Mendez, with whom she'd flown for two rotations, had taken his out and gone home. Now she had a shiny new Chief Warrant Officer at her right, Bill Newell, fresh out of training and looking terrified. Everything felt slightly *off* for Lilli, but she shoved her unsettled feeling aside and focused.

"Your music SUCKS, sir!" Lopez yelled over the lyrics to 'Time Bomb' and the roar of the rotors. Her guys knew she hated "ma'am"; they all called her "sir." It had at first raised some eyebrows with Command, but it was an approved term of address.

She laughed. "Fuck you, Lopez. Fine—you wanna pick, be my guest."

His eyes went wide; she never turned over control of the tunage. "I need me some Angus!"

"Christ, you're such a cliché." She rolled her eyes and put 'Highway to Hell' up instead. The men all reacted favorably, hooting and shouting. No class, no taste.

Just then, the cyclic got gummy, and Donna shimmied hard, rolling slightly to the left. What the fuck? The men shouted their surprise, and in her periphery, she saw Lopez give her a look of sharp concern. Newell looked shocked. Great. Fucking noob.

"We're cool, boys. Donna just got some gum on her shoe." But it happened again, and this time the copter tipped more violently. A copter wasn't a plane. Off its axis, it didn't roll and resettle. It crashed. Period.

Lilli was calm. She was not someone who panicked. "Mr. Newell, take your cyclic. You clear?"

The kid swallowed hard and put his hands around the stick. What skin Lilli could see on him was running sweat, and Lilli was fair certain it was flop sweat, not heat sweat. God DAMMIT. The kid was going to choke. She turned off the tunes.

"Hey, be cool, Newell. Just need to know if you're feeling a fight in the cyclic, too. If you're not, you're going to take over, but we're all right here with you."

Newell maneuvered, and Donna rocked hard, losing noticeable altitude. Now the cabin was quiet but for the sounds of the engine. Everybody was paying attention to what was going on up front.

"Was that you or Donna dancing, bud?"

"I—I don't know, ma'am. Sir. I think I feel something."

Lilli carefully reached over and manipulated the co-pilot cyclic. She felt the same catch. It wasn't the stick, then, it was something deeper. In the engine itself. Donna wasn't taking anyone to the front today. She called it in.

The response from Command was terse and direct. "Negative. Squad on the ground is overrun. Get those troops forward, Major."

She had fourteen men on her ride. She gave it another couple of tries, but Big Donna was getting angrier every time. She barely reclaimed control the last time, and a few of the men actually screamed as the rotors skipped and the engine coughed. "No can do, Colonel. Donna won't fly. Putting her down."

"That's a NEGATIVE, Major. Those troops are needed now!"

She knew full well they were needed. She knew full well what they would all likely lose by not carrying out her mission. But her mission had already failed, and she wouldn't risk these men, too. "Sorry, sir. Mechanical failure. Putting her down. Need new transport."

~oOo~

Within ten minutes, another copter was on the scene, but they were too late. The squad on the ground was wiped out. All of them—Okada, Scarpone, Miller, and the rest, KIA.

Lilli had disobeyed a direct order. She'd done it to save her squad, but she was relieved of flight duty as soon as she hit camp, pending investigation. Captain Ray Hobson, the senior pilot but for Lilli, was put in charge of the investigation. Hobson had never stopped gunning for her—in fact, he'd recently gotten much worse. He'd been passed over for promotion to Major, a promotion Lilli had gotten below the zone. Hobson had one more go, next year. If he was passed over again, he'd be forced out of the service.

Lilli knew his being in charge of the investigation made things even dicier for her, but she didn't care. She'd let a whole squad of men—friends of hers, brothers—die violently, their bodies desecrated. She'd done it to save another whole squad, but it didn't ease the loss. And she'd lost more. She'd lost Colonel Corbett's respect. She'd lost the respect of everyone on base. The men who'd been flying with her, most of them understood. But not all of them. Some had been livid that she hadn't pushed on.

Everyone was questioned. She had no idea what the men with her had said; she had no intention of asking. For her part, she'd told the truth. She went easy on Newell, who'd been no help to her at all, but he was green. She'd been shaky on her first mission, too, and she hadn't been headed to a firefight.

Lilli pushed her papers and waited for the investigation report. For the most part, she kept to herself. For the most part, everyone left her to herself.

The investigation turned up no mechanical faults. Nothing. The cyclic was smooth. Everything worked as it should. Lilli read the report three times and then went straight to

Chief Pettijohn, who glared at her as she approached. He saluted, and then nodded curtly. "Ma'am."

"Chief, is this right? No fight in the cyclic?"

"Checked it myself, Major. Donna's healthy as a horse. No failure." He turned back to his work.

Lilli didn't know what to think. She *knew* there'd been a bad—a potentially catastrophic—failure. She'd never have landed and disobeyed an order otherwise. She *knew* it. But Chief was good. He was thorough. And he'd once been on her side.

Had she fucked up? Had she gotten men killed?

CHAPTER THIRTEEN

Dumbstruck, Lilli didn't answer Isaac right away. He knew Hobson? How did she not know that? She briefly considered lying, but decided against it—and it was too late anyway. Isaac's question had caught her flat-footed, so she'd already given the answer away, simply by standing there, stunned.

But Jesus, she couldn't tell him. And if he knew Hobson, fuck. Would he try to get in her way? She didn't know what to do. Normally, she thought quickly on her feet, adapted to the situation before her. But now, her brain just...*skipped*. Without answering, she turned and headed back toward the house. She had no idea why—it wasn't like there was any chance at all that Isaac was going to turn around and ride away, or let the subject drop. She wasn't avoiding anything. And yet, it took a force of will to keep her legs from speeding into a run.

She was panicking. She didn't panic. Ever.

Sure enough, she heard him coming up behind her, and he grabbed her arm—not roughly, but firmly. He stepped up to face her and grabbed her other arm as well. "Lilli, no fucking way. We are talking this out. The secret ends now."

She fought him. More than anything else, that was a testament to her panic. She broke his hold with a violent swing of her arms, then hit him hard in the chest with the heels of her hands. Winded, he fell back a few steps, and she bolted, thinking to get into the house and lock him out.

None of what she was doing made any fucking sense. Running would not get her clear of this problem. Running was making it worse. But her body would not listen to her brain. She heard him coming up behind her, surprisingly fast, and she felt his hands reaching just before they grabbed her. She spun as he got hold, and they went down, Isaac landing hard on top of her. They were face to face, on the ground, both of them winded.

"What the fuck, Lilli?"

She fought to get out from under him, but he was determined, strong, and probably a hundred pounds heavier than she. He grabbed her wrists and forced them to the ground on either side of her head. There was a fire in his eyes that boded an entirely different kind of passion from the kind he usually had for her. He was enraged.

"Why are you fighting me? Did you fucking know Hobson is connected to the Horde? Is that why the secrets?"

She didn't know why she was fighting. She didn't know why she couldn't stop, but she was still trying to find a way to get free of him. Focused on that, she didn't answer his question. He yanked her arms roughly over her head and manacled both wrists in one of his large, rough hands. With his other hand, he grabbed her jaw. She could feel the tension of his anger in his fingers digging into her cheek. "Lilli, goddammit. You talk to me. *Did you know?*"

"No! I didn't know!" His hold on her face slackened instantly, and he let her arms go. Just like that, he believed her. She pushed on his shoulders, but he still wouldn't move off of her.

"Fuck, Sport. Fuck. We *have* to talk. You see that, right?"

The familiar pressure of Isaac's body on hers was beginning to calm her, and her brain kicked back into gear. She could feel the jangly edge of the panic receding, and she realized that it had fed itself. She took a breath, as deep as she could with his weight on her chest, and nodded. "Yeah. Okay."

"Okay?"

"Yeah." He pushed back to his knees and then stood and held his hand for her. She took it, and he pulled her up and then to his chest, folding her in his arms. Surprised, she didn't return his embrace at first, but she could feel the calm in his body. Responding to it, she relaxed against him and clutched his kutte in her hands.

He kissed her temple. "No lies, baby. It's time to come clean. Fuck the risk. Looks like our lines are gettin' tangled up. We gotta try to get them straight."

Lilli's brain was turning fast, trying to catch up and recover from her freakout. If Hobson was one of Isaac's brothers, then this was a fucking calamity. He was right. Everything had to be out in the open between them. Her head still pressed to his chest, tucked into his kutte, she nodded.

"That's my girl." He shrugged back from her and raised her head. "I love you. Let's work this out."

She nodded again and took his hand. Time to sit down and talk.

When they got inside, she went straight to the kitchen and got them each a beer. She glanced at the digital clock on the range: 12:15pm. Good enough. She considered getting the tequila out instead, but she didn't think getting drunk would improve the situation much. At least not yet.

Isaac was already sitting on the couch, his kutte off and folded over the back of an armchair. He'd sat in a corner, his arm stretched over the back of the couch. Lilli handed him a beer and sat facing him, kicking off her shoes and tucking one leg under her ass.

He took a long swallow from his bottle and said, "Tell me why you're gunnin' for Ray."

Not yet. She shook her head. A hard look crossed Isaac's eyes, and he opened his mouth to protest, but she put her hand up. "You first. I'm sure my story is longer. Is he one of the Horde?"

"Not a patch. A patch's brother. Wyatt. I don't think you met him yet."

"Do you know where he is?"

"Not exactly. I know why he's gone and about when he'll be back. But you're not gettin' that until I hear your story. Talk, Sport."

What Lilli heard first and foremost was that Hobson was still local. She didn't have to leave. That lightened her heart so dramatically that for a brief second she almost forgot that her plan to kill the cocksucker had just had an enormous wrench thrown in it. What would she do if Isaac and the Night Horde got in her way?

Fight one fire at a time. She told Isaac the story of the day she disobeyed a direct order, the day a whole squad was wiped out and she was blamed for it.

He never interrupted her, and she never stopped until the story was told. Her beer had gone warm in her hand. She told it the way she'd told it to Colonel Corbett on the day it had happened, the way she'd told it to the review board, which ruled to discharge her, allowing her the dignity of an honorable discharge and retaining her rank only to keep a lid on the story. They didn't want cable news to get wind of the hotshot female combat pilot who'd lost her nerve.

She told it flat, without emotion. She had to. The emotion was too big, even now, to let loose.

When she'd gotten that far, she stopped and drained her warm beer. She knew she wasn't done, but the rest was something she hadn't told to anyone who wasn't part of this mission. And now she was about to break that seal.

Isaac spoke up during her pause. "Christ, Lilli. That's awful. But I don't understand why you're after Ray."

"Because he fucked with my ride. He got those men killed. And he got away with it."

Isaac stared, his eyes hot. Lilli wished she could know his thoughts. "That's a fucked up accusation. You better know it's true."

"I know it's true. I didn't know it then, but I know it now." She stood. "Fuck the beer. I need tequila. You?" Isaac nodded slowly, and she took their empty bottles and went into the kitchen to pour a couple of tall glasses of Patrón. She came back, handed him his glass and sat down exactly as she had before. Isaac hadn't moved.

After a sip from her glass, she started again. "Lopez, my crew chief, told me that he'd seen Hobson around my copter a couple of times shortly before the mission. He said he'd mentioned it in his testimony, but Hobson must have had some reason queued up, because it didn't make any waves. But a few months after I was stateside, Lopez got in touch. This was before I was fully into this gig, so getting in touch wasn't so hard. He'd just rotated out, and Hobson got wasted at the party and *confessed* to Lopez that he'd sabotaged my engine and then fixed it before the Chief got to it. Would've been easy to undo what he'd done. He knew he'd be in charge of the investigation—he was senior pilot after me, so he'd be OIC."

For the first time, Isaac interrupted. "OIC?"

"Office in Charge. The perfect fucking crime. In charge of the investigation, in charge of the report."

"Why didn't Lopez report what Ray told him?"

Their glasses were empty. Lilli got up and brought the tequila in from the kitchen and refilled them. "A drunk utterance about a closed file? A confession that would tear the battalion apart? It would go nowhere but up Lopez's ass. He did the right thing. The only way for justice to work here is off the books."

"Lilli, you're telling me that Ray let a whole squad of men die because he didn't like you. That's a special kind of crazy. I know this man."

"I don't think he expected the mission to be so dire when he fucked with Donna. I don't even know if he was trying to ruin my career so spectacularly. For all I know, he was just fucking with me. His favorite pastime. Doesn't matter. What he did got men killed. He doesn't walk away from that." The story told, she had a moment to understand something. "Are you saying you don't believe me?"

He didn't hesitate. "That's not what I'm saying at all. I'm trying to get my head around what you've told me, though. I need to make the pieces fit."

"No, you don't. This is my thing, not yours."

"You're wrong, Lilli. This is someone I've known most of my life. This is my brother's brother. A friend of the club. Baby, he's under club protection. You understand what I'm saying to you?"

She thought she did, and it broke her heart. She stood and took his glass from him. "You're saying you're my enemy now. Get out, Isaac." She turned and walked into the kitchen and put the empty glasses in the sink.

Then he was behind her, his hand on her shoulder, turning her roughly around. "No. You got it wrong. I'm not your enemy. That's the last fuckin' thing I want. But I have to take this to the club." He lifted her onto the counter before she had a chance to resist.

The tequila was stirring her sadness and anger into a particular kind of heat, and she could feel her hands shaking with it. She needed Isaac to get out of here. "Then we *are* enemies. That's a confidence you can't break, Isaac. I'll kill you before I let you. It's not just me on the line here."

He wrapped his hand around her ponytail until his fist was against the back of her head. She swung at him, but he caught her fist in his other hand. "You need to trust me, Lilli. You need to let me work this. If you kill Ray while he's under our protection, the club will kill you. I won't be able to stop that. Let me work this. Let me figure it out. Let me help you."

Isaac was panting, his face only inches from hers; Lilli could feel his breath against her cheek and ear. She was furious, but she was also wet and almost writhing with need. She pushed at him with her free hand, trying to make room to get her leg up and kick him, but he sensed her intent and knocked her leg away, spreading her wide and settling his hips against hers. *Oh, fuck.* He pulled hard on her hair, forcing her head back, and then his lips were on her throat, sucking. Gasping, she thrust against him, not even sure herself if she was trying to push him off or just grind on him. She was trying to remember that he was fucking everything up and threatening to put people who trusted her at risk, but the scent of him. The feel of his denim-clad legs against her bare ones, his hands holding her forcefully…fucking tequila.

"Let go of me."

She knew Isaac wasn't feeling the booze the way she was; she'd seen plenty of evidence of his impressive tolerance. But something was on him. His gaze was all but scorching her. "Fight me."

"What?"

"I want you to fight me. C'mon, Sport. You've been trying to hit me since I got here. Fight me now."

They weren't done. They were in big trouble. Everything they'd found together was in jeopardy. Hell, it was probably already over. There was a good chance that one of them would kill the other soon. And he wanted a rough fuck?

But Lilli could feel the hot steel of his erection against her pelvis. Her heart was pounding in her head, and the crotch of her shorts was soaked.

She head-butted him.

"Christ!" Staggering back, he dropped his hold on her fist and put his hand to his forehead. He still had his hand wound in her ponytail, and he'd wrenched her head around when he backed up, but she swung with her just-freed right and punched him in the face. That made him let go of her completely, and she jumped off the counter and backed out of the kitchen.

He charged at her and reached for her arm, but she spun out of his way. She noticed that he was trying to contain her, not hit her. That answered her question of whether this was a fight or foreplay, and she adjusted her defense, ignoring the opening he'd given her. He lunged at her again, and she let him catch her arm. He yanked it behind her back and dragged her against his chest. When he slammed his mouth on hers, she bit his lip, tasting blood.

"Ah! Damn!" He reared back, licking his wounded lip. He reached for her free hand, but she spun again, eluding him and breaking his hold on her other arm as well. She backed up as he came for her. He was grinning wildly. "You are a hot-ass little bitch, you know that? I'm gonna fuck you into next week."

He grabbed her arm again and swung her around so that she was facing away from him. She tried to spin, but he caught her other arm, too. He'd acquired a keen understanding of her flexibility in the weeks they'd been together, and he folded both arms behind her, holding them tight against her back with one large fist. Then he shoved her over the back of the couch. With his free hand, he tore her hiking shorts and underwear down, letting them drop around her ankles. Then his rough fingers were pushing between her legs from behind, shoving into her. "Jesus fuck, baby, you're always so damn wet for me. I love how you love it rough like this."

Needing more from him, she struggled against his hold, and he pushed her arms up higher on her back. "You're gonna have to wait, Sport. I'm not done here."

Then his fingers were on her clit. He was rubbing hard on her, almost violently, and she was ready to come almost immediately. She cried out, "God, yeah! Fuck, Isaac, fuck!"

Then his fingers were gone, and she could hear him opening his belt and jeans with one hand. He hadn't let go of her arms. She was losing feeling in them, but she didn't care. She needed to get fucked, and now. Her bigger concern was how he was going to get a condom on one-handed. She turned her head. "Condom?"

Leaning over her, his mouth against her ear and his cock hot and hard against her ass, he said, "Don't need one." He stood back up, and his hand was between her legs again, inside her, then dragging along her cleft, wetting her. When he pushed his fingers—at least two—firmly past her anus, she gasped and bucked, so close to orgasm she thought the unmet need might actually kill her.

He bent over her back again, his fingers pumping and flexing in her, and he rumbled in her ear. "You like that, baby? You want me to fuck your ass?"

"Yes! Fuck! Please, Isaac, I need to come!" She bucked against his fingers, trying to get enough stimulation to get over. Then his fingers were gone again, and his cock was filling her core. He thrust several times—too many times, taking too much risk without a condom, but she was in a frenzy now, millimeters or milliseconds or whatever measurement was appropriate from the edge of her climax, and she couldn't find breath to stop him—and then he was out and pushing into her ass. He didn't go slow this time; this time he just pushed right in, and it was intense and just over the tipping point of pain. She screamed. And then she was coming, her whole body, even her voice, pulsing with it. He hadn't even moved inside her yet.

She heard him whisper, "Oh my God, baby. God, that's so tight. God. God." But he didn't come. When she was done, he pulled out of her, fast and completely hard, making her scream again in pleasurepain.

Isaac released her arms then and picked her up, carrying her down the hall to the bedroom. He threw her on the bed and dropped down on top of her, claiming her mouth in a ferocious kiss. She kissed him back just as hard, sucking the blood from his lip where she'd bitten him. He growled and pushed back onto his knees, fetching a condom from his wallet. She'd lost her shorts and underwear in the living room, so she spread her bare legs wide and waited for him.

When he was wrapped, he entered her powerfully, fast and to the hilt, making her arch off the bed at the deep fullness of him inside her. Damn, she'd never felt anything like him.

His eyes were intent on hers. "Fucking you is like nothing I've known before, baby. You fit me like you were made for me. I can feel you everywhere."

Pounding away inside her, he yanked her t-shirt and bra up, exposing her breasts. He shifted back to his knees, pulling her partway onto his lap, and worked her nipples the way she liked. He'd known from the first time just what she wanted. Firm pressure. He pulled and pinched just right, until she was bucking on him, feeling another wave of ecstasy mounting.

"Suck me, Isaac. I want your mouth." He growled and gathered her into his arms. She arched backward over his hold, giving him access, and his mouth latched onto her breast like a starving babe. "Harder. Harder. Oh, fuck, yeah." She drove her hips down on him, taking him as deep into her core as she could, holding him as tightly as she could, striving, striving. He groaned loudly, clutching her closely, and bit down on her breast as he came. The feel of his cock pulsing inside her and his teeth bearing down on her sent her over, too, and she sank her nails into his shoulders as she screamed again.

When they could relax, Isaac laid her tenderly down and eased out of her. He got up from the bed and dealt with the condom. Then he stripped—he'd even still had his boots on—and returned to her. He helped her out of her t-shirt and bra and pulled her close to rest her back on his chest.

They were quiet, regrouping together. Lilli felt calmer than she thought she would, after the conversation they'd had— the one they were still in the middle of, in fact. Then, out of the blue, Isaac said. "I'm bringing you to the clubhouse. You and I are going to talk to Showdown. He's the brother I trust most; he's the one I go to for advice. We need a head that's not so deep in this. Because Lilli, I am not fuckin' losing you. We will find a way out of the mess. I need you to trust me, baby. Please."

Lilli was tired. She knew she shouldn't. All of her training, her loyalty, everything told her that it was wrong to bring in anybody else, much less a whole motorcycle club. The greatest risk to a mission like hers was the people who knew about it. The risk increased exponentially with each person. What she should do is eliminate the threat.

What she *would* do is what Isaac asked. She wanted him. If there was a way that she could keep him, then she'd take the risk and trust him. She sent up a little prayer to a god she'd stopped believing in when she buried her father, asking that if she was wrong, others didn't pay the price with her.

She shifted on his chest so that she could see his face—his gorgeous face that she'd come to love so much, with his astute green eyes. She ran her finger along the scar across his cheek. "Okay. But tell me where he is."

"Wyatt and Ray are off on a deep woods camping trip. He's out of reach, but he'll be back in a couple of weeks. You don't have to go anywhere, Sport. He's still around."

CHAPTER FOURTEEN

Isaac parked in front of the clubhouse, and Lilli and he dismounted. Damn, he loved riding with her wrapped around him. Even with all the shit going down, what he really wanted to do right now was pull her back into the nearest dorm room and fuck the sense out of her. Again. He couldn't, of course; the kind of trouble they had wouldn't wait any longer. But when she took off the helmet that was now hers and ran a hand to smooth her ponytail, he couldn't resist dragging her up against his body and kissing her until he felt her almost sag into his embrace.

He had to fix this. He had to find a way to clear a path for Lilli to do what she needed to do with Ray. He believed her story; the first thing he'd known about her was that she was honest—even while she was secretive, she managed to be honest. So he had no doubt that Ray had done the fucking awful thing that she said he'd done. Isaac wanted him dead for fucking with Lilli; he needed no other provocation than that. But it was the squad of lost soldiers that he knew could turn the club to her side. Against one of their own. Because Wyatt? Wyatt would never turn on Ray.

Wyatt was the older brother. They'd grown up in a tough house, with a hard father and a weak mother. A lot like Isaac's house—and not so few other houses in this part of the world. Country life could be hard and austere. Men worked until they were bone weary and drenched in sweat. Then they drank and thought about how they had to do it again the next day. Then they went home angry and spoiling for trouble.

What was different about Ray and Wyatt, though, was that Ray had had trouble keeping out of their father's way. He'd never seemed to learn when to lie low. Sometimes, it had seemed like Ray took pains to *provoke* their dad. And then Wyatt would step between them and take the brunt. Wyatt always took the brunt. He'd been offered a football scholarship to Nebraska, but he wouldn't leave Ray behind, so he'd turned it down. Ray had gone to college instead, going ROTC.

Wyatt worked the family farm with his father and lived in a little cottage he'd built on the property, some short distance from the main farmhouse he'd grown up in. Ray had been in the service for sixteen years, but he'd come home, what, a year or so ago? He'd moved into a ramshackle hut a couple of towns away and kept mostly to himself, making money doing odd jobs as they came up, but mainly letting Wyatt take care of him, seeing to it he had groceries and whatever else he needed. Isaac had only seen him a few times, when Wyatt dragged him to Friday nights to try to get him to have fun. Ray had gotten very weird and twitchy. Everyone assumed it was something that happened in the war. Now Isaac knew that was true.

He took Lilli's hand and headed to the door. Almost everyone was here; work shifts had recently ended, and the Horde always came together for a couple of drinks, at least, before those who had families went back to them. So Isaac knew he was about to create a stir. Most of the Horde had met Lilli and had seen her with Isaac, but it had been at least fifteen years since he'd walked into the clubhouse with a woman. He brought her hand to his mouth and pressed a kiss to her knuckles. She smiled at him.

"It's gonna be okay, Sport. We're gonna work this."

She huffed dryly, not quite a laugh. "One way or another, yeah. We are."

No. Not one way or another. There was only one way. With them on the same goddamn side. He would not lose her. He never thought to have this; he never thought he wanted it. But he had it, this love, this *binding* with another soul, and he was not giving it up. Fuck no. He would not betray her.

He could not betray his club, though, either. These men, their families, this town—all his responsibility, and he would never shirk it. So there was only one way. The club had to believe her, and they had to agree that Ray deserved to die.

He gave Lilli's hand a squeeze and opened the clubhouse door.

When they walked in, heads turned as usual, to see and greet their president. But when they saw Lilli, the room got quiet. Horde, girls, and hangers-on, literally everyone in the room eventually was watching Isaac walk through the room they called the Hall. He turned to see that Lilli was smiling slightly, looking confident. But she was also holding his hand just a tad more tightly. He squeezed back and decided that they wouldn't walk straight through and get to business. Showdown was at the bar; Isaac led Lilli there. The Horde who'd met her nodded cordially or lifted their drinks her way. Slowly, people turned back to what they were doing.

Rover was working behind the bar. When he wasn't around, people helped themselves, but he knew he was expected to serve if he was in the Hall. Now, he came straight up to Isaac.

"Just a couple of Buds, Rove." Rover nodded and turned to the bar fridge. Still holding Lilli's hand, Isaac leaned toward Show. "After this drink, we need to talk." Show gave him a quizzical look, but nodded and took a pull from his own beer. Rover brought their beers; when Lilli took hers with a bright smile and a softly spoken thanks, she turned to lean her back against the bar. Isaac watched her as she took in the Hall. Her expression took on a rapt cast as her eyes fell on the far corner of the room. He realized what she was seeing and turned around himself to look.

For the most part, the Hall looked like a giant rec room where a bunch of mostly uncouth men hung out. The bar, which was a big, ugly thing with tufted orange vinyl up the sides (and for which Isaac was not in any way responsible—it predated him by decades) and stools upholstered with the same orange vinyl; a large pool table with a blue felt top; a couple of arcade video games and an old pinball machine; several big leather couches and chairs arranged in front of an 80-inch TV mounted on the wall; and a few four-top tables and chairs. The wall décor was lighted beer signs, bike posters, sexy pinups, an oversized bulletin board covered in snapshots, and a wall of framed certificates and plaques of town appreciation. The walls were cheaply paneled, the concrete floor covered in peeling, cracked linoleum. Everything well used, nothing remarkable.

But in the corner Lilli was fixed on was a large chess set, the board itself the surface of a table. The pawns were each five inches tall. The kings and queens, the largest pieces, were each ten inches tall. A game was in progress on the board. Isaac could tell that Lilli knew he'd made the set. He was pleased to see her rapt focus; he was proud of that work.

Chess sets were among the work he did that actually made him some real money. Depending on the wood he used and the carving and turning choices he made, he could get hundreds of dollars for a set that took him a couple of days to make and less than a hundred bucks in materials. He'd once done a set on special order that had taken him a week of fairly focused work, and had netted him a couple grand. But the work Lilli was fixed on was a labor of love. Isaac considered it art. The pieces were turned in an abstract style, and no two pieces, not even the pawns, were identical. The woods he'd chosen were elaborately grained and burled, and he'd spent a very long time picking the right wood, the right orientation of grain, for each piece. He'd made the set over months, when he had time to just play in his shop. It had been a kind of therapy, started right after his father died, when he'd taken over the head of the table.

Lilli turned to him, "Jesus, Isaac. That's beautiful. Can I—?" She gestured her desire to take a closer look.

"Sure—that's an actual game in progress, though, so it'd be good to leave the pieces where they are." He went with her as she crossed the Hall.

"Who's playing? You?" She brushed her fingers over the white queen, made of a perfect piece of spruce. She was a beauty; Isaac knew it—all spirals and latticing.

"Told you chess was my game. Show and I have one going pretty much all the time. None of these other assholes has the head for chess." He said that loudly enough for the room to hear him, since he was giving them shit. A lot of the men were smart enough, he thought, but they were mostly the kinds of guys who liked their games loud and drenched in booze. Poker was their game. They all knew to keep their paws off the board, though.

Isaac moved behind Lilli and put his free hand on her hips. He kissed the base of her neck, and she leaned back into him. He knew what the room was seeing. He wasn't touching her rhetorically, but he was glad of the message nonetheless. He kissed slowly up the sleek line of her neck, and she tipped her head to the side to give him full access. When he reached her ear, he whispered, "You play?"

She turned into his kiss, her head resting against his shoulder. "I know how the pieces move, but no, I've never really played."

"You should, Sport. You'd be great at it. Your mind works the right way." The shit with Ray rising again to the fore of his thoughts, Isaac pressed his lips to her temple. "C'mon, let's talk to Show." He put his bottle to his lips and drained it, then he took her hand and led her back. He nodded toward the office to Show, who drained his beer and came off his stool to follow them.

When the three got back to the office, Isaac led Lilli to the couch against the back wall and sat down next to her. Left with the choice to sit three on the couch, stand, or sit in Isaac's desk chair, Show, after a quick pause, sat in the chair. That was okay with Isaac. He had no need to remind Show who was in charge, and he wanted to be close to Lilli.

"We got ourselves a problem, Show. I need you to hear Lilli out. Can't leave this room, though. Stays between us three until we're ready to do what we decide to do." Without a word, Showdown nodded and turned to Lilli, waiting for her to say her piece. With an uncertain glance at Isaac, she did. She told the story almost exactly as she'd told him. Isaac got the sense that it was the only way she could tell it, almost as if she were reading back a transcription.

Isaac watched Show as Lilli spoke. His VP was several years older than he, and the smartest man Isaac knew. He would have made a good president, too, but he was too smart to want it. Getting him to agree to be VP had taken Isaac a lot of effort. But from the time he was a teen, it was Show he could talk to, Show who had the right view on things. He was the kind of guy who sat back and saw everything. He wasn't slow to act when action was needed, but he never acted simply for the sake of the action. He was quiet and thoughtful. He'd been in the club for a long time, and he'd seen some heavy shit, but he was content running the feed store and going home at night to his little house, and spending the evening with his wife and three daughters.

Isaac was thoughtful, too, and he worked hard to lead with his head and not his fists, but his temper was much hotter than Show's, and when provoked, he did things like shove scissors into the hand of a shithead realtor. Said realtor was playing nice now, seemed like, after Show had talked him down and brought him Candy. Distract him with shiny things, indeed.

Now Show sat quietly and listened, never interrupting Lilli as she told the story all the way through to how she knew what Ray had done. Isaac saw his face change, from a look of curious interest, to much more rapt interest, to sympathy and shock, and finally to something Isaac couldn't quite identify—or, rather, something Isaac had never found the apt word for. Show was running the scenarios.

Finally he focused on Lilli and said, "Pardon me for this, darlin'." He turned to Isaac. "You believe it all, then? That's heavy shit to throw down, not much evidence. I'm going to speak plainly and say it needs to be your brain doing the believing, and not some other part."

Isaac would pulp any other man who suggested such a thing, but Show was doing his job. "No doubt, Show. At all."

Showdown nodded. "Good enough for me. Won't be good enough for the club, though. I don't see it. Lilli's new in town and doesn't even know the whole club. Her word against a brother's—won't be enough." He leaned toward Isaac. "Brother, you know that's true. If she was with any other of us and brought this story here, you would need more."

Lilli nodded and started to stand up. Isaac's arm shot out almost without his realizing it, and he pinned her where she sat. He knew what she was thinking. "Easy, baby. We're not done yet. Wyatt and Ray are gone for two more weeks at least. Can't do anything until then. We have time to work this." To Show he said, "Her word and my faith in it is enough for you. Between you and me, it'll be enough for

Bart and Len, too. Don't need a unanimous vote. Just need one more."

Show sat back in the chair. "You're talking about moving to kill a brother's blood on a split vote. That could tear the club apart, right in the face of this Ellis shit. You ready to take that risk?"

"Ray is dead anyway, vote or not. I'm ready to take that risk to save retaliation on Lilli, yes. Right now."

Show's eyes went wide at that, and he turned to Lilli. "You think you could give us a couple minutes, Lilli?"

Isaac was having none of that. "No. She stays. Say it."

"Alright then. You've known this girl what, three weeks? A month? And you're ready to risk the club—the whole damn town—for her? Isaac, that's your dick thinking."

Suddenly, Isaac forgot that Show's job was plain speaking, saying the hard shit and keeping Isaac level. He flipped straight into rage and started to stand, his whole body tense. But Lilli held the arm he still had on her thigh, keeping him in place, and she spoke, her focus intent on Show.

"Look. I understand. You don't know me. What I'm going to do will affect your club, and cause a member pain. Ray is dead, that's not negotiable. An entire squad was gunned down. Their bodies were mutilated, they were burned, and then they were hung from a wall to taunt us. All that happened because Hobson didn't want a woman—me—as his superior. That son of a bitch is dead. I'm sorry if that hurts the club, and I understand you'll do what you have to do. Hell, I won't even fight retaliation, if that's the way it goes."

Isaac jumped at that and grabbed her arm—what the fuck did she think she was saying?!—but she ignored him and went on. "There's no way I can get you proof. I have only the word of an ally I won't pull farther into this. But here's this: get Hobson drunk. He confessed directly to my friend when he was drunk. See if he'll do it again. From what Isaac says, he's a screwy mess, anyway. And I can wait a bit to try to do this as cleanly as I can."

Show considered her; Lilli held his eyes steadily. "You're a badass little beauty, aren't you? You've got sense, too." He turned to Isaac. "I think she's right, Isaac. We wait. We see if we can get Ray to talk. Then we take it to the club. It's CJ and Victor we can get on board, I think. Either or both of them. They're vets. This thing Ray did? They'll want him dead, too. With Ray fessin' up, though, we might get everybody but Wyatt. That's my advice."

Isaac had another idea, too. But he was angry now and done with advice. He needed to calm down. He nodded tersely to Show, who got the message, patted Lilli's knee, and left without another word.

When Show was gone, Isaac got up from the couch and paced the room. He was livid, and he needed to get control. Why was he so angry? Because Lilli had basically said once Ray was dead she didn't care if she lived or died? Yes. Because Show had insulted *the fuck* out of her and him? Yes. Because he was right—to keep Lilli safe, Isaac was ready to blow his club up if he had to?

Yes. No. Goddammit. He couldn't fucking *do* that. Too many people were counting on him. He clutched the tall back of his leather desk chair and sent it wheeling hard across the room to crash into the metal filing cabinet.

"Isaac."

He turned to Lilli, who was still sitting on the couch, looking calm. "Baby, I'm sorry. It's not as bad as it looks. We'll work it, I promise."

She stood and walked to him. She was so goddamn beautiful, her long, dark ponytail over her shoulder, her jeans snug on her hips but not too tight to restrict their sway, just the barest inch of perfect belly peeking out from under her t-shirt. She stopped right in front of him and took his hands in hers, easing them from the fists he hadn't realized he was clenching.

"There's a plan. It's the best plan we've got, I think. Whether it works or not, we won't know until Hobson is back. That means we have two weeks, right? So let's set it aside. It might be the last two weeks we've got."

"No way, Lilli. No way. It'll work. Has to." He couldn't even contemplate what she was suggesting could happen in two weeks.

"Okay, then. We'll have more time. But just in case, let's take *this* time. Okay?" She put a hand on his cheek, stroking her fingers through his beard. It was a frequent caress, and it calmed him. He leaned into her hand.

"You can do that?"

She smiled. "Sure. You learn that on the front lines, love. Don't take out an advance on trouble."

He looked into her eyes. To call them grey was insufficient, but he had no better word. He'd tried to think of a metaphor for the color, but had failed. The best he'd come up with was the color of the sky on an overcast day, but he'd be damned if he said something so florid out loud. They were beautiful. Bright. They glittered when she smiled. "God, I love you, Sport."

"And I love you." She grabbed his belt buckle and pulled it loose. "Show me how you love me."

He'd been hard since she'd put her hand on his face. Now, he chuckled and opened her jeans. "You want it sweet?" Their sex earlier had been rough and intense.

"You know I don't." She had his jeans open, and she slid her hands along his hips and around to grab his ass. Their sex was loud, and he didn't relish the thought of everybody out in the Hall hearing them. It had never stopped him before, but Lilli was different.

Then her hand came around to cup his sack and give him a squeeze. She shifted her hand to his cock. "Oh, damn, you're so hard," she whispered, her forehead on his chest. "I love your cock so much."

Isaac figured the soundproofing in the office walls was good enough.

He lifted her face and kissed her, his tongue plunging into her mouth, tracing her teeth and tongue. She snaked her arms around his neck and raised up high on her toes. Nothing—nothing—felt like her body against his. He wanted their clothes off. All of them.

"I want you naked." Even to him, his voice sounded like a growl. She stepped back from him with a little siren's smile and pulled her t-shirt over her head, dropping it to the floor with a wink. He went to the door and locked it; when he turned around, she had her boots off and was shimmying out of her jeans. He stripped as fast as he could, barely taking the time to hang his kutte over his chair.

When she was wearing nothing but a black lacy thong, her breasts bare and beautiful, her nipples hard with desire for him, he stopped her. "Leave it. I'll get it." She unhooked her thumbs from the thin strings across her hips and stood waiting.

Finally rid of his clothes, her strode to her and pulled her close, taking a second to feel the satin of her bare skin on his coarse body. He pulled the band from her hair, and she shook it loose, the silky tresses brushing over his arms on her back, making him groan. He brought them to the floor.

She wanted it rough; she always wanted it rough. But Isaac found that he was too overwhelmed by love and too haunted by the fear of losing her to be anything but sweet right now, to this woman who'd found a place in his heart he hadn't known was there. He kissed her, holding her close, his hands all over her, but gently, soothing. He slid her thong slowly down her legs, kissing a path to her ankles as he went. Then he pulled himself back up along her writhing body and thrust his hand between her legs to find her wet and ready, as she always was for him. He rubbed lightly over her clit, gently between her folds.

She bucked and moaned, frustrated. "Isaac, come on."

He bent down and kissed her breast, flicking his tongue softly over the hard bud of her nipple. His mouth on her skin, he said, "No, baby. Let me go easy. Easy is good, too." Pushing up onto his knees, he reached for his jeans and grabbed a condom. After it was on, he shifted to lie over her and press into her, slowly inching his cock as deep as he could get. She arched her back, and her eyes rolled up. She moved hard under him, flexing. He brought a leg up to rest on her thigh, pinning her. "Hey, no. We're goin' slow. I want to savor you."

"On the floor of your office, we're going slow?" She huffed and struggled some more.

Isaac liked a rough fuck, too—in fact, he was surprised at his need now to be sweet—but Lilli's resistance to his tenderness was beginning to seem strange. He caught her head in his hands and peered down into her eyes. "Baby, there a problem?"

She stilled and stared back; then, she surprised him with a chuckle. He felt it around his cock, so deep inside her. "No. I'm sorry. Habit." He didn't understand, so he furrowed his brow. She continued, "Self-protection, I guess. Don't make love. It's like a rule I had for myself."

He brushed his fingers over her cheekbones. "Had?"

The look she gave him then, limpid and warm, swelled his heart. "Yeah, had."

"Good." He moved slowly inside her, holding her eyes with his. She wrapped her arms around his back and her legs around his waist, clasping him tightly to her, and, for the first time, they made love.

Even sweet, though, he still made her scream.

~oOo~

Isaac and Show watched Kenyon Berry and Marcus Grant, Berry's right hand, drive off the Horde lot. Isaac's brain was buzzing. He turned to Show; any lingering anger he'd felt about the conversation with Lilli they'd had the day before had been blown away by Kenyon's visit.

Though still backing the Horde, Kenyon was suspending traffic on this pipeline, diverting resources elsewhere until the pressure from Ellis was down. Ellis was making a hard push in St. Louis, too, fully annexing the Northside Knights and looking to eliminate the Underdawgs entirely. St. Louis was open war. Kenyon's point—a good one—was that the risk was too great for the Horde and Signal Bend, too, to keep moving product into such volatile turf. But St. Louis and points east of it represented substantially more than half the revenue the cookers, and thus the Horde, and thus the town, brought in. To the west, they had Springfield, Joplin and Tulsa. Losing St. Louis would cripple them.

That wasn't even the worst news. His attempts to take over Signal Bend through legal channels thwarted thus far by the Horde's success at keeping Mac Evans distracted and vulnerable property owners strong enough to resist, Ellis had apparently decided to use force instead. He was bringing the war to them. The Northsiders were recruiting like crazy, swelling their ranks. Kenyon's intel was that they were looking to move on Signal Bend physically, drive people out. Kenyon thought they had maybe a few months before there was a turf war on the lazy streets of Signal Bend, and the enemy was bigger, stronger and richer—by orders of magnitude.

Show spoke up first. "How we handling this, boss?"

It was clear to Isaac. Nigh on impossible, but clear. "Straight on. Only way. We're gonna need the whole town on the beam, if we have any chance. We have a little time, though. Kenyon'll keep us apprised. First thing, we need to start guard shifts. Get men patrolling town, farm roads, all of it. We're gonna need volunteers, and they're gonna need some training and setup."

Showdown nodded slowly. "We need weapons. These assholes won't be coming in with hunting rifles and shotguns. We don't have the scratch to arm people."

That was how Tulsa and Joplin could help—and it would keep them away from the heat, too, as they wanted. "I'll get with Becker and Dandy. Tulsa's running guns; I'll get a family discount. And I'm calling Sam. Time to call in a marker with The Scorpions." They'd done an array of favors for the international MC over the years and had never needed to call in one. Now it looked like they might need them all at once.

"You bring them in, they might bring heat from law with them. Their brand of outlaw is high profile. Not like our penny ante shit."

"Can't be helped. We're not letting the Northsiders fuckin' burn us out." With that, Isaac turned on his heel and stalked back into the clubhouse. Everything was going to hell at once.

INTERLUDE: 2011

Lilli slid the keycard in and opened the door to her room at the Residence Inn. Home, such as it was. She been back stateside for three months, out of the service for three weeks. No job, no home, no family. Her father had had a generous life insurance policy and had left her everything, and it had all been earning interest while she was in the service, so she wouldn't need to work. She would hate to use that money, but she couldn't imagine joining the world again. She figured she'd just stay put.

Fuck it all.

When the incident report had come back, and Big Donna had checked out clean, Lilli had fought it. She'd fought hard, at first. If Donna wasn't malfunctioning, that meant Lilli had gotten her men killed. Okada. Miller. Scarpone. And eight other men. It had taken them more than a day to get clear and recover their bodies. Twenty-nine hours seeing their burned, hacked remains hanging from a wall.

And she'd done it. Chief had checked Donna out himself. Lilli didn't understand what went wrong, how she could have felt trouble if there had been none. Maybe they were right. Maybe she'd lost her nerve and had some kind of weird attack. She'd gotten her men killed.

So just fuck it all.

The light on her room phone was blinking. She ignored it; probably the front desk or housekeeping, or something. There was no one who'd call her.

Around 3am, she finally checked, just to get the damn blinking light to stop. She didn't sleep much, but that light was getting in the way of even her slim shot at it.

It wasn't an internal call. The message was terse. "Ms. Accardo, you can still be of service to your country. Please call." *Ms.* Accardo. God, that sucked. She recognized the area code and exchange on the number as DC, but not Pentagon.

She erased it and blew it off. Every day for a week, the same male voice left the same message one time. On the eighth day, there was a knock at the door to her suite.

A week after that, she was in training to work with the NSA.

CHAPTER FIFTEEN

Lilli felt the change in the air when Isaac opened the bathroom door. She tended to guard her bathroom privacy jealously. Spending years showering in the desert surrounded by men had made her really appreciate and luxuriate in her time alone in the bathroom. But he'd been on her early and often to shower together. She'd relented about a week or so ago, and hadn't regretted it. She knew there would be regret if she didn't set some ground rules soon, because he had become a shower vampire—expecting unlimited access now that he'd been invited in once—and she was starting to strategize ways to be in here alone.

Like this morning, for instance. She'd had an easy night without the dreams that drove her awake so often, and she'd woken before him, which was itself not an easy task. She'd been tempted to curl up close to him and sleep a little more, but then the thought came over her that she could shower alone. She'd sneaked into her own bathroom.

Normally, she would never be dodgy like this. She'd tell him to turn around and march his naked ass back out of the bathroom and wait his damn turn. But there he'd be. Naked and glorious, the lush long waves of his hair loose, his chest so goddamn broad and cut. And his cock. His brilliant cock, hard and ready for her. They didn't fuck in the shower, but he went down on her spectacularly, and she on him, and they'd be in there forever, wasting water.

She needed to talk to him when they weren't both naked. But now, he was stepping in with her, and her nipples were pebbled in anticipation of his touch. His hands on her hips, he kissed her cheek without saying a word. Then he moved in front of her, into the stream of water, and wet his hair, his head tipped back, the water spraying across his face and beading on his beard. It was among the most erotic images

218

she'd ever seen, and everything between her legs spasmed and clenched. He towered over her, his shoulders broad, his chest wide and rock hard. The muscles in his neck corded and flexed, tightening the leather around his neck, with the Mjölnir medallion lying at the base of his throat.

Yeah, she couldn't quite regret the loss of privacy, when it came in this enticing package.

Lilli put her hands up and slid her fingers into the hair on his chest, then dragged them slowly down, over his nipples—his hips flexed spastically—and the ridge of his pecs, down the banded muscle of his belly, into the nest of black hair. She gripped his cock with both hands and slid him back and forth through her fisted palms. Isaac rumbled deep in his chest, and Lilli looked up.

"I don't like waking up alone in your bed. Or any bed. Not anymore." He thrust against her grip, and she squeezed harder, until he groaned.

"I was just trying to squeeze in a shower before you woke up." She gasped when his hand pushed between her legs and his fingers found her core, flexing inside her. The friction of his callused palm on her clit weakened her knees, and he enfolded her in his other arm, holding her close.

"Why?"

With his fingers moving inside her and his palm rubbing on her, she was having enough trouble remembering to work his cock without trying to remember why she hadn't told him she wanted privacy. Why *hadn't* she told him? So she did. "Sometimes I like to shower alone." Why was that hard, again?

He stopped moving all at once, and she thought she'd hurt his feelings. Oh, that was why. She looked up; he was grinning at her. "Sport, I *crowdin'* you? Why didn't you say so?" He pulled his hand out and away, and she whimpered and clutched his cock more tightly.

"You don't want me to go?" His voice was a mischievous, raspy whisper that she felt in her spine. Jesus, this guy was like a drug.

She pumped him harder, leaning her forehead against his chest as she did. "Well not *now*. But sometimes I just want to hop in, wash up, get out and get my day going."

Even under the cover of his beard, she could see his jaw twitching with the strain of the orgasm she was wringing from him. He grunted and leaned forward, his hands on the back wall, caging her between his arms. "Shoulda said somethin', Sport. I'd leave you alone. For a couple minutes." The last few words came out hard, in wrenching gasps. Watching him near an orgasm was almost better than watching him have it. When it was like this, only about him, he *strove* for it, instead of pushing it away, as he did when he was inside her.

He was close, grunting in time with the drag of her hands on his shaft. She felt his balls tighten, and she dropped to her knees, surprising him. She took him into her mouth, and sucked him as deep as she could manage. He went off immediately, shouting her name and punching the shower wall while she swallowed down what he gave her. It was so erotic and intense to feel that kind of power over him that she almost didn't care if he paid her any reciprocal attention.

But he did.

~oOo~

Later, as they were cleaning up from breakfast—they'd picked up a domestic rhythm, whichever house they'd spent the night in, moving around each other fluidly as they cleared and rinsed and washed and wiped—Isaac stopped her progress in the kitchen doorway, grabbing her by the waist. "Come with me to Tulsa this weekend."

It caught her completely off guard. She hadn't known he was going to Tulsa, and the weekend started tomorrow. "What? Why?"

He tucked a lock of her loose hair behind her ear and leaned down to kiss her neck. "Few reasons. I got some club business to do. And I got a booth at an art show there for the weekend. You could be my booth babe. And I don't want to spend the weekend away from you." He winked, giving her a leering grin. "I usually stay in my camper, but for you, I'd spring for a hotel."

Probably most anyone else would think this was an absurd time for a weekend getaway, in the middle of her plan to kill someone. But Hobson was away, and would be for some time yet. As for her actual work, she'd finish the last project she had today, and she could send word not to send her another until the weekend was over.

She hooked her hands in the pockets of his jeans. "I like the idea of the camper. Romantic."

His laugh was deep and warm. "You haven't seen the camper. But okay. We leave in the morning?"

"Sure." She raised up on her tiptoes, bringing her hands up and around his neck, and he pulled her close and kissed her.

~oOo~

It was dusk before Lilli got her work done and sent the re-encrypted document back through the labyrinthine security channels of the NSA. She'd spent—she checked the clock on her laptop—ten hours hunched over her work. She'd gone into her zone and never gotten up. Not to eat, not even to pee. Her shoulders felt like they'd been soldered to her neck.

She checked her phone to find that Isaac had called twice and texted once. No message—he almost never left a voice mail. The text read *Stay here with me tonight*, and he'd sent it about two hours ago. The last contact, the second call, had been about 15 minutes ago.

She hadn't responded to his attempts to contact her—her phone was on vibrate, and she just hadn't heard them. Isaac lived about twenty minutes from her house. Lilli went out onto the porch, and within a minute or two, he was riding up the gravel road that served as her driveway.

She walked down the deck steps and across the yard to meet him. He was off his bike fast, striding toward her. "Fuck, Sport—you okay?" He reached her and yanked her hard into his arms. "Shit, you had me worried."

"I'm okay, love. I just had my head down with work."

He sighed with evident relief. "You can't do that, Lilli. Not with the shit goin' down around here. I gotta know you're okay."

He hadn't told her what the "shit" was going on with the club, and she hadn't asked. If it was going to get in her way, they'd have to have a conversation, but for now, she said, "I can handle myself pretty well, Isaac."

When he framed her face with his big, coarse hands, Lilli's eyes fluttered shut at the thrill of it. "I know. But I need you to keep in touch. I'm not used to giving this much of a shit about somebody, and it turns out I got a short drive to crazy. So check your phone, okay?"

"Okay. I'm sorry."

He bent down and kissed her. "D'you get my text? You want to stay at my house? We can get an early start."

She'd only need her backpack for a weekend, so she could ride with him to his house. "Sure. Wanna help me pack?"

"I got silk and lace detail." He swatted her ass, and they went into the house.

~oOo~

They stopped at the Chop House for dinner. It and No Place were the only places open for dinner, and Isaac didn't want to get pulled into the scene at Tuck's tonight. The Chop House was, by Signal Bend standards, more upscale, with dimmer lighting, a red and gold color scheme, and the kind of candles that came in red glass covered in white netting. The clientele was a town crowd, pretty much the same crowd Lilli had seen everywhere in the weeks she'd lived here.

People knew her now, and knew her as Isaac's woman, and the suspicion with which they'd first met her had been replaced with a kind of artificial respect and affection. The suspicion had made Lilli feel more comfortable, ironically. It was honest. The near-fawning that happened now, especially from women, was just carry-over from Isaac. In fact, she had a sense that there was no small dollop of hostility from the women, and she suspected she knew why. If he'd been solo for as long as he'd said, then these women were all wondering what the hell made Lilli so special. She figured they were saying what they really thought in the church hall on Sundays, or over the fence while they hung up their washing.

That was a thing that happened in Signal Bend that Lilli found surprising in its preponderance. As if no one owned a clothes dryer, clothes and linens billowed on clotheslines every day throughout the town. The place was trapped in a weird kind of time warp. She'd asked Isaac about it, and he'd given her a lopsided smile and said, simply, "Sun's free."

Now they walked through the restaurant following Molly, the hostess, to the corner booth Isaac liked. It always took them time to get to their table, because everyone they passed at least said hello. Sometimes, they wanted a chat or had a problem to bring up to Isaac—whom almost all of them called Ike. He twitched every time, but let it slide. Lilli had learned that she was right about him—if there was power in this town, it was in Isaac. Even the mayor talked with Isaac before he brought anything to the town council. The Night Horde was both law and order here.

Molly got them to their table at last, and they sat. "You need menus?" They both declined. "Okay, I'll have Beth over in a sec. You both want Buds?"

Isaac nodded, but Lilli said, "Maybe some red wine?"

Molly cast her a glance. "All's we got is the stuff that comes in a box. You want that?"

Mostly she'd been curious to see what Molly would do, so Lilli smiled and shook her head. "No, thanks. Bud is fine."

When Molly left, Isaac gave Lilli a nudge under the table. "Shit disturber."

"What? I thought some wine would be nice with dinner." That was true, but it was also true that she took most opportunities to test the limits of this town's quirks.

"Never seen you drink wine, Sport. You just like sticking a wrench in the works."

"I like wine sometimes. And it's crazy that people around here expect everything to stay the same all the time. It's like some kind of group neurosis. Hell, why even have menus? Or choices? They should do a *prix fixe* thing and be done with it."

"Don't know what that is, city girl. Enlighten me." As he spoke, he reached across the table and stroked her arm. Her heart picked up its pace a step.

"It means fixed price. It's when the restaurant prepares a meal, usually several courses. That's the whole menu for the night, and everybody there that night eats the same thing and pays the same price."

"Yeah, but this way, I get my T-bone and you get your chicken, and everybody likes what they get." He leaned forward, his green eyes catching the light from the flickering little candle. "We're gonna have to work harder at gettin' you countrified if you're gonna live here."

"Don't, Isaac." They only had this brief time before Hobson was back; she didn't want to think about what the future did or did not hold. "And it's not country, it's crazy. I'm sure it's not a thing everywhere." A shadow had quickly crossed his face at her first words, but now he was smiling.

"Maybe. Lot to be said for crazy, though."

Beth came over, and Lilli ordered the chicken parmesan, as she had the three other times they'd been here. Isaac got his T-bone, which was probably his thousandth. While they were eating their garden salads, Isaac looked up, and the expression that overtook his face gave Lilli pause. She turned to see a man she hadn't met. He looked familiar, though, and Lilli scanned her memory to place him. He was tall and very thin, the kind of guy whose Adam's apple was the first thing you noticed, with greying brown hair.

Dressed in jeans and a plaid shirt, tucked in, which was apparently the "dress casual" uniform around town.

Isaac spoke first. "Will."

The man apparently named Will said, "Isaac. Need to talk to you."

Lilli was still combing her memory. She knew she'd get it. If she'd seen him, she'd place him. There it was—he was the guy who'd gotten stabbed at Tuck's place her first night in town.

Isaac set his fork down but didn't move elsewise. "Havin' a meal with my lady, Will. Gonna have to wait."

Will glanced at Lilli. "Ma'am." She smiled and nodded back, and he returned his steady look to Isaac. "Can't wait."

With a terse nod, Isaac said, "'Scuse me, Sport," and got up. He gestured toward the front door, and the two men walked through the restaurant and out.

Alone at the table with her salad, Lilli used the time to people watch. The restaurant had about twenty tables; six besides theirs were occupied. She saw Don Keyes and his wife Lonnie, sitting with the Reverend Mortensen. Ed Foss was eating alone. She recognized the people at the other tables, too—farmers, a couple of shopkeepers—and Mac Evans, who was staring at her. She smiled, and he raised his glass.

He didn't stop staring, though, and Lilli was disquieted. Her instinct was not to flinch from an aggressive look like that, but after a few awkward seconds, she nodded, then moved her own gaze elsewhere in the room, letting him have the victory in their strange, impromptu stare down.

Isaac came back in, looking glum. He strode to the table and sat down. Lilli didn't ask; she could tell that whatever it was wasn't good news, and he knew she would listen if he wanted to tell her. But he gave her a concerned look and said, "What's wrong?"

The question surprised her. "What? Nothing."

"You have a look, Sport. Somethin' happen while I was outside?"
Lilli thought about the weirdness with Evans. Could he read that lingering on her face somehow? Was he already getting to know her that well? The thought thrilled and alarmed her.

She shrugged. "Kind of a strange moment with Mac Evans over there." Isaac turned quickly, and Lilli took his hand and brought his attention back. "No big deal. Caught him staring. He asked me out when I got to town; maybe he's feeling jealous. Don't sweat it." But Isaac looked back, his fists clenching. Lilli glanced over to see Mac looking decidedly uncomfortable now.

"I fuckin' hate that guy." The malice in Isaac's tone was unmistakable. Lilli would hate to find herself on the other end of that emotion, and she was surprised that Mac Evans, realtor, had earned it. She didn't doubt he had, though.

"He's smarmy, yeah. Seems fairly innocuous, though."

"He's not." Beth brought their entrees then, and Isaac sat back. He said no more on the subject of Mac Evans. They ate quietly, Isaac unable to shake off whatever ill news he'd gotten.

They should have stayed in and cooked.

~oOo~

227

Lilli woke standing next to Isaac's bed, her heart racing. The room was dark. When she had her bearings, she checked the clock on his nightstand: 3:21. Then she noticed that Isaac wasn't in bed. Snagging his t-shirt from the floor and pulling it on, she went looking.

After doing a turn of the whole first floor, she checked outside and found him in the yard, sitting in a metal lawn chair—one that would be considered 'vintage' and 'kitsch; if it hadn't been sitting in this very yard for probably fifty years. He was smoking. Lilli didn't smoke, and Isaac never smoked inside except at the clubhouse, so it wasn't unusual for him to be sitting outside with a cigarette. What was unusual was that he'd left the bed she was in to do it. He had a thing about waking up alone when he'd gone to sleep with her, and he didn't do it to her, either.

She pushed open the wooden screen door, and it sang on its spring. He turned at the sound and watched her walked toward him, the glow of the dusk-to-dawn light giving the yard an ethereal glow. The air was still and muggy. The night creatures had quieted, the dawn creatures had not yet stirred, and the silence had weight. As she neared, he stubbed his smoke out on the ground and held his arms out to her. She sat on his lap, her arm across his shoulders.

Wearing only his jeans, he held her snugly, one hand on her hip, the other high on her thigh. "Did you dream, baby?" He rested his head on her chest, and she ran her fingers through his hair.

"Yeah. You okay?"

"I'm sorry." Instead of answering her question, he asked one of his own. "You ever gonna tell me what they are? Afghanistan stuff?"

She sighed. She didn't want to talk about them. She'd never spoken of them. She could say what she always said when he asked, that she didn't remember, but it was a lie. He'd stop asking if she'd just tell him. "I guess. I mean, they started after I came back to the States, so I guess. But it's not like I'm reliving memories from that time. They're death dreams. I dream I'm being killed. Violently. I feel it happening. Sometimes it's pretty gory."

He'd lifted his head to look up at her as soon as she started to answer. "Christ, Lilli."

Fearing he was about to engage in some amateur psychoanalysis, before he could say more, she asked, "What's got you sitting out here in the big dark?"

He smiled, and Lilli saw the weight he carried in the low curve of his lips. "I'll tell you. Soon, I tell you everything. But not yet. For now, I'll say I just got a lot of people counting on me, and I don't know how not to let them down. The whole town is looking to me, and I am outmatched. I'm not who they want me to be."

"Who do they want you to be?"

He blew through his lips. "A fuckin' savior."

"I don't know, love. I think maybe you saved me." She cupped her hand around his jaw, her fingers tracing his scar. She'd yet to ask how he'd gotten it.

His whole body reacted to what she'd said, his arms clutching her more tightly, his eyes intent on hers. "You have to stay. I'm not gonna lose you. You have to stay."

This was the wrong moment to start thinking about what could happen when Hobson and his brother got back, what a club vote might mean for them. "Isaac, we're not talking about that stuff now.

"Fuck." He dropped his head again to her chest. "Just fuck."

Feeling a need to reshape this moment and reclaim the sliver of peace they were supposed to be enjoying, Lilli put her hand over his where it rested on her thigh and pushed it between her legs. He groaned, and she felt the vibration of it against her breast. When she moved his fingers into her wetness and over her clit, he groaned more loudly and took over.

She kept her hand on his, enjoying the way it moved against her palm as his fingers stroked and probed. Just as she was beginning to feel the warm current in her joints that signaled her climb toward release, he stopped and pulled his hand away, setting it on her hip. She whimpered and reached to bring it back, but he shifted her then, seating her square on his lap, facing away. He grabbed the hem of his t-shirt where it rested on her thigh and lifted, encouraging her to raise her arms so he could pull it off. Once she was nude, she turned and put her hands on his belt, but he caught them in his and brought them to his lips.

"Just you, baby. I just want to touch you. Lay back on me."

She did as he'd asked, and then arched hard, with a keening gasp, as he returned his hand between her legs and took her breast in the other. The feel of him took her under, dulled her consciousness as it sharpened her senses—his strong chest against her back, his rough hands cupping her most sensitive flesh, his lips firm and soft against her neck, her jaw, her ear.

As he worked her, his fingers making need unspool in her blood, he murmured in her ear. "Baby, your pussy feels like satin, it's so smooth and soft. Ah, yeah, I love it when you squeeze me tight like that." He pulled his drenched fingers up to swirl on and around her clit, making her hips dance on his lap. She could feel his erection bulging in his jeans, pressed against her ass and thigh. He rested his head on her shoulder with a groan. She wanted him inside her. All of him. She reached behind her and grabbed his belt buckle again, but his hand left her breast and clamped on her wrist, bringing her out from between them.

He spread his hand wide over her belly, pushing her flat against him. "Just let me feel you, baby. That's what I want," he murmured into her ear.

"Isaac, please. I want you to fuck me. I want your cock."

He chuckled, and the sex in the sound made her clench and moan. "I will. When I'm done here, I'll take you inside and give you my cock. Oh, yes, I will. I will fuck you well and truly. But now I want you to lie back and let me touch you." He petted her, long sweeping strokes from her throat to her knee, as his other hand continued to probe and flex inside her. "Just relax and feel it, baby."

She did. She released a long breath and relaxed into the curve of his body, letting him touch her. His hands were everywhere—her breasts, her throat, her arms, tracing the line of her collarbone, her legs, her belly. His fingers plunged deep into her core and her ass, pinched and rubbed circles on her clit. His mouth latched onto her neck and sucked and sucked.

She stayed relaxed and calm as long as she could, giving herself over to his touch, letting herself feel the way her need moved all through her, heating and loosening her joints and muscles all the way to her toes. His fingers were on her, in her, moving faster and harder by degrees until his body was shaking under her with his own efforts, and she couldn't stay calm any longer. As her climax rolled closer, gaining speed, she grabbed his hand between her thighs and forced him to go harder, move faster, until it was on her, and she needed to coil her body up, but he wouldn't let her, he held fast, whispering, "go, go, go, go, go, baby," and she went rigid, ecstasy shooting through her like electricity, her sight going red and starry behind her eyelids, and she screamed.

When it was over, Lilli's body went limp and liquid, and Isaac clutched her tight to keep her on his lap. She was glad; she felt sure she'd have ended up in a puddle at his feet. He'd done that to her—for her—with only his hands.

He kissed the skin beneath her ear and whispered. "I love you, Sport. You're mine, and I'm not letting you go."

Lilli knew she should resist those words; he couldn't know what the next weeks would bring. But the tendrils of ecstasy still held her, and when his arms tightened around her and he stood, swinging her legs into his hold, all she cared about was him making good on his plans for the night.

~oOo~

"Lilli…Lilli…Lilli."

Sweet Jesus, she was going to kill him. She'd just gotten to sleep. Now he was running a finger up and down her spine, saying her name in an extremely life-threatening singsong voice.

She groaned and swatted at him. "No fucking way." She tried to pull the covers over her head, but he blocked her.

"We gotta go, baby. You can sleep in the camper if you want. Rise and shine—or, well, rise, anyway. Looks like the shine's awhile off."

"What time is it?" She turned to glare at him.

"6:30." About and hour and a half since they'd collapsed, sweaty and spent. How could he be so chipper? "Come on, soldier girl, that's practically lunchtime for you, right?" He gave her ass a swat and got up. "Hey—I'm gonna make some coffee. You get up now, you can shower all by yourself. And there's a brand new box of Cookie Crisp on the kitchen table."

Grinning like an idiot, he left the room. Lilli got up. She wanted some room in the shower this morning.

Showered, dressed, caffeinated, and full of sugary cereal, Lilli felt marginally better. When she climbed into the camper, she felt even better. It was awesome. It was a little one, with a van front, a tiny kitchen and seating area, and a bedroom of sorts in the back. The best, very best, part was that it was at least forty years old. Gold shag carpeting. Rust, gold, and avocado floral print upholstery. It was the tackiest thing she'd seen in a long time.

"Holy shit, this is beautiful!" she cried as she opened the side door and tossed her pack on the floor by the banquette. Isaac, standing on the ground leaning into the driver's side, gave her a look that said he thought she was delirious, and she climbed into the passenger seat and grinned. "No, really, I love it. This is gonna be great!"

The way he was smiling at her now gave her a little heart tremor, and she said. "I love you."

He wiggled his eyebrows in response. She liked that he didn't mindlessly repeat it back when she said it. Like her, he valued those words and used them sparingly.

"Hey, come over here and sit behind the wheel for a sec—I need to check the trailer lights." They were pulling a trailer behind the camper that held his show gear and inventory as well as his bike. She climbed over the center console and sat behind the wheel.

The lights checked out, and Lilli climbed back so Isaac could take the wheel. As they pulled away from his house, Lilli realized that she was in a fantastic mood. Despite the lack of sleep, despite the darkness in her past, despite what loomed in the near future, she felt light. She felt happy.

She didn't want to lose it. She didn't want to lose him.

CHAPTER SIXTEEN

Isaac liked to arrive when setup opened; it got crowded once all the vendors were all trying to get their tents and booths together at once. But after their athletics of the previous night, he and Lilli had gotten a later start than he wanted. Not too bad, though, and the setup was going fine.

Isaac loved these shows overall, some more than others. Some, the juried art shows held in the middle of a bigger city, like St. Louis, were a nightmare to get to, expensive, and generally not worth the fuckery. This one in Tulsa, though, an arts and crafts show staged at a big state park on the far edges of the suburbs, was his favorite. It was big, so there was some earning potential. There was a good campground in the park, so most vendors set up camp there, and they'd do a big bonfire each night and party hard deep into the night. It was a good group of folks—mellow, good-natured, a little on the rougher side. Isaac's kind of folks.

They'd dropped the trailer first thing, then parked the camper at their site and walked back to set up his tent. The booth rental fee included the actual booth, a white 10'X10' tent with removable sides. It took awhile to get started, because everybody was glad to see everybody else—a lot of these men and women Isaac called friends, but they only saw each other a few times a year, at these shows. So there was hugging, fist-bumping, and arm-clasping to do with the vendors who were there when Isaac and Lilli got there, and the ones who continued to file in.

Isaac took especial pleasure in introducing Lilli around. Many were surprised; Isaac wasn't known as a tied-down kind of guy. But they recovered their wits quickly upon talking to Lilli for half a minute. She was light and easy, knowing as if by instinct that she could unleash her sense of humor around this crowd, and she had just about everybody she met charmed. She seemed charmed herself. Isaac felt good. He could almost—almost—set aside his cares.

While Lilli went to the campsite to rig up the electric and pay for some bundles of firewood, Isaac was setting up his tent, hammering in the guy wires on the last pole, when he felt feminine hands on his back. Not Lilli—the scent of gardenias was strong behind him. Lucinda. *Fuck*. He hadn't thought about Lucinda.

"Hey, lover." It was her best, silkiest sex voice, whispered in his ear. Her hands crept down his spine and into the back of his jeans. He stood up, removing her fingers, and turned around.

"Hey, Cin."

Lucinda made very pretty sterling silver and gemstone jewelry. Her work more craft than art, she didn't do the juried shows, but she'd been Isaac's fairly regular art show fuck for five or six years. She was a good-looking woman. Mid-forties, about five-six, long hair streaked just about every shade of blonde, but done artfully and attractively. Light brown, almost tawny eyes. Narrow hips, and not much ass, but tits for miles. She dressed in very snug jeans—Isaac knew exactly how snug, since he'd peeled them off scores of times—and flowing, filmy tops that showed lots of shoulder and cleavage. She knew her assets. She also modeled her own jewelry, so she wore rings on every finger, lots of earrings, a prominent pendant, and several inches of bracelets on each wrist. She could be heard coming a half-mile away. And yet, he hadn't heard her. He'd been too preoccupied. Just as he'd been too preoccupied to remember her at all and give Lilli a heads-up about her.

Now, she stepped up against him and hooked her be-ringed hands around his neck, raising up on her tiptoes for a kiss.

236

Luckily, she still couldn't reach unless he bent down, because just then he saw Lilli returning, walking down the lane that was emerging between the tents going up. He put his hands around Lucinda's waist and set her back.

"Sorry, Cin. I'm with somebody."

She snorted. "Right. Like that'll ever happen." She stepped toward him again, and he held her off, giving her a warning look. She drew her brows together. "What—you're serious? You brought a fuck with you?"

The surprising urge to give her a slap for that remark came over him, but he mastered it. Lilli drawing ever nearer, and very obviously paying attention, Isaac leaned down close to growl, "No. I brought my old lady with me. We're done, Cin."

Wait—*old lady*? The words surprised Isaac almost as much as they clearly surprised Lucinda, who drew back, gave him a killing glare, muttered, "Asshole," and stalked off— in Lilli's direction.

Isaac watched as Lilli gave her an absolutely brilliant smile and continued on. Lucinda stopped, turned and watched Lilli approach him. He was suddenly living his own special soap opera, set in hell.

Lilli walked straight up to him, muttered, "Make it good, pal," and yanked his head down to kiss him hard. Feeling a little sorry for Cin, he obliged and wrapped his arms around Lilli, bending her backwards a little and kissing her until she was breathless. He raised his eyes mid-kiss to see Cin spin away and storm to her own booth.

Well, he now knew that his woman was the jealous type. Hopefully, Cin would behave, and the weekend wouldn't become unnecessarily interesting.

He pulled up and set her back. "Feel better?"

Lilli put her hands on her hips. "And she is?"

"Lucinda. Old news."

"Well, next chance you get, you might want to let Lucinda Old News know that I can break her neck with the heel of one hand." She walked into his booth and opened a box of carved flowers. "Will there be more like her?"

Isaac found Lilli's jealousy highly erotic. He'd hated possessive women. He'd learned that early on, and he'd kept to fuck buddies for years, dropping any of them the second he scented possessiveness. But Lilli's possession he found entirely wonderful. It opened up something in his chest to feel *claimed* by her—and that was what that kiss had been. A claiming. He shifted his very erect cock in his jeans, trying to find a more comfortable and more subtle position. "Unlikely. I'm sorry, Sport. I honestly didn't even think about her." As sexy as it was, he didn't want it to turn into a problem. Wanting to pull their boat into safer waters, he stepped behind her and pulled her close. His mouth on her ear, taking in the smell of her, so different, so much more natural, so much better than Cin's cloying gardenias, he murmured, "My head's so full of you, there's no room for anybody else."

She laughed, and turned toward his mouth. "Smooth." He captured her lips in his, and knew in the way she yielded that their weird little moment was over. Her breath tickling his lips, she whispered, "You should know that I always got bad marks in sharing."

He turned her in his arms and clutched her chest to him. "So did I, baby."

~oOo~

238

The first night bonfire, when everyone was feeling energized for the coming show, and happy to be reunited with old friends, was a riotous affair. Isaac had found himself...distracted as Lilli stood in the camper and changed from shorts to jeans, so by the time they got to the fire, Isaac carrying a cooler full of beer, the fire was in full, glorious burn, and people were deep into their cups. This park had a lake and swimming beach, and the bonfire was set up not too far away, so there were some swimmers, clad and not, in the water as well.

There were always musicians in the mix, usually of the folk variety; this night, three people had guitars, someone had a fiddle, and someone else had a set of hand drums. Joints and bags of mushrooms were passed freely, as was beer and booze. Bonfire. Folk music. Artsy types. Booze and drugs. Isaac would never hear the end of it from his brothers if they saw how much he loved this hippy shit.

They said their hellos, and Lilli laid out a blanket. Isaac sat against a log near the fire and pulled her down to sit between his legs. He handed her a beer and opened one for himself, then leaned back against the log and pulled Lilli back with him. He felt calm. He almost wished this could just be his life, riding around in that shitty old camper, selling his work, hanging out with the show bums, riding curvy country roads with his woman behind him, in the deep night. He could be a vagabond. Wouldn't even take much of a push. The road was where he felt right.

Duncan, a leatherworker and good friend, and his wife Mindy, who made beautiful papers, shared the long log with them. They also shared their weed, and Isaac and Lilli shared their beer. Lilli lay quietly on his chest, listening while Isaac talked shop with Duncan and Mindy. When Stan came over, though, and then Tonya, and the conversation became a dishfest, Isaac could feel Lilli getting restless. But he was in the thick of the conversation and didn't really want to get out of it. He hadn't seen these friends in a while.

Eventually, Lilli scooted from between his legs and out of the growing cluster of people gossiping about stuff she knew nothing about. Isaac saw her go and watched her wander toward the bathrooms, listing to starboard a bit. Knowing where she was off to, he returned his attention to the increasingly lively conversation.

But she was gone a long time. Isaac looked around at the empties on the blanket, where she'd been putting hers, and did some math. She'd downed a six pack. And had her share of hits off two good-size doobs being shared among four people.

Lilli was very likely wasted off her ass.

When she was around him, he knew what that meant—completely uninhibited and a little bit freaky. Horny as fuckall. When he was with her, it was spectacular. He didn't know what to expect when she was wandering around on her own.

"'Scuse me folks, I seem to have misplaced my lady." Nobody really noticed, and he got up and went Lilli hunting.

She wasn't at the bathroom; he'd grabbed Julie, a weaver, and asked her to check. He looked everywhere, finally just yelling her name as he walked. He was starting to get really worried, bordering on frantic, wondering if the club's problems could have chased him to Tulsa and caught up Lilli, when he got to the lake. There were more swimmers, more of them naked, now.

And she was one of them.

He'd scanned the water only because it was the last place to look, sure she wouldn't be there. But there she was, standing in waist-high water, her breasts bare and shimmering in the moonlight and the faint light cast from the bonfire. She was beautiful. And completely exposed.

"LILLI!" he roared. She saw him, laughed, and dived under. Her bottom half was bare, too.

Holy fucking Christ. She was wasted and swimming. She was naked, in front of all these people. His woman. On display. He didn't know whether to be worried for her safety because she could drown or because he was going to throttle her.

When she came up again, he roared again, "LILLI! GET YOUR ASS BACK HERE *NOW*!"

She laughed, flipped him off, and went under again. This time she stayed under for a distressingly long time and was farther away when she finally broke the surface again. Then she dived again. When she came up, she was far out and treading water.

Now they were into drowning territory, if she was as wasted as he feared.

He was going to have to go out and get her. Fuck.

Isaac swam, but he did not leave himself vulnerable. Stripping to his underwear in a crowd, even this crowd, leaving himself unarmed and barely dressed? He did *not* do that.

Fuck, fuck, fuck.

During the few seconds Isaac grappled with his quandary, Duncan walked up and stood at his side. "I'll go get her, man."

No. Another man was not bringing his naked woman back to the beach. He toed off his boots. "I got her. Just—grab our blanket for me." Duncan nodded and headed back to their log by the fire.

Now that he'd committed to this folly, Isaac stripped quickly and efficiently, down to his boxer briefs, then strode into the—*fucking cold*—water and dove in. He swam long, strong strokes. Lilli hadn't moved much, just bobbed in place; Isaac took that as a bad sign and put a little more power into his stroke.

She'd gotten even farther out than he'd realized. When he got to her, she was breathing too hard and looked distressed, but she was still above water. As he got his arms around her, Isaac felt a strange brew of emotions: rage, terror, love, relief. He let love and relief have sway. "Hey, Sport. Whatcha doin' out here?"

"Water's deep," she gasped, with a strained little smile. "Cold."

"I gotcha. Wanna head back?" She nodded, and he pulled her close and swam back. She didn't fight at all, and Isaac was glad to be able to concentrate on getting them back to the beach. When he got to water they could stand in, though, she didn't. She'd passed out. Fuck. Thankfully, he could feel her chest moving under his arm, so he knew she was breathing. He swept her naked body into his arms and walked onto the beach.

Duncan and Mindy were both waiting for them. Mindy had the blanket spread wide, waiting to wrap Lilli in it. When she saw that Isaac was carrying her, she shifted her hold so that she could cover Lilli in his arms. Duncan had their clothes.

"She okay?"

Isaac grunted. "Don't know. Gotta get her back to the camper."

"Wait, Isaac." Mindy put her hand on his arm. "She's freezing. Sit at the fire for a few minutes to warm her up. You, too."

He nodded and sat down where they'd started the night. Cradling Lilli in his arms, he checked her over. She was still breathing, so it wasn't that she'd drowned. Her pulse was strong, if fast. But even in the firelight, he could see that she was shockingly pale. He pressed his lips to her forehead; she was deeply chilled. He wrapped the blanket tighter. He was shivering himself, but he didn't care. "Lilli, baby. Come on. What's wrong?"

He didn't understand what the holy fuck had happened. She'd gone to the bathroom, and then she'd been swimming naked and wasted, in the dark, out to the middle of a lake? She'd gone much farther, into dangerous territory, when he'd called for her. Like she was trying to get away from him. He didn't understand.

He had no idea how long they sat there. For the most part, the party went on around them. Somebody—Isaac didn't even notice who—draped a rough woolen blanket over his shoulders. Duncan took their clothes back to the camper. Otherwise, they were left alone.

When she woke, or came to, or whatever, she did so violently, in the way she sometimes came out of her dreams. Isaac took a hard hit to his chin before he could get the right hold on her. He squeezed her close, pinning her arms until she settled. When she did, he pulled back so he could see her.

"Hey, Flipper. You with me?"

After a confused second or two, she nodded. "I don't—I—I'm naked."

Relieved, confused, but no longer angry, Isaac laughed. "Indeed you are. I'm gonna pick you up and carry you to the camper, okay? We're gonna sleep, and in the morning, we're gonna talk."

When he picked her up, she hooked her arm around his neck and laid her head on his chest.

~oOo~

He tucked her close, curling his body around hers. Lilli slept right away, having barely woken at the bonfire, and Isaac was able to sleep, too, once he felt sure she was settled.

He woke at dawn to the sounds and smells of camp waking up—people at neighboring sites speaking quietly, fixing campfire breakfasts, heading off to showers. He was stiff. They hadn't moved all night, and the camper bed wasn't exactly luxurious. He had a bad moment, when he feared something terrible had happened, but Lilli was simply sleeping deeply. She stirred, sighing prettily, when he came up on his elbow.

Her lake adventure had really thrown him. He didn't know whether it was a big deal, or whether he should make it a big deal, but she could have died. Stupidly. And he had no fucking idea why.

They needed to get up, though. He rubbed his hand up and down the firm, satiny length of her arm. He kissed her shoulder. She tasted like lake and bonfire, and he felt his heart cramp at the memory of his fear. And his anger. She stirred again, her beautiful ass sliding slightly against his rigid cock.

He shifted his hips back; she was probably feeling like crap. Not the morning to get anything started. His hand on her shoulder, he gave her a gentle shake. "Time to get up, Sport." She moaned a little and curled up more tightly, her ass coming back to graze his cock again. Christ, he wanted her. He felt a need for her whenever she was near, like a buzz in the back of his head, but skin to skin with her, the urge was almost overwhelming. He flexed against her, unable not to, and then turned and sat up, making some better space between them.

He swatted the ass that was causing him such consternation. "Lilli, baby, up you go." This time she rolled to her back and opened her eyes, giving him a nasty look. The hangover hit her then. "Ow. Fuck."

He couldn't help the grin. "Not surprised. You had an adventurous night. How d'you feel besides your head?"

She sat up and groaned. Her hair was a matted mess, and she looked pained, but otherwise okay. "Like I ran a marathon without training for it first." She rubbed her hands over her face, then dropped them and looked at Isaac. "Did we swim?"

"I guess that's one way to put it. Another way is that you skinny-dipped and almost drowned, and I swam out to rescue you."

She gaped at him. "Jesus. What was in that weed?"

"It was just good weed, baby. You're a lightweight." He brushed her hair off her shoulders and came back with a piece of lake grass. Rolling it in his fingers, he asked, "There something going on with you? Us?"

She furrowed her brow, then winced in pain and relaxed her face. "What? No."

"I think there is. Drunk man's words are a sober man's thoughts. Same with actions. You swam away from me last night, into trouble."

"No, Isaac, I don't"—she stopped and closed her eyes—"No. Truly. And my head hurts too much for a big talk."

That told him there was a big talk knocking around somewhere in her sore head. Of course there was something going on with her, with them. They were facing big shit when they got back to town. He still didn't know whether what happened last night was just a lark or somehow was related to their murky future, but he decided to let it drop. They weren't talking about that shit now, anyway; that was their deal. "I can help you with the hangover. I'll get breakfast started; why don't you take a hot shower?"

She agreed, and Isaac got up and helped her to her feet. He was still hard as granite, and she cast a sardonic look at his crotch. He chuckled. "What can I say? You're hot even when you're a hot mess. But I'm a big boy; I'll survive without getting off."

She looked exponentially better when she came back from the showers, but she was still moving slowly. And now Isaac saw that she had a sizable bruise on her upper arm, as if she'd been grabbed hard. Had he done that? He took her arm and gave it a close look—no; his hand was bigger. "Where'd you get this?"

Lilli looked down, evidently confused. "I don't know. Random drunk bruise, I guess." She grazed her right hand over the bruise, and Isaac saw that her knuckles were red, too. She'd punched someone. She didn't seem to notice her hand, so Isaac didn't say anything more. But he was going to be on the lookout for somebody with a bruised face today. And he had an idea where to start.

For now, though, breakfast.

He gestured toward the picnic table at their site. "Have a seat." He'd laid the table, and fixed her scrambled eggs and toast with honey. A glass of tomato juice. And four ibuprofen. "Start with the juice and pills, then the toast. Eggs last."

She looked up at him, amused. "Kinda bossy."

"Hey, trust me. The juice and bread will help. Work up to the eggs. You'll feel ready for 'em by then."

She smiled and did as he suggested. Isaac made himself a plate and sat next to her, his hand on her thigh.

~oOo~

The show was extra busy this year, and Isaac and Lilli had little time to talk during the day. She was a great booth babe. She'd learned a lot about his work in the weeks they'd been together, and she spoke enthusiastically about it. She wasn't much for haggling, so he took over that part. People liked to haggle at these things.

When he took a bathroom break during a lull, he walked by Cin's booth. She was wearing a pair of big sunglasses, even though the day had gone overcast. She was alone in her booth, so he went in, walked right up to her, and took the glasses off her face. Black eye. Really good shiner, too. Lilli didn't go in for half measures.

"You stirring up shit, Cin?"

She snatched her sunglasses back and put them on. "Fuck you, Isaac. You two can have each other. Little b——." She stopped, thought better of her choice, and continued, "*girl* has no sense of humor."

That filled in the blanks enough for Isaac. Cin had said something bitchy—probably grabbing Lilli's arm to get her attention—and Lilli had…expressed her displeasure at what Cin said, or at Cin putting hands on her. He could see it clearly. He put his elbows on her little display counter and leaned in close. "I know it came as a shock to you, and I'm sorry for that. But, Lucinda, hear me when I say that you need to settle your shit down, and right now. We had good times, but you had no claim. You know that."

She pouted. "If I'd thought you were claimable, I would have."

"I wasn't, Cin. That's what I'm sayin'. Let's leave it on good terms. I don't want you to get hurt." He gave her hand a squeeze.

"Too late, asshole." She walked to the other end of the counter, and Isaac left.

~oOo~

The first day of the show really went well. The weather was good—hovering between sunny and overcast, but no threat of rain, so it was cool for midsummer—and the crowds were thick. Isaac sold several expensive art pieces, got some promising queries about furniture, and talked to a guy who seemed pretty serious about commissioning a piece. Time would tell if that panned out, but he couldn't help but be a little excited at the possibility.

The usual craftsy stuff that always sold well at these shows was flying out of the booth. Isaac was beginning to get a bit concerned that he'd have sufficient stock for the second day. Not a bad problem to have, though. When a small gaggle of elderly women left the booth carrying carved flowers and birds and one fancy little wren house he'd made on a whim, he turned to see Lilli smiling at him as if she'd caught him doing something cute.

"What?"

She walked up to him and pushed her hands under his black t-shirt until she grazed his nipples, heedless of the people browsing the booth. "My big, macho biker is a totally sweet flirt with the little old ladies. Quite the Lothario—had them all giggling. Shameless, really."

He grinned. Also ignoring the browsers, he put his hands around her ribs, his thumbs just skimming the undersides of her breasts. She took in a sharp breath, and her eyes fluttered shut for a second. "What can I say?" he whispered, "I appreciate a woman who can appreciate my charms."

"Then you must appreciate the fuck out of me."

"Oh, I do, Sport. Literally." He kissed the corner of her mouth and let her go.

CHAPTER SEVENTEEN

When the first day of the show wrapped up, Lilli helped Isaac fill in the rest of his stock and then close up his booth. It had floored her at first that he didn't pack everything away and lock it back up at night, but he explained that the grounds were guarded, and the tents were too difficult for anyone to get into before one of the guards came around. So they closed up the sides and walked back to the camper.

She'd thoroughly enjoyed watching Isaac work this fair, or show, or whatever it was. She'd loved helping him do it, too. She loved his work, and she loved to hear and see him talk about it. He was so much more than a biker or an outlaw. She felt proud and protective of him, which turned out to get in his way a little. Within a couple of hours, he'd stepped in and suggested that he complete the sales. She wanted to punch people who tried to dicker his pricing down. Fuck them for trying to cheap out on the fruits of his talent and skill.

He'd pulled her back and gotten close, whispering in her ear, "Easy, Killer. This is the game. Everything's priced with that in mind. I'm gouging the ones who don't play."

But she didn't care. It pissed her off. So instead, Isaac suggested that she hand the hagglers off to him. She did so, gladly. She still wanted to punch them, but she forbore.

He was different here—still Isaac, but more relaxed. Much more. It really hit home for Lilli how much responsibility he carried in Signal Bend. Here, his cares moved back a little and gave him room to stretch out. He chatted with the people browsing his booth, and flirted with the old ladies oohing and aahing over the knickknacks he made. Boy, did they flirt back.

There were lots of groups of older people traversing the park. Lilli didn't know if they came in buses or whether this was just a general draw for the older set, but some of the women, in colorful, coordinated slacks and blouses and big sunhats, literally, actively flirted with Isaac, taking every opportunity to put their hands on him—squeezing his biceps, patting his pecs. One teensy, stooped woman in a purple pantsuit and a red hat, who must have been at least eighty-five, actually rubbed his belly and exclaimed, "Oh, Maeve—it's a twelve pack!" At which point, her similarly clad friends tittered and slapped at each other like high school sophomores.

Isaac took it all in stride, flirting right back, making the most of that sexy, lopsided smile, even lifting the red hat lady's hand from his belly and kissing it. When she left, clutching several pieces of Isaac's work, she pressed her new loot to her concave chest and grabbed his ass in her bony hand.

That shocked him. He even blushed. And Lilli about wet herself laughing.

He didn't wear his kutte here, but he was still a huge, brawny guy with long hair and a full beard. Only the bottom half of the ink on his upper arms showed under the sleeves of his t-shirt, but he did not look like someone with whom to fuck. Normally, people who didn't know him— and quite a few who did—looked on him with fear and respect. Not here, though. Here, he smiled almost constantly, and his smile was a thing of wonder. It made Lilli's heart swell to see it. His aura was warm and approachable, and people approached him.

She really liked his friends, too, the other artists and vendors. They had a true community together. They were a lot like Isaac, the way he was here. They came as they were, without artifice or façade. Lilli's kind of people. She had very little patience for most people, who seemed consumed by shit that didn't matter, and who spent a great deal of energy trying to pretend they were different from their true selves. Lilli liked people who cut the crap. She'd learned that she could find those people on the edges. They were those who lived close to the bone, their lives, for one reason or another, not giving them room for pettiness and triviality. Soldiers. Outlaws. Artisans. Wanderers.

She'd spent some time talking to several people here, especially Duncan and Mindy, who had the booth next to Isaac's, and with whom Isaac seemed especially close. Duncan did beautiful leatherwork. Like Isaac, he did art pieces and also more accessible, and cheaper, craft things, like leather-bound journals, for which Mindy made the paper. She, too, did both art and craft. Lilli was sorely tempted to buy a sensational art piece that at first glance looked like an elaborate quilt. It was lovely at that first glance, but when Lilli examined it more closely and understood the intricacies of the work, done all in handmade paper and natural dyes, she was nearly brought to tears. But she was not in a position to be collecting possessions. She needed to be able to shove everything she owned into her military-issue duffels and take off, on very short notice.

The show wasn't all unicorns and rainbows, though. Lilli was surprised to learn that Isaac had himself a girl here. The violent jolt of jealousy that had charged up her spine when she'd seen said girl—well, woman, more like; older than Isaac, and almost a generation older than Lilli—had surprised her even more. She didn't think she'd ever been jealous before, but seeing some flouncy blonde with her arms around Isaac's neck—yep; that had done it.

Though the previous night at the bonfire was a haze of beer and weed, parts of her memory had cleared throughout the day. At first, she remembered being cozy with Isaac by the fire, then there was a big blank space. She vaguely remembered being in the lake. But as the day advanced, she'd feel a piece of memory fall into place here and there. She remembered getting bored when she and Isaac had become encircled by artists cackling like washerwomen over what the fuck ever, and she'd headed to the bathroom to pee and then maybe wander around a bit.

When another piece of the puzzle fell into place, it was skinny dipping. Well, *that* was totally like her. Dropping trou in public while wasted. There was probably a plaque in her honor commemorating it hanging somewhere at her college. It was why she'd never drunk with her unit. When she was drunk, she followed whatever impulse came on her. Isaac had told her she'd almost drowned, though, and she couldn't remember why she was out there without him. Probably just because she'd come across a lake.

But then, toward the late afternoon, when she was bringing a late lunch back from one of the food vendors, she passed the booth of Miss Lucinda Old News, and they made eye contact. Her fancy blonde hair was pushed back with a pair of sunglasses. She had a nasty black eye. Lilli had a sore right hand, which she'd figured was a consequence of banging it against something last night. Apparently, that something had been Miss Lucinda's left eye.

And then Lilli remembered. She'd come out of the bathroom and met Lucinda on her way in. When Lilli had tried to sidestep her, Lucinda had stepped over, too, staying in her way. She'd smiled up at Lilli, who had three or four inches on her, and said, "You're pretty, no doubt. You think you have him now, but don't get comfy, sugarpie. I've had years to figure him out. I know what he needs. You're just a cute young thing caught his eye. What do you say we wager on who lands him?"

Feeling wasted and mellow, and totally secure, Lilli had just smiled and sidestepped her, but the bitch grabbed her when she passed and tried to yank her back, hissing, "Don't dismiss me, little whore."

Lilli didn't remember thinking anything then. She'd just wheeled around, instinct taking over, and busted Lucinda in the face. Lucinda had dropped to the ground, and Lilli remembered standing over her, snarling, "You lose, bitch."

The rest of the night was still a fog, except for a memory of being in the water. But standing in the grassy aisle between booths, staring at Lucinda and her black eye, Lilli remembered enough to know she needed to be careful at this night's bonfire. Finally, bestowing on Lucinda a confident little smile, she turned and continued down the aisle with falafel and sodas for her and Isaac. She was not thrilled to discover that she could be jealous and catty.

Back at their booth, she uncovered Isaac's plate and handed it to him. He stared down at it for a few seconds. "Um, Sport? What's this?"

"Falafel. Never had it?"

He shook his head. "I ask again: what is it?"

"It's fried chickpea balls in pita bread, with greens and a spicy sauce. It's good." She took a bite of hers. It was delicious, in fact, and the spice in the sauce made her tongue tingle.

"None of the words you just said is a meat." He set his plate aside and opened his Mountain Dew.

She laughed and rolled her eyes. "Dude. You're not even going to try it? I asked what you wanted, and you told me to surprise you. Well, surprise!"

"I thought you'd be picking between a steak sandwich and a bratwurst! Who even came up with a stupid word like falafel? Sounds like a frog with tonsillitis."

"It's Middle Eastern, and you are being a big baby. At least try it. I promise you won't turn into a vegetarian if one meal you eat in your life doesn't have an animal in it."

He pulled his plate back. "Yeah, something tells me this is a gateway sandwich." With an attitude of reluctant experimentation, he took a bite. Lilli watched him consider what was in his mouth and on his tongue. He smiled as he took a second bite and said around his mouthful, "I draw the line at tofu. No way that's food."

She laughed and handed him a napkin. He had sauce in his beard, and she pointed where he needed to wipe. "I'll keep that in mind."

~oOo~

When Lilli and Isaac went to the bonfire the second night, with their blanket and cooler of beer, Lilli did so with the resolve to stay in better control of herself. Like the night before, there were people playing music and singing, weed and 'shrooms were going around, people were talking and laughing. The log they'd settled at was taken by the musicians this time, so they found another spot on a grassy patch a little farther back from the fire. They weren't mobbed this time by fellow artisans. It was almost as if they were being left alone on purpose. Lilli wondered if Isaac had said something.

There was nothing to lean back against, so Isaac stretched out on his side and pulled Lilli to lean back against him. He pulled the band from her hair and combed his fingers gently through it, and she closed her eyes and relaxed.

Feeling soothed, she let her senses reach out. The big fire cast a dancing, golden glow over everything around it; patterns swirled through Lilli's closed eyelids. The warm, woodsy smell of burning pine was almost a potpourri. The sound of sap crackling in the flames seemed to harmonize

255

with the music being played—right now it was 'There but for Fortune.' And then there were Isaac's hands—one playing softly in her hair, the other around her arm, his thumb tracing patterns on her bicep. She loved those hands, big and callused, rough and strong. Tender and loving.

"Baby, you goin' to sleep?" His voice was gruff, little more than a rasp over his tongue. He brushed her hair off her shoulder and ran the backs of his fingers against her cheek. Jesus, what his touch did to her. Everything from her shoulders to her knees constricted in a powerful spasm of desire. Because he'd touched her cheek.

"Nope." She shifted to lie down next to him, on her back so that he loomed over her. He pulled her in more snugly and looked down at her, his ponytail falling over his shoulder. Lilli reached up and took it in her hand, coiling it through her fingers.

"You look good enough to eat, Sport," Isaac growled. "I'm more than half tempted to get you screaming right here by the fire."

She smiled and pulled on his ponytail, bringing him down for a kiss. She'd only had a couple of beers, but she was so overwhelmed by the powerful need she felt for him that she was more than half tempted to let him get her screaming right here. Instead, though, she turned her head away from the kiss, just a bit, and whispered, "I really love you, Isaac. I love seeing you this way."

He smiled, his brow wrinkling a little. "What way?"

"Relaxed. Easy. Getting a chance to set your burden down for a minute."

In the flickering golden light, she couldn't read the look that rolled through his eyes, but then he smiled. "You make me feel easy, baby. You make me feel strong." He kissed her, and she opened her mouth wide, letting him in, taking him into her. He growled and lay on her; she could feel him thick and hard, pressing against her belly. Suddenly, he pulled away, rising onto his elbows and staring down at her.

"Let's get out of here. I want to ride with you tonight."

That came out of nowhere. Lilli loved to ride with him, and that itself was sexy as fuck, but she had a different kind of riding in mind just now. She lifted her hips and squirmed against his cock, making him twitch and groan. "I thought you wanted to make me scream. I want you to make me scream."

"In good time, baby. Ride with me. I'll make it worth your while." He stood and held out his hand. Bemused and frustrated, she let him pull her up. They gathered up the blanket and cooler and headed back to the camper and Isaac's bike.

~oOo~

He rode them out far into the country, taking winding roads, mostly through farms and fields. Some woodland, but not like it was around Signal Bend. Lilli held on tight and laid her head on his back. She felt Isaac's gloved hand squeezing her linked fingers, and she kissed his back, breathing in the smell of his leather kutte.

Eventually he turned onto a gravel road in fairly thick woods. They came to a gate, and he dismounted and opened it. Lilli was curious, and gave him a look that said so, but he just got back on the bike and followed the road, leaving the gate open behind them.

He stopped near a small lake and parked the bike. They got off, and he took her hand and led her to the shore. A stand of pines ringed the lake, and there was a narrow, pale rim of sand circling the shore. It was lovely, the bright moon making the water sparkle, but Lilli was confused.

Curiosity overwhelmed her, and she pulled on his hand. When he turned to her, she asked, "Why are we here? Where *is* here?"

"A friend of mine owns this place. Just a little private lake. Emphasis on private. Since you like skinny dipping so much, thought I'd take you somewhere we can do it together." As he spoke, he lifted the bottom of her hoodie and pulled it up. Surprised and delighted, she raised her arms and let him pull it off, bringing her t-shirt with it. Then she took over the rest of her undressing, and Isaac stripped, too.

There was a little dock jutting out from the slim sand beach. When they were naked, he got a gleam in his eye. He swept Lilli up in his arms and ran down the dock. Lilli laughed and yelled, "Oh, shit!" when she realized what he was going to do. He jumped, she squealed, and they landed in the water together.

The water was deep and cold, and they both came to the surface gasping. Laughing, Lilli swam away and floated on her back for awhile, reveling in the feel of the water lapping at her bare skin. She spread her legs, and the cool eddied over her tender flesh. Closing her eyes, she let the water take her, her hair loose and swirling softly around her.

Isaac came up from below and wrapped his arms around her, her back against his chest. He swam with her, pulling her into shallower water. When he could stand, the water at chest level for him, he swung her around, pulling her legs around his waist. His cock was there, steely and proud despite the chill of the water, pressing against her entrance. Lilli was completely relaxed and completely aroused, and she moved, starting his slide into her core. With a grunt, he grabbed her ass and pushed all the way in.

"Jesus fuck, you feel good," he breathed. She didn't say anything. She was too wrapped up in the amazing feel of this night, of him sliding inside her. Moaning, she tipped her head back, and he latched on, suckling at her throat, then kissing along her shoulder where the surface of the lake lapped at her.

She couldn't stop moaning. His hand was on her breast, under the water. The cool had tightened her nipples to hard points, and every time his thumb flicked over her, she twitched and gasped, and he grunted. He was moving fast inside her, the hand not exciting her breast clutching her ass. God, she could feel all of him. All of him, so hot and smooth inside her, and—wait.

She stopped, resisting his thrusts. "Isaac," she gasped, fighting for focus when she wanted to keep moving. She was caught up in the way the water buoyed them and changed their movements, made them nearly effortless. She wanted more. But she made herself focus. "Isaac. Wait. We don't have a condom. Wait."

He stopped and met her eyes. He was breathing hard, every exhale coming out in a growl. Releasing her breast, he brought his hand up to hold her head, his thumb on her cheek. "I don't want to stop, baby. It's too good to stop." He flexed, thrusting hard and deep, and she cried out.

This wasn't fair. She didn't want to stop either, but somebody needed to be responsible here. She whimpered. "Isaac, come on."

But he was insistent. "No. We'll get you something at the drugstore. I want to feel you. So silky and hot on my cock. God, let me feel you." She was torn. She shouldn't be torn. She should get loose of him, swim back to shore, and get dressed. And then kick his ass for being a fool. But she loved him, she loved *this*, and she didn't want to stop. Still deep inside her, he took several steps into shallower water. When they were just more than waist deep, he unhooked her arms from him and laid her back. She was floating on her back, her legs around his waist, his cock filling her up. He thrust into her with a long grunt, and her decision was made. Or not made. She just let it happen.

She spread her arms out in the water and loosened the grip of her thighs around his hips, letting him move her as he would. She'd always wanted rough sex; sweet and gentle made her feel impatient and unsatisfied. Sometimes her fucks had seemed only a few steps from brawls. That was the case with Isaac, too. They'd literally fought their way to a fuck. But she'd learned something in this time with him. What she really wanted, what turned her on more than anything, was to trust her man enough to give herself over. She wanted his strong hands to move her, demand of her. Sweet and gentle was amazing when she felt tamed by it. Now, floating in the lake, attached so intimately to him, his big hands grasping her, stroking her, making her glide through the cool water as he moved her on his cock, taking this crazy risk with him, she felt something inside her, in her core, in her heart, fold open.

When her orgasm came on, it came like a locomotive. She gasped and lifted out of the water, crashing her body against his, clutching him tight, moving with him now. Isaac crossed his arms on her back and gripped her head, his mouth on hers, devouring her as she devoured him.

He broke from their kiss and tucked her head to his shoulder. She surged on him, driving him into her. Growling in her ear, he urged her on, "Yeah. Yeah, baby, that's it. That's it. Go, baby, go." When he started walking to the shore, his cock shifted in her with every step, and she was done. She cried out, driving her fingernails into his back as the waves of ecstatic release undulated through her.

Then she was on the ground, feeling grass, sand, and pine needles under her still-thrumming body. Isaac hooked her knees with his arms and pushed her legs to her chest. "Fuck, Lilli," he groaned, "oh *fuck*, this feels like nothing I've ever known. Like everything." Their bodies slammed together, the sounds of their joining—their cries and moans, the slap of their slick flesh—driving the night animals to silence. Isaac didn't even try to be gentle now, and she was glad of it, wanted his hard, heavy need. She could feel another climax coiling hot inside her, and she reached out to claim it.

She felt a sudden swell of him inside her, and, still pounding deep into her, he raised up on his hands, looking down at her as if he were surprised. "Oh God, Lilli! Jesus—jeez—oh *FUCK*." He came, his body straining, every muscle flexed and corded with the force of it. She was close, watching him in his throes pushed her closer, and she wrapped tight around him and let her hips free to buck hard on him until she caught it, and she screamed.

Isaac collapsed at Lilli's side, his breathing rough and irregular. Lilli felt dazed and utterly, utterly full. His hand rested on her belly, lightly stroking. She felt sated. Loved. Happy. Damn. Damn, it felt so good. As soon as she recognized that feeling, dark thoughts of what awaited them stole to the edges. She slammed the gate and kept them at bay. Turning away from those thoughts, she curled into the shelter of his embrace.

"I love you, Lilli. So much I'm dizzy with it."

Lilli knew she didn't need to say anything. She simply snuggled closer and let him swallow her up into his arms, wanting to stay exactly like that forever.

But they couldn't, of course. They finally got up, rinsed off again in the lake, and dressed. Just before Isaac swung his leg over his bike, Lilli said, "Let's find a drugstore tonight, okay?"

Isaac put his leg down and turned to her. There was a look on his face that she thought she could read—but it scared her. Lifting his hand to her cheek, he asked, "Would it be so bad?"

Holy God. She didn't hesitate. "*Yes*, Isaac. Fuck, you know it would. What the hell are you suggesting?"

He dropped his hand, and for a scant moment he looked badly hurt. Then: "You're right. I don't know what— you're right. I know where there's a drugstore. Let's go." He pressed a light kiss to her cheek and mounted his bike.

Lilli's heart was pounding. They'd crossed a line somewhere, and now they were in territory she had no map for.

~oOo~

On Sunday, the weather threatened rain, and the show attendance was down because of it. Saturday had been so good, though, that nobody seemed to mind much. They just kept an eye on the skies, prepared to protect their work if the rains came. They didn't.

The show ended several hours earlier the second day, and, with little stock left, they had the trailer hitched, packed and ready to go within an hour of closing. Though a lot of the artists were camping one more night and leaving in the morning, Isaac and Lilli were heading home that night. But Isaac had Horde business in Tulsa, so he left Lilli to pack up their camp while he rode out to conduct it.

As she was packing up the campfire cooking gear, she felt a tingle at the nape of her neck and turned around. Her new friend Lucinda was standing akimbo on the road just at the

262

edge of their site, glaring at her. Lilli walked up to her. "Something you need?" She pointed to Lucinda's face. "A matched set, perhaps? I'm just as good when I lead with my left."

The older woman sneered. "Just thought I'd let you know—if you want to keep him, you better come with him to every one of these things. Because I'm taking him back."

Lilli was done with this sad broad. She smiled and turned away. She was hoping Lucinda would grab her again, but she didn't.

Just then, they heard the roar of a Harley, and Lilli turned back around as Isaac rode up. Lucinda stood pat as he parked and dismounted, setting his helmet on the handlebars. He looked straight at Lilli, strode up to her, and kissed her deeply, his hands on her ass. When he pulled away, he winked at her before he turned to the other woman standing there. "Cin," he said.

Lucinda turned on her heel and stalked away. Lilli had seen the hurt on her face, though, and she felt a stab of pity. She could understand feeling possessive of Isaac. He was something special. And he was *hers*. The ferocity with which she felt that claim surprised the hell out of her.

Isaac turned back to her, his hands on her hips. He drew her tight to him. "You want to tell me what's been going on between the two of you this weekend?"

Lilli thought about that for a moment. She considered blowing it off, but decided to just be straight with him. "Your friend Cin isn't ready to give you up. She put me on notice that she plans to get you back. We're probably not going to be BFFs."

Isaac shook his head, a wry smile pulling up one side of his mouth. "I figured her eye wasn't from a love bite." His face clouded over then, showed an edge of anger. "I'm sorry, Sport. She never had me. You know that, right? I'll talk to her, make sure she backs the fuck off."

"No, Isaac. It's okay. I know we're solid. I'm pissed, not threatened. I've got it handled."

He didn't look satisfied with that, so she repeated herself. "It really is okay. I mean, she gets all up on you again, and I will break several important bones in her body, but you don't need to intervene, at least not now. I got it."

Laughing now, he kissed her head. "Lucinda does not know the hornet's nest she stuck her hand in, that's true."

Lilli nodded. "Exactly." She remembered that he'd been off at a club meeting. "Hey—everything go okay with your thing?"

"It did. Pretty well." She didn't ask more, and he didn't offer.

Isaac slid his arm around her waist. "You ready to hit the road, Sport?"

Whatever had happened between them in that moment at the lake seemed forgotten. Or, not forgotten—Lilli certainly had not—but set aside. She'd taken her pills, and she and Isaac were as they should be. "Yep. All packed."

With another kiss to the top of her head, he went to trailer the bike. Then they went around camp to say their goodbyes. Lilli felt wistful; she liked it here. She liked these people—with one key exception—and she'd liked the way she and Isaac were. She didn't want to face what Signal Bend had waiting for them.

CHAPTER EIGHTEEN

Isaac woke and didn't feel Lilli. He lifted his head, worried, and found her sleeping on top of the covers, her head at the foot of the bed, her feet on her pillow. She was sometimes a fairly athletic sleeper, usually when she was having a bad night. This, though, was a first—and if she'd dreamt, she hadn't woken him, which would also be a first, he thought. She looked relaxed, so he switched his own position and slid up behind her, wrapping his arm around her waist and pressing his face into her hair.

He was done sleeping, but he wasn't done being close to Lilli. She didn't even stir when he brought her close, so he relaxed and let his brain kick into gear. His meet with Becker in Tulsa had gone as well as he could have expected. Becker was unwilling to offer manpower, but they'd cut a decent deal on firepower, and Becker would handle the transport, freeing the Horde up from that expense of time and risk. Then Show had called him while he and Lilli were on the road home with two pieces of critical information: first, that his own meet with Dandy in Joplin had been a bust, and second, that Wyatt had called in—he and Ray were coming home.

That was yesterday. He and Lilli had gotten in late, unpacked the trailer, and gone to bed. He hadn't shared with her what Show had told him; he wanted to keep hold of every possible second with her trouble with Ray set to the side. It had been late when they'd finally turned in, and they had both been tired, so they had simply curled up to sleep.

She sighed and snuggled deeper into his arms. Isaac's cock, alert since he'd lain behind her, swelled full, but he simply held her more tightly, taking in the encompassing sensation of completeness he felt merely being close to her like this, knowing that he had her trust. He moved his hand to press it against her flat, firm belly, his fingers splayed wide. What their weekend away had told him unequivocally was that Lilli was his one true. He wanted a life with her. A long one. He wanted a *family* with her. He'd been surprised, too, at the lake, when the thought of her full of his child had made his heart expand, and he'd seen, bright and clear, the life he wanted. His woman, his child. A family, done right. Love filling his home in a way it never had in his lifetime.

They had Ray to deal with. He had Ellis, too. But he swore a vow right then, mouthing the words, that he would get them through this shit or die trying. He would keep her.

He could no longer be still, and he let his top hand roam her sleek, strong body, stroking the long planes of her legs and arm, cupping the curves of her ass, her tits. He tweaked a nipple, and she moaned and gently scissored her legs.

Nuzzling against the nape of her neck, he murmured, "There's my girl," and moved a little so that he could slide his bottom arm under her head. He felt her make way for him—she was awake.

"Are you faking?" he whispered.

"I never fake." He could hear the smile in her sleep-sultry voice.

He chuckled. "That's good to know." He took her breast in his bottom hand and pushed his top hand between her legs. She was wet for him, and she arched her back, kicking her leg back to hook over his, leaving herself open to his touch. She reached between her legs to grip his cock, already trying to bring him into her.

He took her hand away and rolled over onto her. "Easy, Sport. I'm gonna linger over you this morning."

She huffed. "I thought you liked our wild fucks."

He traced his nose and lips over the contours of her beautiful, clear face, moving down the side of her neck. He loved the little hollow at the base of her throat, and he paused to lap at it. "You know I do, baby. I love it rough with you. It's explosive. You are hot and strong and can take everything I can give you." He groaned and flexed at the thought. But things were about to explode around them. On this very day, in fact. He knew that, but she didn't, not yet. He wanted to linger, savor, love. As he kissed her, all over, down her arms, over her belly, across her breasts, he whispered to her. "But right now, I want to take some time and feel the way we slide together. I want it to build up. I want to fill you up over and over, I want to feel your skin moving under mine."

She stilled, and so did he. He looked up, checking her response. "Jesus Christ, Isaac." She sounded breathless.

Not sure yet whether she was still frustrated, he grinned a little. "You okay, Sport?"

He saw her swallow. "Yeah. That was sexy as hell. Do that. I want to fuck like that."

His lips on her belly, he shook his head. "I'm not gonna fuck you, baby. I'm gonna move you. Let me. Let me have you." She nodded, and he felt her relax completely, like she'd flipped a switch. With a smile, he ducked between her thighs and tasted her. He took his fill.

That morning, he made her come over and over, slowly, with his mouth and his hands and his cock. He made her come until she cried mercy. Then they showered together, and he brought her off again. Always in the back of his mind was the knowledge that this could be their last time alone together, and he did everything he could to make it count.

Then, he took her to Marie's for breakfast. They greeted the regulars, and Lilli had her usual, as did Isaac. He watched her eat her waffles, carefully filling every square with syrup before she dug in. When she looked up and caught him staring, her lips glistening with syrup, he smiled. "I love you, Sport. You're it for me. You fill up a space in me I didn't even know was empty."

She grinned smugly and took another big bite. She looked happy and at her ease. She was perfect.

When they were done, he rode her back to her little house. Not knowing yet that Ray was back, she planned to spend the day working.

~oOo~

For the first time in his memory, Isaac hated walking into the Night Horde clubhouse.

Even before he crossed the threshold, he felt the weight fold over his shoulders like a mantle. Ray Hobson. Lawrence Ellis. So much trouble focused on the club. He couldn't shake the notion that his brief weekend with Lilli had been some sort of last hurrah. The choices he would make this day could determine the fate of his club and his town, and *would* determine the course of his life and Lilli's.

When Isaac came into the Hall, Dan was standing at the bar. He was about to do his shift patrolling the town, Isaac knew. Wyatt was at the bar, too; he and Dan were drinking coffee and chatting.

"Hold up, D. Let me talk to Wyatt a minute; I'm gonna send him out with you."

Showdown had been pondering the chess game, obviously, but his eyes were on Isaac now. "Show, why don't you head back to the office with Wyatt and me. We can get him up to speed on what he missed."

Isaac and Show sat Wyatt down in the office and filled him in about Ellis and the Northsiders, and the new plan for keeping watch against trouble. When Wyatt was caught up and understood the plan for actively patrolling the town and surrounding farms, Isaac leaned back in his desk chair and asked, "How was your trip? Ray doin' okay?" Show gave him a sharpish look but said nothing.

Wyatt shrugged, looking morose. "Trip was okay. Put a pile of fish in the freezer for the next fish fry. Ray's Ray. Ain't really been right since he got back. Thought getting him out in the woods, doing somethin' we always did, tradition or whatever, might shake him loose some. But I don't know. He's got shit goin' on in his head."

Isaac leaned forward. "What kind of shit?"

Wyatt simply shrugged again and said, "War shit," but there was something in his eyes. Isaac saw it and knew: Wyatt knew about what had happened. Ray had told his brother. Isaac wasn't sure how or whether that changed the plan, but it was something to be aware of.

He sent Wyatt out to take off with Dan. When he and Show were alone in the office, he asked his VP, "You ready for this?"

Show nodded. "Are you?"

Isaac was chomping at the bit, in fact. "We got four hours. Let's get it done." They waited until Dan and Wyatt left, and then they took the club van and drove south to Ray's place.

~oOo~

They found Ray in his underwear, already half drunk, barely past noon. They got him dressed and brought him to the clubhouse promising all the booze he could drink.

What he really wanted to do was drag Ray's sorry, drunk ass back to the room and torture the truth out of him. Isaac didn't need Victor for it, either. He was more than happy to get Ray's blood under his fingernails. But Show had talked him down from that idea. They were sticking with the plan. Ply the bastard with alcohol, get him blubbering. The thought sickened Isaac. It was plain that Ray was experiencing some kind of guilt over what he'd done. He was a broken shadow of a man. Good. Fine. Whatever. His guilt, when he'd never made an attempt to come clean and set to rights what parts of his crime he could, was hollow and self-indulgent.

Isaac wasn't sure how he was going to sit next to this guy and drink with him. He had to do it, though, and he had to do it friendly. So he and Show sat Ray between them and got the booze flowing.

For a long time, Ray just blathered. He talked about their trip. He talked about Wyatt. He talked ad nauseum about hot chicks he'd supposedly banged. And he talked plenty about Afghanistan, too, but it was all gloryhound bullshit. Then, finally, when Isaac was beginning to worry that he'd pass out before they could get it out of him, he started moaning about losing his commission and being discharged after being passed over twice for promotion to Major.

In the midst of that pity party, Ray muttered, "Handed that damn cunt her oak leaf on a fucking platter." Isaac's ears perked up and his fists clenched. He looked at Show, who cocked his head and gave it a slow shake, his eyes turning to Isaac's fists on the bar.

Isaac relaxed his hands and took a breath. "What d'you mean, Ray?"

Ray had been staring at his half-full glass. He looked up, startled, when Isaac asked. He seemed to be trying to think what it was he'd said, then, getting it, shrugged. "Hotshot chick pilot gettin' favors, prob'ly cuz she was givin' favors, you know what I mean. Got upped right past me, way before her time. She was supposed to be some big deal, but she got where she did on her knees, I guarantee you."

Nope. Isaac couldn't deal. Torturing the truth out of Ray was suddenly his only possible option. He came off the barstool fast, surprising Ray and Show. Show covered, flashing Isaac a look that said, *you will fuck this up, if you can't maintain*, and then he asked Ray, "Sounds like a shit situation, buddy. Anything you could do about it?"

And Ray started to cry. Isaac stood there, rage jackhammering through his veins, and waited to see if Ray would end this fucking farce and spill. "I tried, man, but it all fucked up. It was s'pose to just be her and that pussy new kid flying with her. She was s'pose to go on a cargo run. Just her and the kid. No big loss. But then we had hostiles, and everything went to shit."

Isaac stepped back, went around the bar and busied himself getting a fresh bottle of whiskey. What he'd heard made him want to bash Ray's head in; he needed a little bit of distance. He let Show keep the lead.

Show put his huge hand on Ray's back. "Aw man, that's tough. You're saying, what, you did something to make her crash?"

Ray was crying hard now; he nodded. "Just s'pose to be her and the kid! Wouldn't have killed 'em, just blown her ride, got her taken her off flight duty. All I wanted—get her out of the damn air. She wasn't s'pose ta be flyin' transport that day."

271

Show, his voice easy, encouraging, asked, "Transport?" And Ray dropped his head to the bar. Blubbering heavily, his head resting on his arms, facing Show, he told the same story Lilli had already told them. Isaac's fist was clenched so tight around the bottle of whiskey he was still holding it was shaking. When he noticed, he put the bottle back on the shelf. This bastard had had his last drink on the Horde.

He came back around the bar and slapped a hand down on Ray's sloped shoulder. "Hey, buddy. What say we take you back to the dorms and you can kick back awhile, wait for Wyatt?" Ray nodded miserably, and Show walk-dragged him back to one of the rooms.

When Show came back out, Isaac asked, "We good?"

Show nodded. "I was already on board, brother. That'll be enough for Victor and CJ both. Bart and Len, too. Probably everybody but Wyatt. That's some bad shit he did. He's got to pay. I'd want him dead even without your girl."

"We need to pull everybody in, get this dealt with." Isaac wanted it done before he left the clubhouse. All of it. Done.

Leaning on the bar, Show asked, "How're we gonna handle Wyatt? This won't go down easy with him."

"We keep Ray, let Lilli deal with him here. That neutralizes Wyatt, keeps him from acting against the club and setting off a whole new set of troubles." Isaac pulled his burner and nodded at Show's pocket. "You call in the club. I need to talk to Lilli."

She picked up on the second ring. "Hey, Sport. Got some news."

"What's up?" He could tell she was distracted, probably deep in whatever work she was doing.

"Ray's back. We did like you asked—got him drunk, he told the whole sick story."

There was a long silence before she responded. "Where is he now?"

"Passed out here. We're calling in the club for the vote right now. Should go our way, baby. We'll keep him here, and I'll call you when the vote's through. You can deal with him here."

This time, there was no hesitation on her end, and when she spoke, her voice was strong and authoritative. He heard the military officer she'd been. "Absolutely not. No, Isaac. It doesn't go down in your clubhouse. You have to stay clear of this. Get him home. I'll deal with him."

"Lilli, there are too many moving parts. It's gotta be here." The only way he could think of to keep Wyatt out of trouble was to keep both him and his brother in sight.

But Lilli was resolute. "I won't, Isaac. No. It brings the club way too far into this. I won't do it."

He tried again. "Lilli—," but then he realized that he was alone on the call; she'd ended the connection. *Fuck.* He also knew she wouldn't pick up again if he called back. She'd made her decision. *FUCK.*

"Show. Hold on. Change of plan." Rover was in the corner, playing Galaga on one of the old arcade games. Isaac called him over. "Rove's gonna take Ray back home and hang out with him until he hears otherwise from you or me." He turned to Rover. "Just keep him home, buddy. That's your job today. Get Ray home and keep him there until you get word from me or Show. Got it?"

273

Rover got it. He and Show went back and roused Ray. When they got him into the van and Rover took off, Show came back to Isaac. "What the hell, boss?"

He shook his head. "God save me from women who think they know better. Lilli doesn't want it goin' down in the clubhouse. She's trying to keep us clear."

"I get that. She's a good girl, but we're not clear. No way we can be."

"I know." But his woman was stubborn and sure she was right.

~oOo~

By the time the club was in the Keep, surrounding the ebony table, Show and Isaac had been able to talk to Bart, Len, Victor, and CJ. All were shocked about what Ray had done and how Lilli was involved. All were dismayed at the way it bore down on a brother and sorry for what Wyatt would face. But all were in agreement that the club should not stand in Lilli's way. Dan had been out with Wyatt, and Havoc had been out on a repair job and late back to the clubhouse, so they would be hearing of all this for the first time at the table, with Wyatt. They were wild cards. Wyatt was not. This was going to be a hard vote.

Isaac took a moment to collect this thoughts, then looked around at the faces of his brothers. "We have a hard vote today, brothers. I need to tell you a story first, so bear with me." Without naming Ray or Lilli, he told the story they'd both told. He watched each man's reaction. Most had heard it once before. Dan and Havoc clearly had not, and he could tell from their reactions that they would most likely vote with the rest to stay out of Lilli's way. But Isaac was especially interested to watch Wyatt's reaction. He looked surprised as well, but not in the same way. Wyatt looked surprised as if a secret he'd held had been revealed.

Isaac had been right. Wyatt *had* already known what his brother had done.

When Isaac finished, he said, "And here's why it puts us around the table today. The female pilot I've been talking about is my Lilli. The bastard who rigged her copter to fail is Ray Hobson. He confessed to me and Show this afternoon. Lilli is here to render justice. Because Ray is family to a brother, we need to vote on whether he remains under club protection."

Wyatt leaned forward, stunned. "Goddammit, Isaac. You can't be saying you're putting my brother's life to a fucking vote! He did nothing to the club. This isn't club business— or if it is, *he* is our business. He's my business, my *responsibility*."

Isaac leaned forward, too. "It's not our retaliation, that's true. And we're not taking it. But we have to decide as a club whether we're prepared to defend a man who got almost a dozen men killed because he thought having a woman doing the same job as him made his dick look small. Defend him against my old lady—*also* family to the club."

There was a collective sense of shock in the room. Isaac was pushing it here; he hadn't even talked to Lilli about this. But the stakes were high, and he had to go all in. Poker might not have been his game, but sometimes he had to play.

Wyatt virtually threw himself out of his chair. "Your *old lady*? How can she be your old lady? You've known her, what, a month? A little more? Fuck, I haven't even seen the bitch yet! She's no family to me!"

Isaac was out of his chair, now, too, ready to fight. Show grabbed him. Dan grabbed Wyatt. Show urged Isaac to sit, but he would not until Dan wrangled Wyatt back into his chair. Then Isaac sat. Still standing, Show spoke.

"Seems to me Lilli's status is between Isaac and her, and it's not on point. The point is this: I heard Ray confess. His side of the story jives right up with what Lilli told me. It's a true story, boys, and it's an awful thing he did. He got away with it, and he let Lilli take the fall. No matter what we vote, I won't stand in the way of her justice. Nothing can bring back the men whose lives ended because Ray didn't like a woman getting up on him." He looked at Wyatt. "I'm sorry, brother. But you know this is how things work. A man pays what he owes."

Wyatt looked stricken but said only, "Vote." Show sat down.

Isaac went around the table. The final tally was eight to one. Ray had lost club protection. Wyatt stormed out of the Keep. Isaac pointed at Dan and Havoc. "Keep an eye on him. He stays put. I don't want him doing something stupid and digging himself a hole." Havoc went straight out.

Dan was set to follow, but then CJ spoke up, his gruff voice filling the room. CJ and Wyatt were close. "Point him at a girl. Wy never turns down pussy, 'specially when he's het up."

Isaac nodded, knowing Ceej was right. "LaVonne's out there. She likes Wyatt." With one quick nod of his head, Dan headed into the Hall.

Isaac held Show and Len back. He needed to get some things straight with his VP and SAA. Now that Lilli had refused to handle her job in the clubhouse, they had to decide how they would proceed. They talked it out fully, Show offering several scenarios. He was a long view guy.

But Len had the simplest, and thus likely the best, take. "Why don't we let her do what she wants to do? I say we stay out of it. If she needs help, I gotta figure she'll ask you for it, boss. We decide then."

Show nodded. "He's right, Isaac. She wants us as far out as we can be. That's not far enough, but it's the right call for the club. Give her the reins. She came in with a plan. Let's let her work it."

Isaac knew they were right. It was the right call for the club. They would have their hands full keeping a lid on Wyatt. But Lilli was his woman. In many ways, ways he'd not thought possible until now, she was his *life*. He had no idea how he was going to sit back and let this happen without offering her his aid. But he'd have to figure it out. "Okay. You're right. I need to call her, tell her we're out of her way."

She didn't answer. He called Rover. He didn't answer, either. He called Ray. Strike three.

Isaac looked at Show. "I need to know what Wyatt's been doing since he left this room."

CHAPTER NINETEEN

As soon as she hung up with Isaac, Lilli got to work. She logged out and closed down the work she'd been doing, changed into hiking shorts, a light tank, and her terrain runners, and quickly loaded her pack—double-checking her ammo supply and attaching a silencer to her Sig. She almost ran to her car, where she fitted her M25 with its silencer as well. This was broad daylight, which had not been part of Plan A, so she wasn't sure she'd be able to use the M25. The situation would have to be perfect to get her all the way to Hobson's on foot with a sniper rifle strapped to her back. But she wanted it fitted just in case.

Most likely, this job had moved to Plan B—up close and personal, with the Sig in play. That was concealed in her pack, allowing her to move freely.

Time was way too short. Lilli had a long hike to get from a safe place for her car to Hobson's shack of a house. Seven miles at least—and she'd have to stay low for the last couple of miles, which would slow her up considerably. If Isaac had done as she'd asked, Hobson would be there well in advance of her. She needed to book it when and where she could. She couldn't imagine she had more than today, at best, before he'd made her.

The clubhouse would have been the safer, for her, arena. But she wasn't going to kill a man in the middle of Isaac's club—it was more home to him than his ancestral land. That wasn't even a momentary consideration. Yet now that her plans were known to the club—to Hobson's brother— her time was short. It was now.

She parked in the rough lot of a well-known hiking area. Nine other cars in the lot. So much for the M25. She grabbed her pack and got to hiking, moving at a trot, as quickly as she could without undue notice, while there were other hikers around. She veered off the path at her first clear chance and headed apace into woods which had become familiar to her over the past weeks.

When she was within a couple of miles of Hobson's place, she slowed and heeded the sounds she made. She had to be alert and ready to hide. Hobson had taken, toward the end of her surveillance, to wandering in the woods; twice she'd almost come up on him, or vice versa, and she'd had to take quick cover. One of those times, he'd passed by her so closely she almost could have touched him.

She almost hadn't recognized him. He was fully bearded, and it was long and unkempt, like his hair. Hair and beard had gone dully grey. He was thin—emaciated, really—and no longer had the bearing of military service. Instead, his shoulders sagged. He looked like a man carrying a heavy load of guilt. As he fucking should have been. It didn't affect Lilli's resolve in the slightest. Remorse was meaningless as long as he drew breath that the men who died that day could not.

The day he'd passed so near her, she'd struggled hard to stay still and not simply handle the situation right then. But they had a plan, and she'd needed to stick to it. Part of the plan was settling into town some before taking action. Another part of the plan was not firing an unsilenced handgun less than a quarter-mile from a working farm. Even in the country, that was an undue risk. So she'd stayed in cover and let him pass.

That was all while Plan A had been in effect; everything had gone ass-up since then. Plan B was more guerilla than sniper. In many ways, she preferred it. Plan A would have resulted in his death, but a clean one he might not even have felt. Plan B put them face to face, made sure he knew what was happening, why, and by whom. She'd told herself—and Isaac—repeatedly that it was justice she and her team wanted, not vengeance. But vengeance would be sweet if she could get it.

Finally, she crept up to a rise over which she could see his ratty little house. It was barely a cabin, really, without even an indoor toilet. The house sat up strangely off the ground, on stilts maybe eighteen to twenty-four inches high. Lilli figured the little creek that ran past it on the far side must occasionally flood, though it was barely a trickle now. A weathered board hut with a half moon in the door stood off a short distance. Outhouse. The place was a literal shithole.

There was a dark grey van parked next to Hobson's beater pickup. She knew that van. She pulled her camera and zoom out and took a closer look. Yes—it was the Horde van. Somebody from the club was still there. Fuck. She lay down on the far side of the rise and waited.

There was no movement or sound for some time—twenty minutes or so—and then she heard the sharp report of a pistol. Nothing more. One shot, and then silence again. Leaving her pack tucked in a cluster of rocks and grass, she took her Sig with her and stole down to the house.

She checked under the house as she sidled up to it—clear. The room in the middle of the house had a large window that must have gone almost to the floor. Curtains closed off all but the middle couple of feet. Her back pressed snugly against the splintered, cracked siding, Lilli tried to get a view into that room. She was barely able to make out a body lying on the floor. She couldn't see enough to know who it was, whether it was Hobson or whoever had been here from the Horde—his brother maybe? She hadn't met his brother. But she couldn't see Isaac letting the brothers leave the clubhouse together.

She had no idea whether the shooter was friend or foe. As she continued carefully along the house, she heard something—a crack or a creak. She paused and listened, trying to place it. The sound didn't repeat. She took another soundless step—and then her feet were yanked out from under her. Her head slammed hard on the rocky ground, and the world got loud and dim. Before she could drag full consciousness back to the fore, Hobson was looming over her, filthy and covered in cobwebs, a wild look in his eyes. Her head cleared then, and she understood that he'd gone under the house to get to her. She'd been colossally stupid not to check again.

Now he was straddling her, one hand holding down her wrist, immobilizing her gun hand. His knee pressed down on her other arm. With his free hand, he had a gun of his own under her chin.

"You fucking *gash*! You come after me? Why won't you get out of my *HEAD*?" He cocked the gun.

In a flash of vivid thought, Lilli made a decision. She could try to back him down, or she could just fucking go for it. Her chances of survival here were nil, either way. One of them was dying today. Perhaps within the next few seconds.

She kicked her legs up and put everything she had into an effort to dislodge him and come up on top of him.

She succeeded, but he pulled the trigger. The gun had shifted in their struggle, though, and instead of going through the soft underside of her chin and into her brain, the bullet glanced off the side of her neck, taking a painful, hot gouge with it. She could feel the blood soaking her top, but she ignored it. She slammed his hand down then, and the gun skidded from his grasp. He still had her wrist in a desperate, iron grip, so she punched him hard in the side of the head. She felt something break in her hand, but she'd dazed him at least momentarily. He moved to roll her.

He was still dazed, so the move didn't have the power it should have had. As he tried to get her back on the ground, his grip on her loosened, and Lilli took the opportunity to flip over and away. She ended up on her knees, free of him but unarmed. He'd dislodged her Sig from her hand; her right side, where the bullet had slit her throat, was going weak. She was losing blood, and the fight wasn't helping. She was concussed. But she pulled it together, not bothering to fret about how hard it was to do so. She saw his pistol—an old Colt revolver—and stood to go for it.

The standing did her in. She went to her knees as her vision swirled and glittered. She looked down and found herself fascinated by the dark crimson dyeing most of her top.

It was going to be her that died.

She didn't even care enough to try to get off her knees.

Hobson limped up to her. "You know what? I don't want you dyin' fast. You been torturin' me for years now. I want you goin' slow. There's shit you owe me, cunt." He bent down and tied something snugly around her neck, like a bandage.

Her last thought was disappointment.

CHAPTER TWENTY

Isaac charged into the dorm room. Len had Wyatt against a wall. LaVonne was curled into the corner, cowering, her mouth bleeding heavily. Isaac spared her a glance, then turned to Dan, coming up behind him.

"Dan—get her outta here. Get her some ice or something." He advanced on Wyatt. "What the fuck did you do, Wyatt?"

"So I hit a woman—back the fuck off!" Wyatt struggled hard against Len's grip, but Len was bigger and stronger. Len handed Isaac a phone; must have been Wyatt's. Isaac checked outgoing calls—none recent. He checked outgoing texts—one, to Ray. It read: *get out now pilot after u cant explain go back 2 camp.*

He tossed the phone on the bed behind him. Leaning down into Wyatt's face, looming over him, Isaac snarled, "That's the stupid shit I wanted to keep you from doing. If Lilli gets hurt because of this, I will end you slow." He shifted his eyes to Len. "Put him in the Room. Chain the fucker down. We'll deal with him later."

Isaac felt panic. He didn't think he'd ever felt panic before, but it was on him now, compelling him to move, move now, find Lilli, keep her safe. But he had to think. He'd tried to call her several more times, to no avail. Something bad had gone down, he could feel it in his very cells. The question was where.

Wyatt's text hadn't given Ray any information about where Lilli was. Rover had taken him back to his place. Most likely, then, that was where trouble was. But he needed to be sure. His men were at his back, waiting to know what he wanted. No one had made any suggestions, not even Show.

283

They were waiting for him to work it through. When Len came back from the Room, Isaac knew what he wanted.

"CJ—you stay with Wyatt, make sure he's contained. Show and Bart—you go to Lilli's place. Don't think she's there, but I need to be sure. Be careful—she'll be on alert and maybe suspicious of anybody but me right now. She doesn't know how the vote went. The rest of us, we're going to Ray's. I think there's trouble, and I think it's there." He met each brother's eyes. "We clear? We good?" They nodded as one and geared up.

~oOo~

They didn't bother with stealth; instead, they roared up to Ray's house and ran in, full-bore. Isaac didn't have the patience for stealth.

The door was standing open; Isaac was first in. Rover was lying at the far end of the short hallway, a thickening pool of blood making a crimson halo around his head and shoulders. Isaac went to him and squatted to check his pulse; the rest of the Horde fanned out to check the small house. Rover was dead, shot just to the side of his right eye. Isaac hoped he'd gone instantly.

Len was standing immediately behind Isaac. "We're clear here." Isaac looked up at him, and Len nodded at Rover's body. "You think that was Ray or Lilli?"

Standing and turning fast, Isaac almost grabbed Len. "It was Ray, and you know it. No way Lilli would've shot the kid."

"Not on purpose, but we don't know what went on here."

Isaac did. He could see it clearly. He'd put Rover on watch detail, and Ray had taken him down after Wyatt warned him about Lilli. Jesus Christ, this was a mess.

He needed to find Lilli. She wasn't in the house, and Ray's car was in the yard. He knew damn well she wouldn't have just driven up—she'd given him enough detail about her surveillance to know that her car was probably several miles away. It all added up to bad, but Isaac was convinced she had to be close. But where? Pushing his panic and worry back so that he could fucking *think*, he went through the narrow back door and out into the overgrown yard.

Like any good country boy, Isaac was an experienced hunter. That made him a decent tracker. But good tracking skills weren't required to be able to see that a major fight had gone down at the far corner of the house. The tall grass was flattened and matted and, as Isaac investigated, he saw blood staining the trampled growth—a couple of smaller but still noteworthy smears, a trail of drips and streaks, and then a much more sizable stain that had clearly been a pool before the earth had taken it in.

Squatting at the largest stain, Isaac breathed slowly, fighting for calm. It was Lilli's blood. No earthly way he could know that, but he felt its certainty like he felt the ground under his feet. If it had been Ray's blood, if Lilli had bled him like this, the Horde would have come upon a vastly different scene, he just knew it.

Ray had Lilli, and she was badly hurt. She was either already dead, and he was disposing of her body, or she would die soon. Despair was crowding in with the worry and panic. Isaac dropped his head to his knees and pushed it all back. *Focus. Focus.* If he had her, where were they be? With a deep breath he lifted his head and looked around. There—a vague trail of displaced grass and weeds. He went toward it and saw that it looked like someone had possibly been dragged in that direction. Maybe it was wishful thinking, Isaac seeing a lead where there was none, but he had no better options, so he followed. He didn't even call his brothers.

But Len saw him go; Isaac heard him hailing the rest of the Horde to follow. Now, though, now he wanted stealth. If there was a chance Lilli was alive, Isaac didn't want to blow it because Ray saw most of the MC bearing down on him. Isaac turned and gestured for his men to fan out and stay quiet.

They followed the trail for almost ten minutes before Isaac understood where they were headed. By then, it had become much more obviously a trail, and had, in fact, begun to show signs that Ray was following what had been an actual trail trodden into the reedy grass and wildflowers of the lightly wooded field. Soon, they were in a thick stand of trees, and Isaac followed Ray's progress easily. He came across one of Lilli's running shoes in the path, and his heart skidded.

They were headed for an old deer blind. Isaac knew it because he'd hunted the woods all around here his whole life, as had all the men behind him. The blind was on Corin Petersen's property—which was now a bank's property. When they came upon it a few minutes later, Isaac ducked behind a cluster of wild growth, and gestured for everyone to stop and be still. He cocked his Glock. The rest of the Horde followed suit.

The blind was sized to accommodate four men for a day of waiting. It was elevated, its floor about four feet off the ground, and had once been painted in a camouflage pattern. Age, weather, and disuse had taken its toll, though, and its color was almost uniformly the grey of dying old wood. Most of the windows were still closed, their board shutters latched with hooks. Weeds had grown up all around it, and it was the weeds that told Isaac they'd found Ray's destination. The growth was disturbed in a path directly to the basic set of steps leading into the blind, and tall, strong weeds had been broken sharply off at the point where they grew up in the empty spaces between each step.

At first, Isaac neither heard nor saw anything. Then, just as he was preparing to step out of cover and advance on the blind, its floor creaked, and he saw the building shimmy slightly. He stopped. He had to get in there, and he needed to surprise Ray when he did so. He had no idea what state he would find Lilli in. He needed to think.

Len sidled up to him then and whispered, "Hav and I will divert him. When we start making a din, you get in there." Isaac nodded. It was a good plan.

But they didn't get a chance to put it in play, because just then Ray shouted, loud enough to be clear to the Horde's ears, "Scream, you fucking cunt! Scream!"

All plans evaporated, and Isaac just ran.

He charged up the steps and slammed through the door; the dry-rotted wood gave way almost instantly, and Isaac nearly lost his footing. He caught himself, aimed, and shot twice before Ray could get his own gun up. Ray went down, two bullets in his chest. He didn't move at all.

Except to kick Ray's gun away, Isaac ignored him and went straight for Lilli. She was lying on the floor, her hands bound with Ray's belt, her clothes badly torn, as if—Isaac stopped that thought. There was blood everywhere, pulsing slowly in a dark ooze from her neck, where a soaked bandana was tied. Except where it was doused in her blood, or bruised, her skin was waxy white, almost blue. But she was conscious and looking at him. She seemed...calm. He dropped to his knees, undid the binding around her wrists, and gathered her up. She was cold. Jesus.

"Baby—God, baby." She blinked up at him. There was so much fucking *blood*. She smiled a little and tried to lift her arm, but it only came up a couple of inches, and then she let it drop back to the floor with a thud. Her eyes fluttered shut. "Lilli!" He shook her, and a wrinkle crossed her brow, but she didn't open her eyes.

He checked her pulse. Thin and fast. Turning to Dan, who was standing at the door—somehow they'd pulled Ray's body out already—Isaac said, "We have to get her help! NOW!"

Dan nodded and called out the door. "We need the van up here—close as you can get!"

Isaac was frantic; he couldn't push it off any longer. "She's bleeding out. It's too much—it's too fucking much!" Dan knelt next to him and put his hand on his shoulder. He reached out and checked Lilli's pulse, gently holding her wrist.

"She's in shock, Isaac. Nobody's got cell service out here, so we need to take her in the van." He pulled his kutte off and shrugged out of his grey cotton button-down, leaving him in nothing but a wife-beater t-shirt. He put his kutte back on and fashioned a bandage with his shirt, wrapping it around her neck. "We need to get her in the van and get her legs up, keep the blood to her organs. You carry her, I'll apply pressure, boss. She's already lost too much blood. She's got to keep what she still has."

Isaac heard the van coming fast through the brush. He stood, Lilli's limp body in his arms. Dan walked backwards down the steps, his hand pressing into Lilli's neck. They climbed into the back of the van, leaving Len and Havoc to clean up and rid the world of Ray Hobson's remains.

The hospital was 20 miles away. Sitting on the floor of the van, Dan sitting in front of him, keeping pressure on her wound, Isaac bent over the still body of his old lady and, for the first time since his sister left him alone with their father, he prayed.

~oOo~

He told the people at the hospital she was his wife. He didn't hesitate at all. He knew they wouldn't question him, and he needed to make sure they gave him access to her. But they'd whisked her away from him almost immediately, and now he and Dan were in the waiting room. Waiting. Isaac was losing his fucking mind.

He had been wearing a rut in the waiting room floor for almost three hours, with no word whatsoever, when Show and Len turned up. Show caught him in the middle of his circuit and pulled him aside.

"Ray's handled, the site is clean, and your bike is at the clubhouse. I know this is a shitty time, but we need to talk about Wyatt."

Isaac had only one thing to say about Wyatt. "That motherfucker is dead. Leave him for me."

Show shook his head. "Not without a vote, boss. You need to think clearly."

The taut wire of control holding Isaac together snapped, and he grabbed Show by his kutte and slammed him against the nearest wall. "Do you see the blood? There was so much blood! She could die—she could be dead already!—and Wyatt did it. I will tear him apart with my bare fucking hands. I will gut him."

Dan was at his back, pulling him away. He released Show and stormed to the far end of the room. He couldn't think about this shit now. He could only think of Lilli. What was *happening*? Why wouldn't they tell him anything? He dropped to a chair and put his head in his hands.

Steady as ever, Show came back up to him and sat down. "Focus on her for now, boss. I'll make sure Wyatt's held until you're ready. I got the rest. You focus on your old lady."

Isaac nodded and went back to waiting.

~oOo~

When a doctor finally came out and called, "Lilli's family?" Isaac was so tightly wrapped in his own hell of worry and guilt that Dan had to nudge him. He stood, and the doctor, a woman who looked too fucking young to be entrusted with his old lady, gestured to a small grouping of chairs in a corner.

When he brought her in, he'd said only that he'd found her bleeding out, which was true. Now, the doctor, whose name, R. Ingleton, was embroidered on the right side of her coat, asked him, "Is there nothing else you can tell us about what happened?"

Isaac shook his head. "Sorry, Doc. She was lying on the floor, bleeding. She was conscious, but barely. She was cold."

Dr. Ingleton nodded. "She'd gone into shock." She sighed. "Let me tell you where she stands now, since I imagine that's of most critical importance to you, and then I'll explain to you what her injuries tell me—my best guess, at least."

Isaac nodded, but said nothing. He didn't want to distract her from telling him what the fuck was going on.

"She lost a great deal of blood—as much as forty percent. This is an extremely dangerous situation, which could result in serious organ damage. She's very fit—really in quite good shape, with a strong cardiovascular system—so that will help her. But now, she's in a coma. She's breathing on her own, and her vitals have shown signs of

290

improvement, which indicates that her organ function is recovering. But we can't know whether there's been lasting impact on her brain function until she wakes—if she wakes."

"Could she die?" Isaac had to force the words to leave his throat.

The doctor was direct. "Yes. I'm sorry to say that her condition is very critical right now. But she is, again, showing some signs of rebounding. That she's breathing on her own is a good sign."

"When can I be with her?"

"She'll be in the ICU for a couple of days at a minimum. Visiting hours there are very restricted. I'm sorry."

"Fuck that, Doc. I'm not leaving her. I'm not. Drag me out if you can."

She sighed and considered. "I'll make some arrangements for tonight and tomorrow. Then we'll have to talk." Looking suddenly awkward, with a glance at his kutte, she cleared her throat. "There are some other issues I need to discuss with you. I've had to call the Sheriff's office."

He'd expected as much. Lilli's injuries were obviously violent. The Sheriff would not be a problem. "It's fine. Why?"

"The laceration to her neck is most likely from a bullet. She has other injuries, though—broken bones in her hand, a badly sprained ankle, serious bruising, and other, smaller lacerations. She looks as if she's been bound and beaten. Some of the wounds cause me to believe that she's been...tortured."

Isaac put his hands over his eyes. He had seen her, lying on the rotting wood floor of the deer blind, her clothes torn open, covered in blood. He shouldn't have been surprised. And he wasn't, not really. But he was sickened. He needed to dig Ray back up and kill him again. He needed to make Wyatt pay.

But *he* was the one who'd exposed her plan. It was him. Maybe, if he'd let her handle it the way she'd originally intended, she would simply have made Ray disappear, and the Horde would never have been the wiser. In the end, this was on him.

"We did a rape kit."

He dropped his hands and looked at the doctor. She shook her head. "It was negative. But I need you to understand that her injuries are extensive. The next half-day or so will be crucial. She'll be getting transfusions at least through tomorrow. If we can get her stable, then it will be a matter of waiting for her to regain consciousness. If that happens, we'll know more whether there has been lasting brain damage from the blood loss."

If. If she wakes up.

Isaac sat and let all that sink in. He tried to, anyway. All that really stuck was that Lilli could die. "I need to be with her, Doc."

Dr. Ingleton nodded. "She'll be brought to the ICU shortly. I'll have someone bring you to her once we get her set up."

~oOo~

It was another half hour before someone came and led Isaac to a small room with glass walls. He stopped in the doorway, cut down by the sight of her, small and frail, connected by wires and tubes to all kinds of apparatuses.

She was so *pale*. As if she were already gone.

There was a single chair in the room. Isaac pulled it as close to the bed as he could get and sat down. Taking her cool, unresponsive hand in both of his, he laid his head on the knot their hands made.

"Stay with me, Sport. You stay with me."

He got no answer but the whir and beep of the machines surrounding her.

~oOo~

The next morning, Show came to the door of Lilli's room. Isaac was sitting, watching her chest move, taking what reassurance he could from that. Show knocked on the door jamb, and Isaac turned.

"Any change?"

Isaac shook his head. "What's up?
"
"Got everybody here, boss, waiting in the chapel. We brought the meeting to you. Can't leave Wyatt in the Room indefinitely."

"Everybody? Who's watching him now, then?"

"I got Victor's proxy. He's babysitting."

Isaac didn't want to leave Lilli even for the time it would take to go down to the chapel and have this meeting, but he knew Show was right. Feeling a pull of conflicting loyalties, he stood, kissed Lilli's still too-cold forehead, and followed Show out.

The men were arrayed on pews in the small chapel, roughly in the same order in which they sat around their table. Isaac and Show went to the front. Show sat, and Isaac turned and faced his men.

"I need to get back, so I'm gonna get to it. We need to vote on Wyatt. Two votes: his patch and his life. He went against a club vote. That action got Rover killed, and it got my old lady badly hurt. She might die." His voice cracked, and he paused and collected himself. "Fuck, she might be dying right the hell now, so let's get on this. All those in favor of taking Wyatt's patch."

The vote was unanimous. No one even hesitated.

"Carries. Next vote. Does he meet his maker? Betrayed the club, got a 24-year-old kid killed, got Lilli shot and tortured. All those in favor of sending Wyatt to his maker. Gotta be unanimous."

It was, though CJ dropped his head as if in prayer before he looked up, steely-eyed, and said, "Aye."

Despite the anxiety wrapped around his spine like iron bands, Isaac felt relief. He hadn't known what he would do if the vote had gone the other way. "Carries. I want him. Hold him until I can get to him."

"Boss, wait." Show stood, and Isaac turned on him, ready to fight. Show put his hands up. "I know you want the kill. I understand. I'm gonna ask you to take a breath. We got girls and hangarounds in and out of the clubhouse. There's only so long we can keep Wyatt on ice. Longer we go, bigger the risk. Do you want to deal with him and leave Lilli? Or do you want to stay with her and let us deal with him? Your call."

Show's job was to pull Isaac back. That was why he wanted him as VP, to temper his temper. And he was right.

But right now, Isaac just wanted to bloody his face. He turned and picked up a vase of flowers, hurling it across the chapel, where it hit the wall and exploded. Leaning on the small altar, Isaac strove for control. He needed to kill him. He needed to feel that fucker's life draining out of his traitorous body. He wanted that life force for Lilli.

He couldn't leave her. He wouldn't.

Isaac turned back to his men. His eyes on Len instead of Showdown, he said, "You and Victor—bleed him. I want him to die slow, and I want it to hurt. I want him to watch while his ink is sliced off. I don't want him ending up anywhere near his brother. And burn his goddamn kutte."

Len nodded, and Isaac walked out of the chapel and back to Lilli's bedside. He would not leave her again.

~oOo~

The days clicked past, and Lilli didn't wake. He didn't go farther from her than the waiting room at the end of the hall. His brothers brought him food, but most of it he left untouched. The nurses—a formidable bunch—forced him to drink and occasionally coerced him to eat, but he tasted none of it.

Twice, the Horde held a brief meeting in the waiting room, and daily, Show came in to give him an update. Victor and Len had taken care of Wyatt. The guns from Tulsa had arrived. The Horde was elevating three hangarounds to Prospect status. They'd never had three Prospects at once before—they'd rarely had more than one—but a Prospect could be called upon to do things they couldn't trust a hangaround to do, and, frankly, they needed the manpower. They weren't a big club, and they were facing a powerful enemy.

295

Mac Evans, currently playing for the home team now, had gotten a pointed phone call from one of Ellis's associates and had called Show immediately. The next day, Will Keller's children had been followed home from the school bus stop by a blacked-out SUV no one recognized. Will was standing firm, but the Horde had paid to send his wife and kids to Florida to stay with her parents. Things were heating up.

And Isaac could barely find space in his head to care. Show updated him, and Isaac nodded. Show suggested next moves, and Isaac nodded. He watched Lilli breathe and he nodded. Then Show would squeeze his shoulder and leave him be.

They'd moved her out of the ICU as soon as she was stable. For almost three days, she'd been in a private room, and they'd brought in a sleeping chair for him. He didn't bother with it. He sat as close as he could get to her and waited, willing her to wake. When he slept, he dozed at her bedside, holding her hand.

The first day or two, Dr. Ingleton would stop and talk to him after she'd checked Lilli. She'd explained what she was seeing, what it meant, what she thought Lilli's prognosis was. The last couple of days, she'd only smiled grimly and left, as if there was nothing more to say.

And there wasn't. No change. She just wasn't waking up.

He kept his mind busy and his heart strong by imagining a future with her. He was going to marry her, mark her, bring her into his home. He imagined coming home to her, curling up on the sofa with her to read or watch movies, taking her into his bed, *their* bed, and filling her with his child. He thought of her sitting on the tall stool in his woodshop and watching him turn and carve. He thought of traveling with her in that shitty old camper that he loved so much more now, watching her glare at people wanting to dicker down the price of a burled wood vase. He thought of her holding their child in her arms.

That was the only life he wanted. He needed her to wake so he could make it happen.

Late on the fourth day, not long before Isaac would update the count in his head to five, Lilli's hand twitched in his. He'd been drifting on the plane between waking and sleep, and he jerked to alertness when it happened. Then he doubted it had happened. He sat up and waited for her to do it again. For long, tense moments during which he tried to see every part of her body so that he wouldn't miss any change, he waited fruitlessly.

And then she took a deep breath.

"Lilli?"

She was still.

Jesus Christ, Sport. Wake up. Wake up, wake up.

CHAPTER TWENTY-ONE

It seemed to Lilli she'd been awake for some time, because none of the sounds she heard seemed unfamiliar. She knew she was in the hospital. She knew she was connected to machines—she could feel the faint pinch of tape on her wrist and the stiff intrusion of an IV stent, and the pull of adhesive on her chest from a heart monitor. She could hear the unique sounds of a hospital at work, beeps in her room, conversations outside. Definitely a hospital. But she wasn't sure why.

Before she'd opened her eyes, she knew that Isaac was holding her hand, his hard, rough palms warm and gentle on her skin. Isaac. Her love. He was here; he was with her. She tried to understand what that meant. There was something she should know, something she needed to know, something important. But it eluded her.

The room came slowly into focus. The light in the room was bright and hurt her eyes, but before she could close them again, Isaac's hands closed around hers. "Lilli? Ah, Sport. Are you with me? Are you here?" She heard the clang of desperation in his voice, and she tried to answer him, but she couldn't make sound pass through her throat. She tried to nod, but her neck shouted in protest. Instead, she fought to really open her eyes and see, and she curled her fingers around his.

"Oh, fuck. Lilli, thank God. Oh, Jesus, baby!" He rose up closer and kissed her forehead. He smiled down at her; then, as if that first kiss hadn't satisfied his need, he kissed her cheeks, her nose, her chin, her lips, and, again, her forehead. By the time he was done and looking down at her again, she could see clearly. He looked awful, his bright eyes sunken in shadow. She lifted the hand he wasn't holding and was surprised to find it in a cast.

As consciousness settled in more completely, so did pain. She realized that she hurt everywhere. She tried to think what had happened. Car wreck? What did she last remember? Isaac stroked her face and then picked up something near her shoulder.

A voice came through a speaker somewhere in the room, asking, "What do you need?"

Isaac answered, "She's awake!"

The voice responded, "Somebody'll be right there."

He lifted her hand to his lips. "You're gonna be okay, Sport. You're gonna be okay." She had no reason to disbelieve him. She closed her eyes.

~oOo~

Lilli woke with Isaac almost lying on her, his hands pressing down on her shoulders, his chest heavy on hers. "Wake up, baby. It's okay. Shh. Don't hurt yourself."

The dream receded quickly, becoming broken pieces of image as she understood where she was. She squirmed under Isaac's weight, feeling irritated at his words, which sounded condescending to her ears. She felt helpless and weak enough without Isaac treating her like a child.

"I'm fine." She shrugged again, and he released her and sat back in the chair at the side of her bed.

"The dreams are bad—worse—now, Sport."

She shrugged again. He was right—they were a lot worse. Still death dreams, but now they were shaded with memory, and death had a face: Hobson. But they didn't stay long after she woke. She'd learn to deal with them the way she'd learned to deal with everything.

By her second day conscious, Lilli had remembered what brought her there. Hobson. She'd let him best her. Again. She'd let him hurt her. She'd failed.

She knew he was dead, and that Isaac had killed him. So the goal of the mission had been achieved. But she had failed nonetheless. Hobson had still managed to take everything he could from her. He'd wanted to take more, but he'd been unable. She remembered every second, until the one in which Isaac had pulled her into his arms. After that, four days of blankness.

Hobson had done a lot of damage. But Lilli was recovering. After three days awake—a week since she'd gotten hurt—she was feeling her strength return. She was able to be awake for longer stretches of time and no longer felt lightheaded even as she lay in bed. She wasn't yet able to stand for more than a few seconds before the world went grey, but she knew it would come. Her ankle was still gimpy, anyway.

She had a nasty wound on her neck, which was the root cause of her weakness. The sundry cuts and bruises making motley of the rest of her body were fading, even if the memory of them would not. Her left hand was in a cast, and that would probably be the thing that caused the most lasting nuisance. All of it, though, would heal. She was expected to make a full recovery.

She wasn't sure how to get her head on straight, though. Fate had taken her family. Hobson had taken everything else, even her strength. She didn't know what was left.

~oOo~

"Where are you, Sport?" They were sitting outside in the crappy little 'courtyard.' Lilli was in a wheelchair, which was more a precaution to make sure she didn't get lightheaded and keel over than a necessity, but it still made her feel like an invalid. Isaac had his hand on her knee, and he'd given it a squeeze as he'd asked.

She came back to the moment and smiled at him. "Nowhere. Just spacing."

"That brain doesn't slow down enough for you to space. There's something goin' on, Lilli. I can see it. Been like this since you woke up. Talk to me." He pulled the wheelchair so it turned on its axis and she faced him. "Talk to me."

He was staring intently into her eyes, like he was trying to see what it was she was holding back. Since she'd woken up, he had a new way of looking at her. It was…naked, somehow, like he was holding nothing back, like he was offering her everything. It scared her, because she didn't have anything to give him in return. She felt empty.

When her mother killed herself, she'd had her father. She'd had him when her nonna died, too. When her father died, she'd had the Army. When the Army kicked her away, she'd had vengeance. Always something to focus on, always something to distract her from her loss. In the space of weeks she'd lived after her discharge and before she'd found out about Hobson, she'd felt empty like this, and she'd just stopped. The sense of loss she'd been running from since she was ten had begun to converge on her. And then Lopez had contacted her, and she shoved it all back into its box.

Now, she had Isaac. But since she'd woken, she could only see him through her failure. Her connection with him had complicated her mission. She had made decisions because of her feelings for him which had put him and others at great risk. And then she'd failed. She'd needed rescue. She'd been at Hobson's mercy. Again. Two men had died who would not have if she'd stayed away from Isaac and

301

the Night Horde. There was a mountain of dead men between her and Hobson.

"Lilli. Please talk to me," Isaac repeated his plea, caressing her thigh.

A strong voice in her head was telling her that this was her opportunity to break free from him. She could end it now, tell him that what had happened had changed her thinking. She could lie low for a while and then move on. She opened her mouth to answer.

But she loved him. She didn't want to leave. She didn't know what was left of her, but if there was anything, it was here. Between them. He smiled at her and put his hand on her cheek, feeding his fingers into her hair. "I love you, Sport. Lilli. I know you have secrets. I understand. But don't shut me out."

Feeling selfish and lost, she didn't. She opened up. She needed him, if only to stave off the emptiness. No. It was so much more than that. She needed him for him, for what they were together. She'd given him trust, and he'd never betrayed it. Now she needed to lean on that. She told him what she was thinking, how she was feeling. She let him in. She'd been letting him in almost since she'd met him.

When she was finished, he had her hands clasped tightly in his. "Lilli, you're wrong. Ray didn't take everything. Don't give it to him now. I don't know any other woman like you—as strong as you, or as smart. You make me stronger. It's when we're not working together that we're weaker. We make a good team. We fill each other out. We fit. I feel that. Do you?
"
She'd felt a fit with Isaac she'd never felt before, almost from the first day. Did they fill each other out? Is that what it was? "I don't know what I fill, Isaac. Or where I fit. I

don't know what's next. My permanent address has been a storage locker for most of my adult life."

"Here, Lilli. You fit here. With me. Make your home with me."

She shook her head. This place was a cover story. "I'm not even my real self here. I can't even claim my own name."

He smiled and curled his big hands around her thighs. "Claim a new one, then. Take mine."

Stunned, Lilli didn't answer. She stared at him; his gaze didn't falter. "Isaac, what—?"

"Askin' you to marry me, Sport. Be my old lady. Fuck, you *are* my old lady. I want you with me."

Her heart pulsed hard at the thought. But it wasn't a solution. "No. Getting lost in you doesn't help me figure myself out. It's not the way."

Isaac sat back on the bench and looked away. It was the first time since they'd come out to this courtyard that his hands weren't on her, and she regretted the loss of his touch. "You're wrong, Sport. For a smart woman, you've missed something huge. I don't know anyone with as strong a sense of self as you have. You know who you are. It's clear in everything you do. The only thing you don't know is what you know."

She was feeling tired and sad now. Not understanding his point and not in the mood for a puzzle, she sighed. "Don't talk in circles. How could I not know that I know who I am? That doesn't make any fucking sense."

He turned back to her. "You're right. But I think maybe you've spent so much time focused on the next thing, the mission or whatever was ahead of you, that you never even stopped to consider how fucking amazing you are. But you also never stopped to wonder if you could do any of the amazing things you've done. Because you *knew* you could. You knew yourself enough to know you could. You never doubted it. I think that's why Ray getting ahold of you is screwing with you like it is. But, Lilli, he's dead, and you're alive. We did it together. You held on. You didn't let him win."

Taking her hands in his again, he leaned forward. "We have something in common, you and me. A lot of things, actually. But one that's really important. We do what we set out to do. We get what we want. So, Sport: what do you want?"

Lilli closed her eyes. She was tired, but mostly she wanted to try to put into some kind of order the clamoring thoughts in her head. She didn't know. She didn't know. And then one thought emerged from the cacophony and clarified. Not even a thought—an image, a memory. She remembered leaning back against him as he lay on their blanket at the second bonfire in Tulsa, the touch of his hands on her. She had felt complete, and calm, and fulfilled.

She'd felt at home.

She opened her eyes; his green gaze was still intent on her. With a smile, she answered, "You. I want you."

His lopsided grin was clear and open, the relief palpable in it. "Well, that's convenient, then. I'm askin' again, Sport. Marry me."

She nodded.

~oOo~

She was walking on her own power and well on her way to healing by the time they released her. Only the cast on her

304

arm and the dark red scar on her neck served as lingering reminders. She was feeling antsy already to start running and working out again, but she knew she had some weeks left before she could.

Isaac brought her to his house, where he could take care of her. It was a permanent move. He'd been able to pack all of her belongings—at least all those she had here in town—into the Camaro and drive it over. She was no longer staying in the little pre-fab house. Now she lived in Isaac's family home.

Work had been a problem to solve. She'd given him the key to her office, and he'd brought all of that over as well and set up an office for her on the second floor of his house. She trusted him not to look at any of it, and there were no classified documents in her files, but it was still a major breach of protocol. She'd had fires to put out, though; her absence while she was in the hospital had caused alarm, and she couldn't wait any longer to get things straight.

Getting things straight with the NSA had turned out to be easy—they had not contacted her until two days before her release, so the big guns hadn't begun yet to worry about secrets getting out. They were only just beginning to think twice about her silence. Rick, on the other hand, her contact for the Hobson project, had been about ten seconds away from triggering their failsafe when she'd connected with him. She owed that boy something to calm his nerves.

It was over. Hobson had been brought to justice—the only kind they had still available to them. It was strange to Lilli to contemplate facing something like a normal life—a home, a partner, a community. She had no idea whether she'd even be good at it.

She wanted to find out, though.

CHAPTER TWENTY-TWO

Isaac parked at the house and went inside. Everything was quiet, which generally meant that Lilli was working. He hung his kutte up on the hall tree and went into the kitchen to grab a couple of beers, then headed upstairs.

In all the years since he'd moved back after his father died, and until Lilli had moved in weeks ago, Isaac could count on his hands the number of times he'd been on the second floor of this house. There were two bedrooms up here, and a tiny bathroom tucked under the eaves. He and his sister had grown up on this floor. For Isaac, whose childhood had few good memories, there'd been nothing for him here. So he'd closed up the rooms and ignored their existence.

But Lilli was here now, and she'd needed a private place to work. He'd given her his old room. Except that the bed was stripped to the mattress, it looked the same as it had when he'd lived in it, and Lilli had been stung by its austerity. So had he, buffeted about by memory. There hadn't been much patience in his father for frivolous things, so there were no posters or albums, no models or amusements. Except for books. Books he'd been allowed, though he'd not been allowed to keep them in his room. He'd learned to work on bikes, and to carve, because they were ways to work, and work passed muster with his father. He had not begrudged an enjoyment of work. Or booze—for himself, at least.

Isaac had enjoyed helping Lilli turn this room into something better. He'd done most of the work while she was recovering, but she'd sat up here and managed him. He'd taken out his old furniture and built her a desk and bookcases. She didn't actually need bookcases for the kind of work she did, but he fancied making a room for her to do whatever she wanted with, and he knew she had a lot of books stored somewhere. He'd painted, too, a color she'd picked from the Pantone book he had in his shop. A kind of sage green.

He didn't want to do more yet, because she had no idea what her taste even was, and he wanted her to find that on her own. She was nesting for the first time in her life. He found that to be bittersweet. Even he had a home, such as it was. To think that Lilli had not—it made his heart ache. But she was making one with him, and they were turning nasty old memories inside out to do it. Isaac felt a focus and clarity about his life he had not felt before.

He knocked on the locked door. She'd told him more than she should have about what she did, but she kept the door locked while she did it. When she wasn't working, he was welcome. Normally, he wouldn't come up here now, but he needed to talk to her.

It took a couple of minutes, and he knew she was closing everything up before she opened the door. When she did, she was smiling. "Hey. You're earlier than I thought."

"Yeah. I want to talk, if you have some time." He handed her a beer.

"Always for you, love. Let's go downstairs, though." She led the way down to the living room, and they sat together on the old-fashioned sofa. Isaac picked up her hand and linked fingers with her.

The cast on her hand had come off the previous week, and she was almost back to a hundred percent, two months after the confrontation with Ray. She'd started running again about a month ago, which had driven Dr. Ingleton into paroxysms, but she'd done okay. Isaac had been surprised she'd waited that long. But the blood loss had taken a lasting toll on her, and she was frustrated even now at how long it was taking to get her strength really back. She'd come back from her run this morning simultaneously excited and frustrated that she'd hit five miles for the first time since.

He saw her always clamoring—to be strong, to make a home, to claim herself—and he stood back out of her way and let her. He'd wanted to get married right away, not because he was insecure about the firmness of her decision, but because he wanted to be fucking married to her. But she would only marry him as herself, as Lilli Accardo, not Lilli Carson. It meant they had to elope, and Isaac couldn't leave Signal Bend right now. Ellis was getting positioned to make a real move, and the Horde, and the town, needed to be ready to repel it if they could.

And that was what he needed to talk to her about. He needed to tell her everything, bring her all the way in. He needed her help. Because he was scared.

"I want to tell you what's going on with the club. It's big shit. Too big for me. I need you."

She lifted their linked hands to her lips and kissed his knuckles. "I'm here. I'll help however I can."

"I just need some perspective. Show's got his ideas, and I've got mine, but I think we're both looking at this from too far inside." She knew about the meth, because she'd done her own research into the club when they'd first gotten together. But now he explained why they did it. He gave her more history of the town, and then he told her about Lawrence Ellis and what it looked like he wanted in Signal Bend.

When he was done, Lilli was quiet, staring out the window into the yard. She wanted chickens, and he wondered if she was imagining them pecking around out there. Other than a few almost-feral cats who fed on mice and voles, he hadn't had animals on the property since he'd taken it over. But Lilli, who'd never had even a goldfish, was discovering an affinity for animals. Isaac was pretty sure one of the mousers was knocked up, and he feared the house would soon be overrun with kittens. She wanted the chickens, too, and a dog. She wanted horses. She showed no signs of being satisfied with all that, either. He'd resisted at first, a knee-jerk reaction, because he hadn't wanted to be pinned down by the responsibility animals presented. But that was what making a home was—setting in stakes. He wanted that now.

And he'd loved to ride horseback. Almost as much fun as a Harley. He wanted to get her a bike of her own, too, though he sure did love having her behind him on his.

For several thoughtful moments, Lilli stroked the long, pink scar on the right side of her neck. It was a habit she'd picked up; Isaac wasn't sure she even knew she did it, but he noticed every time. She turned back to him. "What happens if Ellis wins?"

Isaac had thought about that a lot, so he had a ready answer. "He builds a full-scale factory in Will Keller's woods, takes over the meth production, and turns Signal Bend into the worst kind of company town. Northsiders crush the Horde, kill us all, take over the streets. The good people who've been hanging on finally give up and leave. The ones who survive and stay are either cooking or tweaking. Probably both. Ellis takes over the meth pipeline throughout the Midwest. The people trying to control it, be sane about it, get flattened."

She nodded slowly, considering what he'd said. "I'm going to say this, and I want you to hear it for what it is, okay? Don't get defensive." Isaac nodded, knowing that whatever she said, it would be thoughtful. "Meth is nasty shit. Is there a way for you to just get out of it? For the whole town to?"

"I wish there was. I hate it. That's why we won't have it in town. We push it through to the cities, let them deal with it." He really did hate it. He rubbed his hand over his beard in frustration. "There's nothing else bringing real money in. That nasty shit keeps Tuck's place open, and Marie's and every other business in town. The money the cookers and the Horde bring in is all that's keeping the lights on. The Horde has no love for the law, but this isn't the kind of shit we'd be doing if we had a choice. Best we can do is move it out of town, keep our people straight."

She took that at face value and didn't push him further. He loved her even more for that. She didn't make judgments; she made observations. She didn't make pronouncements; she asked questions. "Okay. Say you win. What prevents Ellis from doing the same thing fifty miles down the road and crushing you anyway?"

"He's gunning for us partly because the Northsiders beef with us, and they put him on our scent. But Signal Bend is in a special situation. We're a good distance from the highway, and we are very remote from the nearest police station. Hell, we're just remote. Nobody even passes through Signal Bend to get somewhere else." He laughed bitterly. "It's a fuckin' brilliant move. We are uniquely qualified for less-than-legal activities. And Will's property has unique qualifications of its own. Anyway, fifty miles in either direction is still Horde turf. We run the whole corridor, St. Louis to Tulsa. We'd have to fight him at any point."

"Doesn't seem like the Horde is big enough to manage so much."

Isaac nodded. Indeed. This shit was too big for the Horde, too big for him. "And there we have our problem. We're not. When things are smooth, it's not a big deal. But we're not strong enough to take on a guy with this kind of reach. We have friends who can help us, but they have their own issues. We'll get some manpower, and we got some guns at a discount, but the favors I'm calling in aren't going as far as they need to." The problem explained, Isaac leaned in, taking Lilli's ponytail in his hand and sifting it through his fingers. "Any ideas, soldier girl?"

She barely hesitated before she nodded and said, "Yeah. You need to flank this guy. You can't beat him head on. You're asking for the wrong kind of favors. The guns are good, for the patrols you're doing. But a shootout on Main Street is just going to blow up Main Street. I'm going to get in touch with Rick. Maybe my team broke up too fast."

She was giving him an answer he hadn't expected. She was pulling herself into the fight. His first inclination was to reject that, but he realized—she was skilled, smart, and experienced. She was more of all of that than he was. He needed more than her opinion. He needed her. "What do you mean?"

"You have no idea the kind of damage a top-shelf hacker can do. The best can rewrite history. Rick is the best. If he's game—and he will be; he loves this shit—I'll hook him up with Bart. Bart's good, but he hasn't been playing in the majors."

Another answer he hadn't expected, one that went against Isaac's very DNA. "What—you're saying we bring Ellis down with the *internet*?"

She smiled, apparently hearing the disappointment in his voice. "What, you thought I was going to fly a Black Hawk in over his house, blow it up? No. I'm saying you can certainly weaken him or at least find out where he's weak that way. If he's a big enough player, that works against him, because too many people have dealt with him. He's known. No matter how well he shields himself, every person with an insight is a little dent. This is where being small works in your favor. Flank him. He won't see you coming."

She was making sense, and Isaac wanted the others to hear it. "I want us to sit down with Show, Len, and Bart."

"Good. I want to work out at the clubhouse, anyway."

He laughed at the matter-of-fact way she'd changed the subject. Very little got her rattled. "You sure you're ready for weights?"

She rolled her eyes. "Yes. Yes. I have a brace for my hand. I'm ready. And I want to go at the bag, too. Enough of this sitting around getting flabby shit. Let me get Rick in on this Ellis thing, though, before we say anything."

For the first time since Kenyon Berry told him how big a threat Ellis was, Isaac felt a small hope that they'd be able to save the town. "I love you, Sport. I want to put my ring on you. I want to put my ink on you. I want to make a baby with you."

She got serious at that, quickly. He knew he pushed it any time he brought up a baby. She'd never thought about kids before, and she'd told him she needed time. He understood, and he would wait, but he wanted it. She grabbed his chin and looked pointedly at him, her grey eyes flashing. "You need to slow down, love. I'm feeling my way here."

He wrapped her hand in his and kissed it. "I know. I'm just puttin' my pieces on the board. Play your gambit."

"Your chess metaphors elude me sometimes. You know I don't know how to play."

"I'll teach you. You've definitely got the head for it." He grabbed her legs and pulled her flat on the sofa, lying over her. "But right now, I gotta say, I'm more interested in the rest of you."

THE END

The Signal Bend Series continues with

BEHOLD THE STARS

ABOUT THE AUTHOR

Susan Fanetti is a Midwestern native transplanted to Northern California, where she lives with her husband, youngest son, and assorted cats.

Susan's blog: www.susanfanetti.com

Susan's Facebook author page:
https://www.facebook.com/authorsusanfanetti

'Susan's FANetties' reader group:
https://www.facebook.com/groups/871235502925756/

Twitter: @sfanetti

Made in the USA
Middletown, DE
11 August 2024